D0610231

To Jonathan, with all my love

In memory of
Christopher Charles Goodson
(29th September 1965–6th May 2013)

First published 2014 by A & C Black,
an imprint of Bloomsbury Publishing Plc
50 Bedford Square
London WC1B 3DP
Bloomsbury is a registered trademark of Bloomsbury Publishing Plc

www.bloomsbury.com

ISBN 978-14729-0540-6

A CIP catalogue for this book is available from the British Library.

Printed and Bound by CPI Group (UK) Ltd, Croydon CR0 4YY

1 3 5 7 9 10 8 6 4 2

MIX
Paper from
responsible sources
FSC® C020471

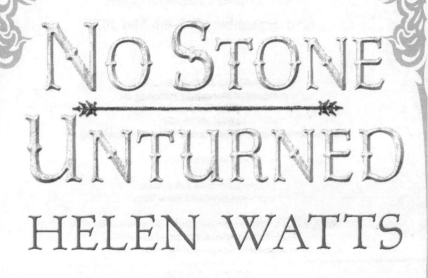

No Stone
Unturned

Helen Watts

A & C BLACK
AN IMPRINT OF BLOOMSBURY
LONDON NEW DELHI NEW YORK SYDNEY

To Jonathan, with all my love

In memory of
Christopher Charles Goodson
(29th September 1965–6th May 2013)

First published 2014 by A & C Black,
an imprint of Bloomsbury Publishing Plc
50 Bedford Square
London WC1B 3DP
Bloomsbury is a registered trademark of Bloomsbury Publishing Plc

www.bloomsbury.com

Copyright © 2014 A & C Black
Text copyright © 2014 Helen Watts

ISBN 978-14729-0540-6

A CIP catalogue for this book is available from the British Library.

Pr   *t*

Contents

PART 1
Chapter 1 – July 2013

'There are angels up there,' whispered Kelly.

When you have spent the entire thirteen years of your life living in a caravan with your parents and a less than tidy older brother, buildings of any size can feel cavernous, so when Kelly first stepped in through the doorway of Westminster Hall, it was perhaps not surprising that her jaw dropped, her face turned skywards, and she stopped dead in her tracks. Her arms fell to her sides and her black and white striped beanie hat slipped silently from her fingers to the floor. She gazed in awe at the solid oak beams arching almost thirty metres above her head.

'Yes,' she murmured, as she made out the delicately carved shapes that clung to the roof beams, each holding a shield as if to protect their wooden bodies. 'Those are definitely angels.'

'Earth calling Kelly,' chanted her friend Leanne, swooping down to pick up the fallen hat and plonking it unceremoniously back onto Kelly's head, messing up her long, wavy, dark-brown hair. 'We haven't even started the tour yet and you've already zoned out!'

'No I haven't!' retorted Kelly. 'It's just, well, look at this place! It's massive...it's stunning...and this is the oldest part, as well. Do you know, they sentenced King Charles I to death in here? Think about it. He could have been standing right where you are now when they told him they were going to cut off his head.'

Leanne laughed, linking her arm through her friend's. 'Honestly, Kel. The things you think about. You're such a weirdo. Come on, let's catch up with the others.'

Kelly, Leanne and the rest of their Year 8 English group were on an end-of-term trip. For the last few weeks, they had been learning about public speaking and how to hold a debate. So to cap it off, their teacher, Miss Shepherd, had organised a visit to London and the Houses of Parliament. They were going to take part in a special workshop, and they would each write their own manifesto—just like real politicians—and present it to the others. Then they could vote on whose ideas they liked the best.

Kelly didn't particularly like public speaking, and she definitely didn't want to be a politician, but she had her own reasons for jumping at the chance of a tour of the Houses of Parliament. It hadn't been easy to talk her parents into letting her go but she had been given a good Year 8 report, so Kelly had argued that she deserved a reward.

The girls hurried down the length of Westminster Hall and ran up the stone steps beneath the huge stained glass window at the far end, to catch up with their school group just as they moved into St Stephen's Hall. A tingle went down Kelly's spine. This was part of the entrance to the Palace of Westminster, which Sir Charles Barry had built after the great fire of 1834.

You did a good job, Sir Charles, she thought to herself as she walked past the statues of former MPs, their smooth marble faces frozen mid-debate.

As Kelly's thoughts drifted back to the present, she realised that the tour guide was speaking. He was pointing to a statue of William Pitt and explaining that this was the Prime Minister who had led Britain in the Napoleonic wars. The rest of the girls in the group were hanging on the guide's every word, which probably had more to do with his uncanny resemblance to the singer Ed Sheeran than his knowledge of the country's former leaders. Kelly adored Ed Sheeran, but even so she found it hard to concentrate on the guide. She was far more interested in the building, and while everyone else stared up at the statue or lovingly at their guide, her eyes wandered around the hall. She was taking in all the details—the vaulted ceilings, the intricate mosaics and the multicoloured stained glass windows. Her gaze lingered on the tiled flooring, patterned in rich reds and blues, interlaced with rectangular pieces of black slate.

After pausing in front of two further statues, Miss Shepherd and the tour guide eventually ushered the group into the octagonal Central Lobby—the crossroads between the chambers of the House of Commons and the House of Lords.

'We're going into the House of Commons first,' announced Miss Shepherd, as she led them into the Members' Lobby. 'Now, listen. Once we are inside, we will only have five minutes, so I want you to have your question sheets and pencils at the ready. I don't want you all spending half the time riffling through your bags and missing what there is to see.'

There was a surge of noise as everyone got themselves organised, and chatted excitedly about the famous room with the green leather benches, which they had seen so many times on TV and were now about to enter. Only Kelly fell silent, eyes fixed to the floor once again. No patterned tiles in here, only smooth, plain limestone paving flags.

Instinctively, she crouched down and laid the palm of her hand flat in the centre of one of the slabs. As her skin touched the cool, polished surface of the stone, Kelly's breath caught in her throat and an image filled her mind. His face. So familiar and yet now so distant. That fluffy, golden hair as untidy as ever. Those piercing blue eyes. The gentle smile. Was it really almost a year since she had last seen him, on that crisp and sunny September afternoon?

'Kelly Hearn, what *are* you doing?'

Miss Shepherd's voice pierced through Kelly's thoughts and the boy vanished from her mind as quickly as he had appeared.

'Nothing, Miss.' She stood back up. 'It's just... It's this stone floor, Miss. I was wondering if this was some of the limestone that came from my village.'

Miss Shepherd seemed confused. 'What do you mean? Which village? Why?'

'When the Houses of Parliament were rebuilt, Miss, after the fire in Queen Victoria's reign, they used limestone from Wilmcote quarry for some of the new floors.' Kelly could see Leanne smirking at her. She blushed. 'Well, that's what I found out, anyway, when I did that local history project for Mr Walker.'

Miss Shepherd was impressed. 'That's fascinating, Kelly. Who would have thought? A tiny village like Wilmcote, supplying the floors for somewhere so magnificent. Imagine all the famous politicians and prime ministers who have walked on it over the years. Well done. I think you should ask the guide about that, after we've finished the tour. There will be some time for questions, I'm sure.'

In spite of her teacher's praise, Kelly remained rooted to the spot, staring down at the flagstones while everyone else began to move towards the door to the House of Commons.

'Why the sad face? Can't be that bad, being the teacher's pet,' teased Leanne, playfully boxing her arm.

Kelly forced a smile and gave a little sniff before squeezing her friend's hand. 'Nah, it's not that. It's just... well, I was so desperate to come here, you know? To see this place. But there's someone else I *so* would have liked to be here to see it all with me.'

'Oh, right,' sneered Leanne, feigning offence. 'I'm not good enough company, am I?'

'Of course you are.' Kelly laughed. 'I don't mean it that way. I'm just missing someone, that's all. An old friend.'

Leanne took Kelly's hand and began to pull her towards the doorway into the House of Commons. 'I know what'll cheer you up.'

'What's that?'

'A foot rub.'

'What?' Kelly looked at her friend as if she had gone mad, then laughed as she realised what Leanne meant. Standing to the left of the arched doorway leading into the House of Commons was an impressive bronze statue of Sir Winston Churchill, hands on his hips, purposefully stepping forwards as if to show off a fine pair of shiny new boots.

'You're supposed to rub his boot for luck,' said the tour guide, as he caught Kelly's eye. 'New MPs like to touch Churchill's foot before making a speech in the Commons for the first time.'

'Go on,' urged Leanne, nudging Kelly.

Kelly laid her hand on the tip of the statue's foot, polished to a shining gold by the hands of decades of hopeful politicians. 'What is it about me and old boots?' she whispered.

Chapter 2 – July 2012

Twelve months earlier, Kelly Hearn was reaching the end of her first year at The Shakespeare Academy. As she emptied her locker outside her tutor group room on the first floor, a wave of relief overcame her. She had made it through three whole terms—two terms longer than her brother Perry had bet she would—and a smile spread across her face as she thought about the summer holidays ahead. Six weeks of not having to get up early and run for the bus. Six weeks of not having to wear a tie and go everywhere dressed like a stick insect in a stupid bottle green blazer. Even better, six weeks in which the only skirt she possessed could stay on its hanger in her wardrobe.

Kelly stuffed the last of her books into her bag, swept the stale crisps and biscuit crumbs out onto the floor with her hand, threw the empty water bottles into the bin and headed outside to join the queue for the bus. With any luck, she would avoid seeing Charlotte, her tutor group's resident bully, and her sidekick Leanne, who followed Charlotte everywhere like an adoring puppy. That was something else Kelly wouldn't miss over the holidays: all those so-called accidents, where Charlotte would knock Kelly's pencil case off her desk, sending her pens skidding across the classroom floor, or bump her arm just as she was pouring her juice in the dinner hall. Nor would she miss Charlotte's pathetic name-calling. *Dirty pikey. Smelly tinker. Thieving gypsy.* They weren't the worst of the insults that had been hurled at Kelly—or muttered under the breath—at one point or another during her first year.

Although she never gave Charlotte the satisfaction of seeing it, the bullying upset Kelly badly. She knew she ought to report it, but she didn't want to draw attention to herself. Instead, when things got bad, she would hide in the toilet and stuff her tie into her mouth to stop the sobs from escaping, or retreat to a far corner of the Learning Resources Centre and duck down behind a PC screen until she could control her urge to cry. The LRC was one room where Kelly knew she was safe. Charlotte never went there. To Charlotte, studying outside of lessons was definitely not cool.

Kelly took her usual seat three rows from the back of the bus: far away from the geeks in the front seats, close enough to the in-crowd at the back to enable her to hear what they were up to, without being in their direct line of fire. Thankfully, the 'cool' kids had stopped staring at her, nudging one another and giggling, a long time ago. Mum had been right about that. 'Don't react, love,' she had said, when she met her off the bus at the end of her first week. 'If you ignore them for long enough, they'll just get bored of it.'

And they had. Kelly spoke to no one and kept herself to herself and her bus journeys became quite tolerable. Kelly wondered how she would have fared if she'd followed her dad's advice. The Hearns had a reputation for being useful with their fists, and Kelly knew that her dad's approach to dealing with someone like Charlotte Kennedy would be physical.

Kelly cooled her forehead on the glass of the bus window and smiled as she pictured the look of surprise on Charlotte's usually smug face if Kelly laid a punch on the end of her podgy, spotty nose. *No*, she thought. *Somehow I don't think that would help. Not unless I wanted a fast ticket to the head's office.*

Kelly had had to stand her ground with her dad about taking the school bus. At first, he had wanted to drive her there and back every day, but Kelly knew that would only give Charlotte an even bigger excuse to tease her. 'No,' she had argued. 'You need to let me do this my way. I have to try and fit in, do what everyone else does.'

In the end they had reached a compromise. Kelly agreed to let her mum meet her off the bus for the first few days, until she settled in. But even that gave some of the other kids something to laugh about. Thankfully, Mum saw how uncomfortable Kelly felt, and soft-talked Dad until he relented and let Kelly walk home from the bus stop unchaperoned.

It wasn't nice being an outsider. It was a lonely place to be, and as she watched the streets of Stratford-upon-Avon make way for the fields and hedgerows lining the lanes leading towards Wilmcote, Kelly felt more than a little sorry for herself. She had found a way to survive school, but after a whole year she hadn't made any friends. The Shakespeare Academy wasn't like any of the primary schools she had been to, where everyone was kind other children didn't seem to care where or how she

 did like her form tutor though. Could she count him as a friend? Yeah, why not? Good old Mr Walker. He was also Kelly's history teacher, and quite early on he had told her that he considered himself a bit of a traveller too. His father had been in the military and had been stationed all over the world so, as a child, Mr Walker had never stayed in one place or at one school for very long. Secretly Kelly thought Mr Walker looked pretty hip, considering he must have been nearly fifty. He rode a motorbike to school and arrived each day clad in black leather, and although he would change before lessons, he always had a slightly greasy, scruffy look about him. Kelly liked that. He wasn't perfect.

The thought of the disapproving looks that some of the other teachers gave Mr Walker when he roared into the school car park on his old motorbike made Kelly snigger, and she shook her head, throwing off her earlier gloominess. After all, what had she expected? She'd known when she started at The Shakespeare Academy that she was going to be the only Traveller in Year 7. She'd known it was going to be tough.

She had fought so hard to get there, too. It hadn't been easy, convincing her parents to let her go on to secondary school. Her elder brother Perry, who was fifteen, hadn't been to school since he was eleven and now worked with their dad in his tree-cutting business. That was the norm in her family. Boys went to work with their dads and girls learned to clean and cook with their mums. That was just the way it was. But Kelly had been determined to carry on with her education—and so had begun a long campaign to convince her parents to let her.

Kelly's mum and dad loved her dearly and it wasn't a case of them wanting to hold her back. It was more that they worried for her, knowing how tough life could be for Travellers who tried to carve a place for themselves in regular society. They had experienced plenty of prejudice in their lifetime and wanted to protect their children as much as they could.

But what finally swung it for Kelly was her final primary school report. 'Dazzling,' her headteacher had called it, arguing that it would be a crime if Kelly did not go on to secondary school. So Kelly's parents gave in, and their daughter's place at The Shakespeare Academy was confirmed.

As the school bus came over the humpbacked railway bridge into Wilmcote and pulled up at her stop, Kelly thought of all the lovely long walks she would have time for over the summer holidays with her dog, Tyson. She hurried to the front of the bus and got off without a backward glance at her schoolmates. She sucked in the fresh air and heard the whoosh of the bus's doors as they closed behind her. Six weeks of freedom had just begun.

Chapter 3 – Summer 1839

The elegant hands on the mantelpiece clock were pointing to half past five when architect Charles Barry swung his legs over the side of the four-poster bed in his room at the Arden Inn. He groped for his boots, feeling on the rug with his toes. Although dawn had not yet fully broken, Barry was wide awake and anxious to get on with the day.

He had arrived in Wilmcote the night before in the company of two of the country's leading geologists and a highly acclaimed stone carver. The men were nearing the end of a four-week tour of England, visiting the six quarries bidding for the contract to supply the building stone for Barry's latest project. One hundred and two quarries had originally been identified, and many months of paperwork and studying rock samples had been devoted to the task of narrowing the shortlist down to six. It was essential that they made the right choice.

It was now three years since Barry had won the commission for what was likely to be the greatest project of his career. It was a venture of such immense scale that it gave him recurring nightmares and stretched his abilities—and his patience—to their limits. But the rewards should be huge and would mean that Barry, his beloved wife Sarah and their six children could live for the rest of their days in luxurious comfort. Barry had no intention of working into his fifties. His eldest son, Edward, was now sixteen and was proving himself to be a brilliant student, with an ability to learn fast and a keen eye for design. He had made clear his wish to become an architect in his father's practice. Confident that the future of his business would be in safe hands, Barry already had retirement in his sights.

The extensive land reclamation and ground works that formed the first part of the project on the Thames in the heart of London were now nearing completion, and the foundations for the building were already being dug. A decision on the limestone, the main construction material, had to be made—and swiftly.

Today's visit to Wilmcote Quarry and Cement Works was the last of their tour, and Barry was looking forward to making his decision, placing his order and moving on to the construction stage. The owner of the quarry, Richard Greenslade, was not expecting Barry and his colleagues until nine o'clock, when he had promised to give them a full tour of the quarry so they could assess the quality of the stone and his company's production capacity, as well as their ability to deliver the material on time.

Barry was always an early riser, needing only four or five hours of sleep a night, and quite used to heading out for an early morning promenade before any of his colleagues had surfaced. He didn't mind at all. For him this was valuable thinking time, when his ideas could flow uninterrupted. Some of his best decisions had been made before breakfast.

He was the only guest up and about when he descended the stairs at the Arden Inn that morning. Putting on his top hat, he slipped quietly out of the front door then paused on the steps of the inn to get his bearings and decide which way to walk.

In the soft, early dawn light, Wilmcote was a peaceful and pretty place. The Arden Inn had pride of place right at the heart of the village, facing a small triangular village green bordered by orchards, a thatched blacksmith's forge and an old Tudor farmhouse. But its rural beauty and tranquillity were lost on Charles Barry. He disliked being away from London and detested the thought of a quiet country life. He preferred the hustle and bustle of the city, and fared far better in a man-made urban architectural landscape than in a rural, natural one.

Barry decided to turn left and, leaving the village green behind him, walked up the main street, following the road between two identical, parallel rows of quarrymen's cottages built from the local stone. He came to a stop when he realised he had, by chance, found the lane which led to the quarry. He glanced at his pocket watch. Six o'clock. There was still time to carry out a bit of reconnaissance before breakfast.

He quickened his pace and headed across the road and up the lane. A couple of minutes later he reached a fork, where a small sign on a rickety wooden gate indicated that the right-hand track went to Stone Pit Cottage. To the left was a wider lane with a larger sign pointing to the quarry and to Stone Pit Farm, which Barry recognised as the home of Richard Greenslade. He followed the latter route and walked on for a few more minutes, enjoying the early morning bird song, until he came to a large, imposing set of metal gates. Unsure whether this was the entrance to the quarry works, Barry hesitated for a second before lifting the latch and passing through. The gate was heavy, and as he let it go, it swung to a close with a loud clang. Undeterred, Barry continued, following the track around the side of a stable building. Then he suddenly realised his mistake. He was standing in the rear garden of Stone Pit Farm house.

'Can I help you, sir?' A gruff male voice from an upstairs window.

'Oh. My apologies. Er, Mr Greenslade is it? I was not intending to disturb you at this early hour. It's Barry. Charles Barry. We are due to meet a little later this morning. I was taking a stroll and I lost my way.'

'Ah, yes. Mr Barry. I am so sorry, I thought you were an intruder. Do excuse me shouting at you like that from my window. Please, let me come down and invite you in.'

Barry held up his hand. 'No, no. No need. We have an appointment for which I am decidedly early. I will come back.'

'No, I insist. You are most welcome here. Please do me the honour of joining me for breakfast—that is, if you haven't breakfasted already?'

Barry smiled. 'No I haven't, and thank you. That would be delightful. How very kind of you.'

* * *

Richard Greenslade had bought Wilmcote Quarry and Cement Works, along with nearby Stone Pit Farm, three years previously. Since then the quarry had gone from strength to strength.

Greenslade was a fair and astute businessman, well-liked by his employees, and highly ambitious for his company's future.

He always kept his ear to the ground for the next business opportunity and so, when he heard that Charles Barry was looking for quality limestone, he had put a proposal forward. He knew he had some way to go to convince Barry of his company's ability to deliver sufficient quantities at speed. So it was crucial that this visit went well.

He hadn't expected to be wearing his undergarments when he first met his potential new client, and he felt embarrassed about suspecting him of being an intruder and verbally accosting him from the bedroom window, so he was determined to redeem himself by making his guest feel welcome in his home.

Dressing as quickly as he could, he dashed downstairs and instructed his housekeeper, Alice, to prepare toast, eggs and bacon and strong fresh coffee, leaving his wife, Florence, to keep their six children out from under their feet. Then he ran to the back door to let Barry in from the garden. He shook Barry's hand a little too vigorously and then led him inside and showed him to a chair at their dining room table.

Helped by a hearty breakfast and several cups of hot, steaming coffee, Greenslade's nerves soon subsided and the two men took a rapid liking to one another. Despite Barry's intimidating reputation and his high social standing, Greenslade found him easy company and surprisingly talkative. He had feared that Barry might look down on him for his lack of airs and graces, but it seemed that his warm welcome and honest, down-to-earth ways were appreciated. Not that Barry came across as anything but tough when it came to business. In that respect, Greenslade sensed that Barry would not suffer fools gladly.

By the time their breakfast things had been cleared away, it was well after eight. Greenslade instructed one of his daughters to call in at the Arden Inn on her way to the village school, leaving a message for Barry's party that he would meet them at the quarry at nine.

So it was that just before nine o'clock the group of five men, with Richard Greenslade in the lead, began their tour of Wilmcote stone pits. The quarrymen had already begun their day's work at the quarry face, and Greenslade gestured to one of them to bring a rock sample up to the pit side to show to his guests.

'You can see straightaway that the stone has a really rich, natural buff colour,' Greenslade said proudly, turning the piece of stone over and over in his large, rough hands.

'Hmm,' said one of the geologists, assuming a non-committal expression. 'It's quite pale compared to the sand-coloured limestone we saw at the Anston Quarry in Yorkshire. We liked that. Their prices were good, too.'

'Well, let me show you what else is so good about *this* stone,' replied Greenslade. 'Follow me, I shall take you to the saw mill.'

Greenslade was keen for Barry and his men to see some of the limestone blocks being cut to make paving slabs. They watched the stonemasons pouring sand and water onto the stones as they were split into perfect sheets, each just a couple of inches thick. Greenslade raised his voice so that he could be heard clearly over the noise, and explained: 'These are going up to Ragley Hall to replace the flooring in the front portico. You'll notice that we've got all the latest equipment. Our saws are powered by our brand new beam engine and you can see how easily the stone splits. It's a natural choice for paving and flooring as it's hard and can be quarried in such big slabs, but it's an excellent general building material. You'll find Wilmcote stone in churches and country houses all over the county and beyond. Bridges too.'

Barry and his party were impressed, particularly when Greenslade showed them the quality of the finish on some of the slabs which were ready to be despatched to Ragley.

'There's no doubt you have a good product, Mr Greenslade,' Barry commented, 'but from what I have seen of your pits and your set up here, you're simply not big enough. Your quarry can't possibly meet an order of the size we're talking about.'

Greenslade's disappointment must have shown itself on his face, for Barry added swiftly, 'But I like you, and I like your limestone. So I will make you an offer. The stone we saw in Yorkshire is relatively cheap and they can supply it in blocks up to four feet thick so it lends itself to the kind of elaborate carving we have in mind for the exterior walls. So I'm going to offer them the contract for the main structure. But, unless my colleagues here disagree with me, I'm inclined to offer Wilmcote Quarry the contract for all the flooring, the main staircases and the external paving.'

Barry paused and glanced towards his advisers, who nodded in agreement. 'Now that's a big contract on its own, so you stand to make a lot of money from it, if you can serve us well.'

'That will not be a problem,' said Greenslade, smiling, unable to conceal his pleasure.

Barry held up his hand to signal that he had not yet finished. 'But I have one more concern.'

'Whatever it is, you know I will do my utmost to allay it,' Greenslade assured him, taking a step forward. 'I can promise you, Mr Barry, we will give you the finest floors you ever did see.'

'I am sure you will. But your challenge will be speed and efficiency. Your stone will need to be delivered to us in phases, towards the end of each main construction stage. So I will be requesting different quantities each time and you will need to fulfil each order pretty quickly. I might require some of your masons to work on site too, now and again, perhaps at short notice. Now, a lot of quarries already have the advantage of a railway link. You don't, and I remain to be convinced that your business will cope with the added demands of this contract as long as you are still transporting by canal alone.'

'But that will change,' replied Greenslade, a tiny note of desperation in his voice. He couldn't let this contract slip away from him. 'There's talk of a new railway. A branch line, linking Stratford-upon-Avon to Hatton. Once that's built Wilmcote will be linked to the main Birmingham to Oxford line, and from there into London.'

Barry raised his eyebrows and rubbed his chin as he took in this piece of news. 'Talk, you say? How certain is it that the line will be built?'

Greenslade shrugged. 'It will be dependent upon the speed at which the Stratford-upon-Avon Railway Company can get the Act of Parliament they require. I am aware that they are still looking for some additional financial investment, but I believe that once they have the funding in place, they are ready to put a proposal to the Member of Parliament.'

Barry nodded. 'I want you to speak with the railway company as a matter of urgency. Tell them what impact this deal could have on your business and on employment in this area. Trust me, the rail company will find it a lot easier to get the financial backing and a charter from Parliament if they can demonstrate a clear need for the branch line.'

Greenslade was about to speak but Barry once again held up his hand. 'And if your MP doesn't move fast enough, let me know. I have contacts—people who can help remind the Members that this decision could influence how soon they will find themselves sitting cosily in brand new chambers. I am sure they will see the need for a new branch line, then, don't you?'

Greenslade smiled. 'Quite right, Mr Barry. Your offer of support is most appreciated. But I would need a signed contract from you before I could argue my case to the rail company with any force.' He could tell that Barry was impressed by his tenacity, so he dared push his luck a little further. 'And if it will help to show my commitment to the project, I would be happy to invest in the railway myself. That might hurry things along a little, also.'

'You are absolutely right, my good fellow,' said Barry, holding out his hand, 'and I believe that I can trust you to make this all happen. If *you* are happy, then *I* am happy. I think we should shake on it, don't you?'

Chapter 4 – August 2012

Kelly's optimism about the fun that her summer holidays would bring didn't last. By week four, she was bored out of her skin. Not having to face Charlotte Kennedy every day didn't outweigh having to stay around the site with little else to do but help her mum clean the caravan. Kelly missed the stimulation of school and, even though she had no real friends there, at least she was among people of her own age. There was no one over the age of seven left on the site to keep her company. Everyone, including her brother Perry, had gone travelling for the summer.

In the past, Kelly and her mum and dad would have gone too, but this year was different. Her dad and his partner had won the contract to clear the railway embankment along the line between Stratford-upon-Avon and Hatton which ran right through Wilmcote. There were some big trees to fell and others to lop, plus about ten miles of hedges and overgrown banks to maintain. It was a steady contract, with the prospect of more railway work if they did well. It was good money, too, as well as being convenient. Their Traveller site was on the road just outside Wilmcote, set apart from the village by farmland, and was right on the side of the railway—so the morning commute was an easy one.

After helping her mum in the mornings, Kelly's afternoons were her own. To keep herself entertained, she went on long walks with her dog, Tyson, a stray who had wandered into the campsite earlier that year. Kelly had found him sitting on the caravan step when she came home from school. He wasn't wearing a collar and no one had any idea where he had come from, but he latched onto Kelly straight away and followed her everywhere. Kelly's dad reckoned that he was only about a year old, and probably a cross between a Jack Russell and a Staffordshire Bull Terrier.

Whatever his background, Tyson was a spirited little mutt. He wasn't very sociable, so Kelly had to be careful to keep him on the lead when other dogs were around, and he didn't like people very much, either. Tyson was fine with folk he knew—soft as putty, in fact—but he would growl, curl up his lips and show his teeth at strangers, especially anyone he thought could be a threat to Kelly.

It was this feisty nature that led to the name Tyson. 'It's a good fighter's name,' Kelly's dad had said, though he was referring to the British boxer Tyson Fury, who had good Irish Traveller blood in him, rather than the American Mike Tyson.

Tyson's fiery temperament brought Kelly a lot more freedom than she otherwise might have had to go out and about on her own. As long as she took Tyson with her, Kelly's mum and dad were happy that she would be safe.

One particularly hot afternoon, Kelly was walking along the canal that curved gently around the outskirts of Wilmcote village before straightening up to tumble down a long series of locks that led in the direction of Stratford-upon-Avon. Tyson was off the lead and was cheekily chasing all the ducks into the water. About half a mile out of Wilmcote, they reached a crossroads where a footpath crossed the towpath and led up to a footbridge over the railway line, which ran parallel to the canal.

Kelly was just wondering which way she felt like going when a rabbit shot out of the long grass on the canal bank, almost ran over her toes and raced across the grass to her left towards the railway. Tyson set off in hot pursuit.

'Tyson!' Kelly shouted sharply, but the little dog was having too much fun to stop. 'Tyson, no! Leave!'

The rabbit reached the hedge that ran along the top of the railway embankment and, with a flash of its little white tail, scurried through the nettles and brambles and disappeared from sight.

'Don't you follow him!' Kelly called out, running through the grass after her dog. 'Tyson! Stop!'

It was too late. Kelly's commands fell on deaf ears as Tyson, tail held high in the chase, disappeared through the hedge after his prey.

Panic rose in Kelly's chest and her throat tightened so that the next time she called Tyson's name it came out as a squeak. The hedge was far too thick to see through, so she had no idea how far Tyson had gone or whether he had run onto the track. 'Oh, you stupid dog,' she muttered through gritted teeth, her fear mixed with frustration.

Desperate to see where Tyson was, Kelly raced along the hedge to the footbridge and looked over the side. Relief flooded through her. There he was. Thank goodness, he had stopped. 'Tyson. Come here, now!' she called.

But Tyson didn't budge. With his tail wagging furiously and his nose down to the ground, he was frantically pawing at the stones next to the track. At first, Kelly was horrified, thinking that he had caught the rabbit, but then she realised that whatever he was sniffing at was definitely not alive. It looked like something buried in the ground.

Kelly's panic returned. She knew how determined her companion could be and knew that he wouldn't give up his mini excavation until he had unearthed his prize. What if a train came?

Kelly looked up and down the track. She couldn't see anything coming but behind her the line curved around a hill, so if a train was approaching from the Stratford-upon-Avon direction, she wouldn't be able to see it anyway. And what was that noise? Was that the rumble of a train in the distance?

Kelly looked back at Tyson and shouted his name again, but he was still pawing away at the ground, stopping every few seconds to tug furiously at the object before resuming his dig.

The distant rumble began to pick up a rhythm. A stomach-churning pattern of metal rattling along lengths of track.

'Oh my God, Tyson!' Kelly screamed, tears forming in her eyes. She felt helpless. She knew she couldn't reach him through the hedge, and climbing over the bridge would be suicide. In desperation she looked for something to throw. If she could startle and distract him, perhaps she could make the stubborn little dog move.

Louder now. The oncoming train sounded like it was just round the bend.

Scrabbling around on the ground, Kelly's fingers closed around a stone. She threw, letting out a desperate sob as it bounced off the rail and over to the far side of the track. Tyson didn't even notice.

Kelly quickly found a second rock and lifted her arm to take aim, the approaching train now terrifyingly loud. 'Tyson!' She let out one final scream and drew her arm back. But before she made her throw, she saw Tyson stagger backwards as the object of his obsession popped out of the ground. Then, as if nothing at all unusual had happened, Tyson gripped the object in his mouth, and trotted triumphantly back up the embankment, his chin in the air.

Kelly raced down from the footbridge just in time to see Tyson emerge from the bottom of the hedge, proudly carrying his prize. He stopped and sat down, dropping the object at his feet just as the train thundered past.

Kelly ran up to him, tears streaming down her face. 'What were you doing, you stupid little dog?' she cried, swooping him up into her arms. 'You scared the life out of me. I thought you were going to get killed!'

Tyson's little body wriggled in Kelly's arms as he wagged his tail happily and licked her face.

Kelly wiped away her tears with the back of her hand and looked down to see what it was that had nearly cost her beloved Tyson his life.

There on the ground was nothing but a soil-covered, mangled old leather boot.

'Is that all it was?' she asked in exasperation, as she put Tyson back down on the ground. 'What on earth did you want that for?'

Tyson looked up at Kelly expectantly, still panting from his adventure. His tongue hung out and his tail swept from side to side on the grass.

'You can wag your tail all you like,' said Kelly. 'I think you've had enough fun for one day.' She bent down to put the dog back on the lead. 'Come on, let's go home.'

She turned, ready to head back to the towpath but Tyson had other ideas. He dug his feet into the ground and refused to budge.

'What?' asked Kelly.

Tyson looked down at the boot.

'Surely you don't expect me to take that home?' She tugged on the lead. 'Come on!'

This time, Tyson did spring to her heel, but not before he had picked up the boot with his teeth.

'Oh, for heaven's sake!' Kelly shook her head in disbelief.

The boot was half as big as Tyson, but the little dog insisted on carrying, or dragging, it across the grass. Kelly had to admit he looked hilarious, and by the time they had reached the gravel path again, she had taken pity on him.

'Oh, go on then, if it matters so much,' she sighed, as she took the boot from Tyson's mouth and tucked it under her arm. 'You know you can always win me over, don't you?'

Chapter 5 – August 2012

That evening, Kelly was sitting outside the caravan, helping her mum to peel the potatoes for tea. Exhausted from his adventure by the railway, Tyson was stretched out in the shade of his kennel, tied to a hook on a long lead. There was still plenty of warmth in the evening sun so lots of people were outside and there was a happy and contented bustle around the site as families prepared and enjoyed their evening meals, or relaxed while their small children played. As Kelly's mum chopped the peeled potatoes and dropped them into a pan of water, she hummed along to a Take That track playing on her iPod inside the caravan. She was about to launch whole-heartedly into the chorus of 'Rule The World' when she and Kelly heard Dad's Nissan Navara coming through the gate.

'Here's your dad,' said Mum, getting up out of her chair. 'Better get these potatoes on. He'll be hungry.'

Kelly smiled and waved at her dad as he got out of the four-wheel drive.

'Hi, love!' he piped cheerfully. 'Good day?'

'Well, it was interesting.' She gave him a kiss as he bent over her before flopping down in the chair Mum had just vacated. 'How was yours?'

'Good.' He wiped his sweaty hands on his jeans. 'Bloomin' hot and sticky but we're making good progress. We've cleared all along the track up the slope from Stratford-upon-Avon and we're not far from here now. We're working near that hill where the track bends round before the final stretch into Wilmcote station. I reckon we'll be finished by the end of September if we keep going at this rate.'

Just then, Mum appeared at the caravan door holding two ice-cold beers in her hand. She came over to greet her husband and handed him one of the bottles.

'Ooh thanks, love. I've been dreaming of this all afternoon.'

Mum chinked bottles with him then went back inside, taking her own drink with her.

'You must be working just round the bend from where I was with Tyson today,' said Kelly. 'I was on the footbridge. You know? The one you have to cross to join the canal towpath, the other side of the station.'

Dad nodded as he took a long swig from his beer bottle. 'So what was so interesting about it, then?' he asked, smacking his lips. 'You said your day was interesting. That makes a change from the usual moans about how bored you are.'

Kelly told Dad about Tyson, the rabbit, and his close escape.

'Well, good for you for not trying to follow him,' praised Dad. 'You hear crazy stories about people getting into trouble trying to rescue their dogs. People walking out onto frozen lakes and falling through the ice and drowning, that kind of stuff.'

'I know. But you can understand it though, Dad. I was so scared. I thought he was going to get hit by that train.'

'Well, keep him on the lead in future. Unless you're one hundred per cent sure he can't go anywhere he shouldn't.'

'I know. I will.'

They both fell silent while Dad drained the rest of his beer and wiped his mouth with the back of his grimy hand. 'That didn't touch the sides, that didn't. It's thirsty work, clearing that embankment in this heat. Anyway, what did you say it was that Tyson dug up?'

'I'll show you.'

Kelly jumped up and ran over to Tyson to retrieve the mouldy old boot which he had been lying with, protectively, ever since he came home. She sat back down next to her dad, holding it out in front of her, and turning it over and over in her hands.

'Why on earth would you let him bring that home?' asked Mum, as she came out to join them. 'It's just a mucky old work boot. Don't you think about bringing it inside my caravan, will you?'

'I didn't intend to bring it home at all,' replied Kelly. 'But Tyson wouldn't come without it.'

'You spoil that dog,' moaned Mum.

'Well, dogs love leather chews, don't they?' laughed Dad, nudging Kelly's arm with his elbow. 'I guess that's, like, the crème de la crème of dog chews!'

Kelly chuckled. 'Ha ha. Good one, Dad. We sure know Tyson's always liked the smell of sweaty old feet, don't we? Just think of all those times when he's licked the sweat from between your toes when you've had your socks off.'

The two of them laughed loudly while Mum turned her nose up in disgust. When she'd finally stopped giggling, Kelly peered inside the boot again.

'For goodness sake, put it down!' cried Mum. 'It's filthy! You don't know who's had their foot in there.'

'Actually, I think it's really old.' Kelly was trying to peel back the tongue, which was stiff with mud and fused in place. 'I mean, it could be Victorian or something.'

'Nah,' said Dad. 'It's probably just made to look old.'

'Maybe. Perhaps there's a label inside. I'm going to clean it and see if I can see anything that might give me a clue.'

Mum shook her head in disbelief as she watched her daughter head off to fetch an old washing-up bowl.

Kelly brought out a kettle and filled the bowl with some warm soapy water. She used a sponge to gently clean all the mud and silt from the boot. It took quite a time, and a couple of changes of water, but eventually the leather began to regain some of its original colour and started to soften so that Kelly could open it up and have a good look inside the boot. She could see where there had been an imprint in the leather sole on the inside, but it was far too faint to make out clearly.

'I definitely don't think this is a modern boot, you know, or even a replica of an old-fashioned one. I think it is old,' she said to her dad as he returned from his shower, rubbing his hair with a towel. 'It's not that big, either. I don't think the owner could have been very tall.'

'It still just looks like a smelly old boot to me,' said Mum. 'What on earth is the fascination with it?'

Kelly couldn't answer that straight away. It puzzled her too. But there was certainly something about the boot that fascinated her. Something that made the hairs tingle on the back of her neck.

'I guess I'm just curious to know whose foot it might once have been on. It might have belonged to one of the old steam train drivers, or one of the men who built the railway in the first place. When was our line built, Dad? Was it Victorian?'

Dad laughed. 'Don't ask me, love. History's not my thing. I never learned to read and write at school, let alone learn all those dates and boring old facts. I'd be interested to know if your boot was worth something, though. You sometimes hear on the news about people digging up old coins and daggers, and ancient Roman sandals and all that, don't you? They must be worth something. So you never know, Kel. You might have struck lucky there!'

'Don't be ridiculous,' scoffed Mum. 'I think the sun's gone to both your heads. Anyway, supper's ready. Come inside, both of you.'

Mum was probably right and the boot was unlikely to be anything special, but somehow Kelly couldn't bring herself to throw it away. Quickly, she climbed up the ladder attached to the back of the caravan and slid the boot onto the roof where it could dry off safely in the sun. At least Tyson wouldn't get hold of it up there, and when it was dry she could add the boot to her treasure chest under her bed.

Although it was only a cheap plastic toy crate with a clip-on lid, Kelly's treasure chest was full of special objects—things she had found, been given or collected, which had taken on special meaning to her. Tucked into a corner was one of Uncle Dave's old Rizla tobacco tins, still secreting its vanilla-sweet scent, in which Kelly kept a small collection of old buttons. Her favourite was one of Nana's old cardigan buttons. It was navy blue with gold patterned edging and Kelly always thought that it looked royal in some way, as if it belonged on the robe of a king or queen. Then there was the sparkly butterfly hairclip that Dad had bought her when she was tiny and which she had dreamed once belonged to a fairy princess, and an old piece of glass, worn smooth by the weather, which Kelly had spied poking out of the soil on their campsite near Malvern. It had a beautiful aquamarine colour and was oval in shape. Finally, tucked among this random collection of odds and ends were some old family photographs and an envelope of used tickets and receipts from places Kelly and her family had visited.

Everything in the chest had a story and, as Kelly went inside for her supper, she wondered what the story of the old boot might be. One day, perhaps, she could tell it.

Chapter 6 – 2 February 1852

It was a cold, stormy, winter evening and the fireplace in the study in Sir Charles Barry's London home on Clapham Common was stacked high with logs. The fire crackled and roared as the high winds sucked the flames up the chimney. But even the heat of the raging blaze did little to soothe the tension in Sir Charles' tired, aching body.

He was working late, as usual, having headed back to his study immediately after supper, asking his wife Sarah to excuse him from her company while he tied up a few loose ends from the day. How ridiculous that was, he thought to himself as he uttered those words. He wasn't sure he would ever tie up all the loose ends on this project. They were more like gaping holes.

What had first been an enviable prize had turned into a burdensome weight around Barry's neck. His designs for the new Palace of Westminster had been chosen as the favourite from ninety-seven entries, submitted by top architects from all over the world, so the news that he had won the commission had left him bursting with pride. Now, six years beyond his original target completion date, Barry felt suffocated by the pressure of it all and wrung out by the challenge of overcoming one unexpected setback after the next, and answering to so many masters. Lately, even Prince Albert had begun to take an interest in the building by chairing the committee which vetted the choice of sculptures and paintings. While the support of such an important figure was flattering, the Prince's involvement meant there was yet another voice to listen to, another body of opinion to be seen to consult.

And the pressure was mounting. Tomorrow was the official state opening by Her Majesty the Queen. Preparing for the event had been a living nightmare. Although the House of Lords and the House of Commons were both now in use, large sections of the building were still incomplete, with months if not years of interior work still to come. Barry and his team had spent the last few weeks focusing on the route that the Queen would take through the building, making sure that royal eyes would not see a single bare wall, unpainted ceiling, or even the tiniest speck of dust. His team had done a marvellous job of preparing those rooms, but Barry still felt like a reluctant party host, caught out by guests arriving too early.

Not that he was in the mood for a party. How could he be, when just one month before he had buried his dear friend and partner, Augustus Pugin? An esteemed designer, Pugin had worked with Barry successfully many times in the past and had proven himself to be an unsurpassable talent. Over the years, the two men had formed a firm friendship, and Barry's affection and admiration for his friend was summed up by the nickname he chose for him: Pugin was his Comet.

The shared stresses and strains of the Westminster project had cemented the two men's friendship, but what Barry loved most about Pugin—his attention to detail and quest for impossible perfection—had been the poor chap's undoing. Achieving perfection on the interiors of a building as large as the Houses of Parliament had proved impossible. Pugin's vision had been compromised all too often and the project had driven his sensitive soul quite mad. In a state of high stress and fragile health, Pugin had finally been admitted to Bedlam, the huge asylum for the insane in Southwark, and had died there before the month was out. Grief at the loss of his friend, and the fact that he felt partly to blame, lay heavily on Barry's mind.

Barry bent over his desk and studied the latest drawings for the Members' Lobby on which he had pencilled some of the most recent amendments. His eyes were scratchy and sore and, in the gloomy evening light, he struggled to read the tiny notes that he had scribbled all over the margins during his last site visit.

'Come in,' he croaked, as he heard a gentle knocking on the door. It was his wife, carrying a glass of brandy on a silver tray.

'I thought you might like a little refreshment, my love,' she said softly as she put the tray down on the end of her husband's desk. 'Do you have much more to do? It's getting so late.'

'Oh my dear, I could work through the night and still not complete everything.'

'Well, I simply won't allow it.' Sarah placed her hand tenderly on top of her husband's. 'Tomorrow is a day to celebrate what you have achieved. You should enjoy it and be proud, and to do that you need a good night's sleep.'

Barry had aged at a frightening rate since the construction of the Palace began and Sarah had nursed him through long bouts of illness. Although she tried to keep his home life free from worry and stress, she could not protect him from events beyond their door. The rush to prepare for the state opening, Pugin's death, and even his recent knighthood had added layer upon layer of pressure upon him.

'The work doesn't stop when the building is officially opened, Sarah,' snapped Barry, then immediately felt bad for taking his frustration out on his wife. Sarah flinched at his abrupt tone but did not move from his side.

'It became necessary to change the dimensions of the Members' Lobby,' Barry explained, pointing to his drawings. 'So we have had to alter the size of the floor slabs also. Each one needs to be a few inches smaller or we won't be able to lay them without cutting them. Normally that wouldn't matter, but on a project like this, everything has to be just so. Only whole slabs will do. It might sound like an insignificant change but it has resulted in a delay at the quarry in Wilmcote—and their deliveries are still coming by canal, which means a further wait. I need the new slabs right away.'

'But did you not say that there was to be a new railway line through Wilmcote? I thought that was all part of the original agreement?' Sarah enquired.

'It was indeed,' said Barry. He looked his wife directly in the eye. 'Sarah, I apologise, but there is something I have not shared with you. I invested some money in the railway company too—our money—to speed the whole thing along. They needed £150,000 for a charter, and I gave them a significant sum towards it. Our friend Sir Francis invested too—as did the quarry owner, Richard Greenslade, so I can't hold him responsible for the delay. But we all underestimated how the waterways company would respond to the threat from the new railway. Holding the keys to the quarry's only existing transport route, the owners of the Stratford-upon-Avon canal had a lot of power to wield. So they launched one appeal after the next.'

'I suppose one can't blame them for trying to protect their business,' remarked Sarah.

'No, but they have become a thorn in my side. I should have given the flooring contract to a quarry that already had rail links.'

'Is it too late to change? Could you get the Yorkshire quarry to take over the whole contract, perhaps?'

'Unfortunately, that's not possible. Even if we did terminate the contract with Wilmcote, there is a difference in the colour of the stone. It is far paler than the sand-coloured stone from Anston Quarry. And my goodness, Pugin would turn in his grave if he thought that his floors wouldn't all match perfectly.'

Barry sighed. 'Anyway, I have sunk too much money into the Wilmcote deal to back out now. No, I shall have to fall back on Sir Francis and his political contacts if I am going to make that railway happen soon.'

Sarah smiled at her husband. 'I am sure you will succeed, my dear. I have every confidence in you. But you also need to look after yourself and to do that you need sleep. So promise me, no more than half an hour more.'

Barry nodded at his wife. Kind, gentle, sweet-natured Sarah. It would break his heart to let her down.

Chapter 7 – August 2012

It was Sunday morning, and Kelly had just finished her morning chores. She had been helping her mum to wash all the lace curtains, which had to be done outside by hand as they were so delicate, and she was now pegging them out on the washing line to dry. It was a perfect day for the job, as the sun was shining and there was a warm, gentle breeze. The curtains would be fresh and dry and back up at the windows in no time.

Tyson, whose lead was looped around the washing line pole, was watching Kelly avidly, yet every now and then he was unable to resist the urge to jump up and snap at a passing fly. As Kelly bent down to take the last curtain from the washing basket, Tyson caught her eye and wagged his tail hopefully, knowing that it was almost time for his walk.

Kelly decided to take him down the road into Wilmcote to the village shop where she planned to buy her favourite magazine.

'You can have a run in the playing field after. As long as there are no dogs about,' she whispered to Tyson, as she put him on his lead.

The two of them set off down the lane that led to the main road into the village. About a quarter of a mile on, the road crossed first the railway and then the canal. The village centre, with its small green, shop and pub, the Mary Arden Inn, was straight ahead, but when she reached the kissing gate that led onto the canal-side, Kelly automatically turned and headed down the slope onto the towpath. She was about a hundred metres along before she realised what she had done.

'Oh!' She stopped in her tracks, looking down at Tyson by her side. 'I didn't mean to come this way. I wanted to go to the shop. Must be force of habit, from last time we came.'

Tyson was panting happily, his tongue lolling out of the side of his mouth. He looked like he was smiling.

'You little monkey. You didn't stop me, did you? I reckon you wanted to come this way. Oh well, we might as well carry on now. We can cross the canal at the next bridge and circle round into the village from that direction. I'll pick up my magazine on the way back.'

They carried on. Tyson was pulling at the lead, desperate to charge at three fat little ducks sitting on the grass at the side of the water. 'Sorry, mate,' said Kelly, reining him in. 'Not today. After what happened last time, I'm keeping you on a lead. It's your own silly fault!'

After a few minutes, they reached the spot where the footpath from the village crossed the towpath and went on over the railway bridge. Kelly glanced to her left towards the footbridge, and noticed a boy standing exactly where Kelly had when she had been calling to Tyson.

The boy was staring down at the track, but he must have sensed Kelly's presence, because he turned his face towards her and smiled. Kelly half nodded and raised her hand to acknowledge him. She was about to turn right to carry on towards the village when Tyson, who had been sniffing around at the base of a tree, suddenly noticed the boy too, and nearly yanked Kelly's arm out of its socket in an effort to reach him.

'Tyson!' Kelly cried. 'Don't pull me like that!'

But Tyson seemed desperate to get to the stranger and, equally desperate not to let go of the lead, Kelly had to let the little dog drag her along the path and up onto the bridge.

'I'm so sorry,' she panted, as Tyson put his front paws up on the boy's trousers, leaving two muddy streaks down his knee. 'I think he just wants to say hello.'

The boy, who was wearing a dark green checked shirt tucked into his now filthy brown trousers, laughed and bent down to tickle Tyson behind his ears. 'It's fine, really. I like dogs. He's a friendly little chap, isn't he? What's his name?'

'Tyson,' said Kelly. 'Like the boxer.' The boy looked blank. This was when Kelly usually had to explain that it was Tyson *Fury* not *Mike* Tyson, but as the boy didn't offer any comment, she quickly moved on. 'He's not usually this friendly with strangers. He can be a bit of a fighter.'

'I find that hard to believe,' the boy said with a laugh, as Tyson sat down in front of him and held up a paw as if wanting to shake hands.

Kelly thought what a nice face the boy had. He looked friendly and kind, and when he laughed his blue eyes twinkled. That, combined with his fair hair, which flopped softly about his face, gave him an altogether angelic look.

'I'm Kelly, by the way.'

'And I'm B…Ben.' The boy briefly stumbled over his name.

Kelly wondered if he had a stutter, so to try to put him at his ease, she made a little joke. 'Ben and Kelly.' She laughed. 'Sounds a bit like Ben and Jerry.'

Ben looked at her, clearly confused.

'You know, Ben and Jerry's? The ice cream? I just thought… oh, never mind. Ignore me.' Ben must think she was bonkers. She quickly changed the subject. 'I haven't seen you around here before. Are you local?'

'Yes. My family has a cottage on Stone Pit Farm, out on the other side of the village.'

'Oh,' said Kelly, surprised. 'It's funny I've not bumped into you before, then. Tyson and I come out walking every day. I think I've been past that farm and I come up the canal quite a bit.'

'Well, you wouldn't have seen me here before. I'm not supposed to be here, you see. I mean—my mother would go mad if she knew I was anywhere near the railway.'

'Yeah, they're not the safest places to hang about. I'm with you there,' snorted Kelly, leaning against the side of the bridge. 'I nearly lost Tyson here the other day.' She told Ben all about the rabbit and the boot, and how Tyson had come very close to being hit by a train. 'I was so relieved to get him back,' she finished. 'He climbed back up that embankment just in time.'

Ben gave Tyson a pat on the head. 'You're a clever dog, aren't you?' he cooed. 'You knew exactly what you were doing.'

'So why *are* you here?' enquired Kelly, as she looked down at the top of Ben's head, covered in gentle golden waves.

'I'm waiting for a train.'

'Then you're in the wrong place.' Kelly pointed in the direction of the Wilmcote road. 'The station's back down there, don't you know?'

Ben gave her a sarcastic look. 'Yes, I know. I'm not daft. No, I mean I'm waiting to *see* a train.'

'You're in luck. There's a steam train that comes though roundabout now on a Sunday. The Shakespeare Express. Should be here any minute.'

Kelly was happy to stay and watch with Ben. He seemed nice and, although she had heard the whistles of the steam train passing through at the weekend, she had never been there at the right time to see it.

As they waited, they chatted some more. Ben explained that there was something about trains that fascinated him.

'Is that why you risk getting into trouble to see them?' asked Kelly.

'I suppose so.'

Kelly sympathised, since her parents could be over-protective too. When she told him that her dad was working on the railway, Ben looked startled.

'What's he doing? Laying track?'

'No,' said Kelly, giggling. 'He's clearing the embankment. He does landscape work. Tree surgery and all that. He's clearing the vegetation and overhanging trees along the line up from Stratford-upon-Avon.'

'Oh, I see,' said Ben. 'Yes, I suppose it *has* got a little overgrown, hasn't it? You know, being the summer and all that.'

They carried on chatting until they could hear the rumble of the approaching steam train.

'You might want to pick Tyson up,' Ben advised. 'The bridge isn't half going to rattle when it passes underneath. He might get scared and bolt off again.'

Kelly scooped Tyson up and hugged him close to her chest. She could see the engine coming round the bend now, its grey-white smoke leaving a trail like cotton wool in the air.

Louder now, and Kelly noticed how white Ben's fingers were, as he gripped the railing of the bridge. He was obviously holding on tight.

'This is the scary part,' he shouted, as the noise grew deafeningly loud.

Seeing them from the cabin, the engine driver waved and pulled on his whistle, adding to the din. The sheer volume of the noise, and the bone-rattling vibrations, flooded all of Ben and Kelly's senses and left them whooping and screaming with delight.

'Phew! That was fun,' said Kelly, falling into step alongside Ben as they set off together along the towpath back towards the main road, with Tyson trotting happily at their heels. She felt so at ease in her new friend's company that the next few words came out without thinking. 'You know I said that my parents could be a bit over-protective sometimes? Well, that's partly because we're Travellers—'

She stopped. Why had she said that so soon? It was usually at this moment that people walked away, or remembered

51

something they had to do, somewhere they needed to be. But to her relief, all Ben said was, 'What do you mean, travellers?'

Kelly smiled at him. 'You know, *Travellers*, with a capital T. Gypsies. Lots of people don't like us because they don't understand our way of life. They always jump to the wrong conclusions, so they can be a bit unfriendly sometimes. I think my mum and dad worry that I'll be exposed to that kind of thing. Prejudice, I mean. So they wrap me up in cotton wool. Well, they try to.'

'Ah yes, some people can be narrow-minded,' Ben sympathised. 'I suppose your parents are doing it for the right reasons.'

He asked Kelly to tell him some more about her family and where she lived and Kelly explained about their caravan and the permanent site they were staying on, just outside the village.

'So how about you?' she asked, when she had finished. 'Did you say that you live with your mum and dad?'

'Er, yes.' Ben paused and seemed to think, before adding, 'In Stone Pit Cottage. Just me and my mother and father. No one else.'

'So which school do you go to then?'

'Wilmcote.'

'But that's a primary school! You're too old to go there.'

Ben shook his head. 'I mean, I *went* to Wilmcote School. Now I just stay at home. My dad thinks you learn more out of school anyway.'

'You're home educated?' asked Kelly, surprised. Some of the Traveller parents she knew had chosen to home educate their children as it suited their roaming lifestyle but it was the last thing she had expected Ben to say. He looked so ordinary. Traditional somehow. There was something about his manner, and the way he was dressed. He looked like he came from a pretty conventional family.

'Yes, that's it.' Ben stuck out his chin with pride. 'My mother teaches me everything I need to know.'

Kelly let out a tiny giggle, forcing a little air from her nose. 'There's nothing wrong with that at all,' she assured her new friend. 'I just think it's really funny. Here I am, the Traveller, and I go to school whereas you stay at home. No one can say either of us is conventional!'

At that, Ben, who had seemed a little prickly over the subject of school, suddenly seemed to relax. He began to ask Kelly about The Shakespeare Academy. He had so many questions about what it was like there, her teachers, how she got there every day and what lessons she had, that Kelly began to wonder if Ben secretly wished he went there himself.

As they reached the point where the path climbed up the slope to join the main road, Kelly remembered her original plan to go down to the village shop.

'Do you fancy coming to the shop with me?' she asked, silently hoping that Ben would agree. She was enjoying getting to know him. 'I'll buy you an ice cream. Hey, maybe even a pot of Ben and Jerry's!'

Ben smiled and hesitated, as if weighing up his options, but to Kelly's disappointment he announced that he had to get back for Sunday lunch.

'I have to be home on time or I'll be in trouble,' he said, already starting to jog away along the towpath. 'I'd better go this way. It's shorter than going down the road. I can cross the canal further down and cut across fields back to our cottage.'

'Oh, okay.' Kelly knew her voice sounded a little flat.

'I'll see you some time in the next few days, I promise,' shouted Ben, as he picked up his pace.

'Yeah, I'd like that,' Kelly called back. Then she realised that she didn't know how to get in touch with him. 'Wait! Ben!' she yelled, but he couldn't hear her. Jogging along the towpath at quite a pace, he had already put too much distance between them.

Kelly watched his silhouette growing smaller and smaller before finally disappearing from view. Then she looked down at Tyson, who gave a little bark and wagged his tail at her as if to try to cheer her up.

'Come on then, Tyson. Looks like it's just the two of us for ice cream.'

PART 2

Chapter 8 – Summer 1859

After years of wrangling with the canal company, parliamentary approval was finally forthcoming and, by the summer of 1859, the long-awaited Stratford-upon-Avon to Hatton branch line was under construction.

For quarry worker William Denton, the new railway meant a fresh start and a new job—a chance to dust off his pit boots and join the ranks of railway construction workers who preferred to spend their days above ground, rather than down in its muddy depths. William's new job would still involve hard manual labour, but it paid a little more and, away from all the dust, was a little healthier. All that aside, he would do anything to prove to his father-in-law that he was capable of bettering himself, no matter how small a step it was.

As he walked home in the direction of his cottage on the edge of Stone Pit Farm, William passed the time of day with his three workmates, Ted, Lewis and George, all of whom had changed jobs at the same time as him. Exhausted from their hard day's work digging out a section of the new railway cutting, they trudged back into Wilmcote. As they skirted around the edge of Stone Pit Farm, their path crossed one of the tramlines which was still being used to move stone from the quarry to the canal.

'That lot'll move a bit quicker once our job is done,' remarked Ted, nodding his head in the direction of a horse-drawn truck.

'Ay, it will that,' replied William. 'And they don't let us forget it, do they? If that foreman of ours tells me once more how we've got to be all done and dusted by this time next year, I'll wring his neck.'

'Ah, leave him alone,' said George, who always tried to see the best in people. 'He's only doing his job. The top brass are putting pressure on him because old Mr Greenslade at the quarry is sitting on their backs, and the toffs down there in London are leaning on Greenslade. So we're all in the same boat. Everyone's waited a long time for this railway line.'

Whether or not there was a good reason for driving the construction workers so hard, William found the long days tough to deal with. He was usually good for nothing in the mornings, and he'd been late to work a couple of times already. He was worried that if the foreman kept picking on him, he might lose his job and end up, cap in hand, back at the quarry.

* * *

Billy, William's twelve-year-old son, was familiar with his father's grumbles. As they sat down that evening to a supper of mutton stew prepared by his mother Alice, Billy listened to William recount his conversation with his friends.

'I'm fed up of that foreman of ours being on our backs every minute of the day,' he complained. 'We can't work any faster.

I blame that toffee-nosed Sir Charles. He just wants that line completed so he can have his stone floors done faster. They've given him a bloomin' knighthood and he hasn't even finished the building yet. Do you know, Lewis said it's twenty years since Barry came to Wilmcote to visit the quarry? That can't be right, can it? What's he building down there, a palace?'

'Actually I think that's exactly what they are calling it,' said Alice. 'I'm sure it's very grand. And we should give thanks for it. It's helping to put this food on the table.' She reached across to take her husband's hand. 'Hush now. Let's say Grace.'

The instant he finished mumbling 'Amen', William resumed his complaining. 'I heard that Barry is a nightmare to work for. He has a fit if anything goes wrong. No wonder that chap of his...what was his name? Pullen or something.'

'Pugin,' Billy chipped in.

'That's right, Pugin. No wonder he ended up in Bedlam, having to work alongside someone so highly strung. It would drive anyone mad.'

Billy's mother sent her husband a look of disapproval. 'William!' she said sharply. 'Please don't speak so unkindly of others. Besides, you do not know these people well enough to judge them. Let us change the subject or we would be better to eat our supper in silence.'

For a few moments, the only sound in the Dentons' modest little cottage was that of knives and forks scraping on their plates as they ate their stew. Then, keen to lighten the atmosphere, Billy piped up, 'I had an arithmetic test today. I got full marks.'

'That's wonderful, Billy, well done,' said Alice warmly, touching her son on the arm. 'I am so pleased that you stayed on at school.'

'Pah,' snorted William. 'If you ask me, he should have left when he was ten like most of the other lads. He ought to be learning a few real-life lessons by now.'

'Well, he didn't,' snapped Alice. 'Besides, what would you prefer? Would you really rather see him working in the quarry, as most of his old schoolmates are, or getting the education he needs to make something of himself?'

'Make something of himself?' snarled William, pulling a piece of meat out from between his teeth with his fingers. 'You mean, make himself a better man than his father? Is that it? The quarry was good enough for me, but not for your precious son?'

Billy looked down at his plate. 'It's not that, Father. There's nothing wrong with working in the quarry—or on the railway. I admire anyone who does. I just, I want to do something less physical. Use my brain more, if I can.' William said nothing, but Billy could see the hurt in his father's eyes.

Alice tried to reason with her husband. 'You know, Billy is one of the brightest pupils they have ever had at Wilmcote School. It would be such a shame to waste that.'

'I am not saying he should waste it. I'm saying that he's old enough to be out earning a living.'

'Well, he will be, soon enough,' replied Alice. 'He doesn't have long to go at school now.'

'So what are you planning to do when you leave, Billy, if you're too clever for the stone pits?' William put down his knife and fork and looked directly across the table at his son. 'Work in a dingy old office, pushing papers around your desk? Please God, tell me you're not planning on joining the clergy, like your grandfather! One man of God in the family is already more than I can bear.'

Alice pushed her chair back from the table. Its legs scraped loudly on the stone floor and her face flushed red as she got to her feet. 'William, that is enough! Why do you insist on being so hostile? Surely you want the best for your son?'

'Best? What does that mean, Alice?' William was shouting now and he, too, stood up so that he was face to face with his wife. 'All I know is that my best is never good enough—not for you, and certainly not for your holier-than-thou father!'

Alice's jaw dropped as her husband stormed out of the room. Billy heard the front door slam and then the crunch of his boots on the gravel outside as he strode off up the path.

His mother's shoulders dropped. All of the air appeared to drain out of her body, and she crumpled into her chair and stared silently at the uneaten food on her plate, the gravy now cold and congealed.

Billy reached over and took her hand. 'I'm sorry, Mother,' he said softly, fighting back the tears.

'Don't be sorry, Billy. It's not your fault. Your father doesn't mean what he says, you know. He loves you. It's just that he wants so badly to do better by us, to look after us properly, in his own way. He's not a bad man, Billy.'

'I know.' Billy squeezed her hand. 'I just wish he wouldn't fly off the handle like that at you. He does it every time Grandpa's name comes up. I shouldn't say this, but I think Grandpa's a lot to blame. He makes Father feel worthless.'

Alice let go of Billy's hand and moved her plate to one side. She ran her fingers around the circular imprint left behind on the tablecloth as she spoke. 'It's true. My father doesn't think William is good enough for me. But your father works so hard and he does love us both. Grandpa will see that he's a good man in the end, as I did.' She paused and smiled. 'You should have seen your father when I first met him. He was so young and handsome.'

'How did Father persuade Grandpa to let him marry you?' Billy liked to think about his parents being in love, back in happier times. But when he asked the question, his mother suddenly drew herself up in her chair. It was as if a dark curtain fell down across her face.

'You shouldn't ask so many questions, Billy!' she snapped.

'But I was just…'

'I need to clear the table.' Alice spoke over him. 'Fancy us sitting here looking at dirty dishes for all this time. Run along now, I am sure you have schoolwork to do.'

Billy knew better than to keep on pushing. Disappointed, he got up from the table and left the room. What had made his mother change the subject like that? Whatever it was, it was likely to be a long time before he could find out. She rarely spoke of the past.

Picking up his satchel from the hall, he hooked it over his shoulder, and retreated quietly to his room.

Chapter 9 – Summer 1859

William had marched all the way down the path, along the lane and to the main street into Wilmcote before he was able to calm down. With his hands shoved hard inside his trouser pockets and his shoulders hunched, he kicked several stones into the hedge along the way to help vent his rage.

But as he emerged onto the village street, the sight of distant lights in the windows of the Mason's Arms soothed him. As his anger subsided, he became more defiant. Arguments flew round inside his skull. So what if the cottage they lived in belonged to his wife's father? It didn't make him less of a man. And what did it matter if he was only a lowly railwayman? He worked hard for a living and he was the one who put the food on the family table and the clothes on their backs. His father-in-law could go to the devil and take his pompous views with him.

Trust me to have fallen in love with the daughter of a vicar, he mused. Yes, who would have dreamed it? His father-in-law, the Reverend Frederick Knott. William would never forget the look on his face when they had told him that Alice was with child.

William had assured Alice that honesty was the best policy and had persuaded her that they should tell her father of her condition right away. Fair enough, at twenty-two he was five years older than Alice and should have known better, but he was willing to do the right thing now and stand by her. He had hoped that her father would give him credit for that, at least.

But breaking the news had gone even more badly than he had predicted. William had thought that Reverend Knott was going to have a heart attack on the spot. He was left in no doubt that, while the vicar would agree to William marrying his daughter in order to protect her reputation, he would never, ever forgive him.

Nothing that William did was good enough in the eyes of Reverend Knott. The vicar could not bring himself to praise William for anything, instead undermining all of his son-in-law's achievements.

'You have never done anything on your own merit,' he had scoffed at him, over a family lunch the other weekend. 'You only got out of that stone pit and into a job on the railway because of my daughter. They would never have employed you otherwise.'

That had cut to the quick. William had been so proud to be starting a new job. And even if Alice *had* asked her employer, Mr Greenslade, to put in a good word for him with the railway company, he had still had to impress the foreman, who had warned that only the hardest workers would keep their place on his team. William was pleased to be able to bring home a better wage, too. With a son with a growing appetite, who didn't seem in a rush to leave school and help bring in some wages, they had been struggling financially.

William's solution at times like this, when his own failings were paraded so cruelly before him, was to head for the nearest cask of ale and drown his sorrows. That usually meant joining his friends in the warmth of the Mason's Arms, where he would throw back several pints before staggering home and falling asleep in the boxroom in a sweet, soothing stupor.

That evening, when William entered the public house, his three companions, Ted, Lewis and George, were already seated around the fireplace among several other railway workers. On the far side of the bar, like opponents on the opposite side of a chequers board, was a group of pit workers, still grey and grimy from their day at the rock face.

Friendly banter passed between the two sets of drinkers, who nicknamed one another Pitheads and Steamheads.

'Well, look who the cat dragged in!' remarked one of the Pitheads, when he saw William heading for the bar. 'You'd better watch your step, Denton. Don't come any closer or your Steamhead friends'll think you've gone over to the other side. We know how you like to do that, eh? Or do you think you're too good for us, now that you work above ground?'

William shrugged and raised his glass to his challenger. 'Hey, you know me. I'll go anywhere for a good pint of ale.'

The Pitheads laughed. 'Come and join us for a while,' said one, a jolly, round-faced chap who had worked alongside William when he had been at the quarry. 'I want you to meet my son, Gabriel. He's just started in the pit.'

William sat on the end of the bench and the men chatted congenially while they supped their ale. The Pitheads were keen to brag about the vast quantities of stone they had quarried since Christmas and how much had already gone down to London.

'I can't remember a time when we were so busy,' William's old friend told him, 'and it's only going to get worse when that railway of yours opens. We will have a devil of a job to keep up the pace then.'

'Have you heard? That architect, Sir Charles Barry, is going to honour us with his presence again next year for the official opening,' said William. 'Alice told me that he and Greenslade have both sunk their own money into the railway. So I suppose they have their own reasons for wanting the line finished, besides being able to get to London quicker.'

'I remember that Barry chap as clear as a bell,' said one of the older Pitheads, leaning up against the wall in the corner, sucking on his pipe. 'I was working in the pit the day he visited. 1839 it was. He was travelling all over the country looking for the best stone he could find. Mr Greenslade asked me to bring him a rock sample. Barry struck me as quite a decent gentleman. A bit of a toff, in his top hat and shiny boots maybe, but he asked me a fair few questions, about working conditions and the like. Of course, that was before he was made a Sir. I'll wager he wouldn't give me the time of day now he's rolling in luxury.'

William agreed, thinking of someone else he knew who thought himself a cut above the rest. Suddenly he needed another pint.

Chapter 10 – Summer 1859

That evening, Barry was also enjoying a drink, but rather than a mug of ale, his was a crystal snifter of fine French brandy. He was standing in the recently completed office of Sir Francis Throckmorton MP, where the smell of fresh paint and wood varnish still filled the air.

After raising his glass to his friend, Barry took a moment to look around. Although small compared to some of the more impressive rooms, the office was a serene and satisfying place to be, with beautifully carved oak panels on three walls and a velvety flock paper on the fourth. Barry recognised the pattern as one of Augustus Pugin's favourites—a rich colourful design of floral motifs, with red roses and golden daffodils on a pure white background, bordered by navy-blue ribbons edged in gold.

'So we finally got our charter. Our Stratford-upon-Avon branch line is well underway.' Throckmorton smiled knowingly at his friend and fellow shareholder over his glass.

'Yes. By this time next year the line should be fully open,' replied Barry. 'But at what cost? I don't know about you, but I have invested more than I intended and this whole deal has taken far longer to secure than—I think it's fair to say—you led me to believe. I may well see the return on my investment in the railway but I didn't expect to have to help the rail company buy the canal company too! I shan't see a return on that investment, I doubt. The canals are a dying business, if you ask me.'

'Well, it was bound to take time, my good man.' Sir Francis swirled and sniffed the brandy in his glass. 'You can't blame the canal industry for putting up a fight. Their business has been hit hard since the railways came. Like it or not, buying up that stretch of canal was the quickest solution in the end.'

'Indeed, and it will ease at least some of the delays on the build if I can have access to Greenslade's stone—and his masons—at short notice. But it still leaves me with a mighty headache. This project should have made me financially secure yet I fear it has the potential to destroy me.' Barry shook his head and looked down into his glass. 'It certainly causes me plenty of worry. I can see myself heading for Bedlam, like my poor old friend, Pugin.'

'I am sure you exaggerate, Sir Charles. But speaking of funds, how's the bottom line looking on this project?'

'Disastrous. Do you really want to know?'

'Well, I can help to keep the wolves from your door more easily if I know what I'm defending. You realise I can put in a good word for you in Parliament.'

Barry sat, as if the financial burden was physically weighing him down. 'I won the bid based on an estimated project cost just short of £725,000.' He paused and looked Throckmorton in the eye. 'At the latest review, we are already over £2 million.'

'Hell's teeth, Sir Charles!' Throckmorton swallowed hard.

Barry reminded Throckmorton of the delays and huge additional expense caused by the problems with ventilation. After the fire that had destroyed the original building in 1834, Barry had been asked to ensure that the building could breathe properly. He had, on Parliament's advice, been required to bring in a ventilation expert, who had amended his drawings to include a 300-foot high tower above the Central Lobby. The tower would act as a chimney, the expert had assured him, drawing up stale air and allowing it to escape through vents in its spire. But his design didn't take into account the direction in which the stale air would flow. MPs constantly complained about the cooking smells and the dreadful reek of manure that wafted by from the kitchens and nearby stables. As a result, Barry was forced to find another solution—and another ventilation expert.

'Then there was the problem with the bells for the Clock Tower,' Barry added. 'Do you recollect? The casts kept cracking. The workshop had never had to make anything of that size before. Then of course I had to find a solution to stop the limestone on the outer walls from decaying in all the blessed London smog. All these things have all added up, you know. Not that any excuse seems to wash with the Treasury. You're aware that they are trying to cut my fees, I suppose?'

Sir Francis remained silent.

'They are refusing to pay anything beyond the fees I originally quoted—but those were based on a six-year project time span. Next year it will be twenty years since we laid that first foundation stone, but no one can blame me for over-running this far. It's not fair that I should be so heavily penalised.'

'Yes, yes, I know. I understand. And other people will too, Sir Charles, I will do my best to make sure of that. Besides, name me an architect who could have done this any quicker.'

'Thank you, Sir Francis. I am for ever in your debt,' said Barry, raising his glass to the MP.

Throckmorton inclined his head slightly in acknowledgement, then added, 'But take my advice as a friend, Sir Charles. If there is even the slightest chance that something else could go wrong, particularly if it could place you in even deeper financial difficulties, then you have to start putting some insurance policies into place—and fast.'

'What do you mean?' Barry asked.

'Protect your investments where you can. Tell the chairman of the railway company that we will both withdraw our support if the branch line is not open within the next twelve months. And by that I mean financial support, of course. Look out the time clause in the contract and threaten to use it. And make sure you tell that quarry owner that he won't get a penny more until you have every last piece of stone that you need from his quarry.'

Barry's thoughts went back to that morning, all those years ago, when he had taken breakfast in Richard Greenslade's dining room. Greenslade was a good, honest man. Barry liked him, and he was aware that Greenslade had almost as much at stake in this whole railway line affair as he did. But Throckmorton was right. Barry had to protect himself, for Sarah and the children's sake, if nothing else. Yes. He would have to start making some ultimatums.

Chapter 11 – August 2012

During the days that followed Kelly's Sunday morning encounter with Ben, she returned to the railway bridge several times on her walks with Tyson, hoping that she might bump into her new friend again. But so far there was no sign of him. She had walked along the canal in the other direction too, to see if she could work out the route he had taken back to his cottage. She remembered him saying that it was on Stone Pit Farm, on the other side of the village, but she wasn't sure where that particular farm's land started and finished, so she didn't really know where to begin looking.

By Friday, she had pretty much given up, and decided that it was about time she took Tyson somewhere he could have a good long run off the lead. She took the footpath that led south from the caravan site and crossed first over the railway, then over the canal, by way of a narrow old stone bridge, before winding its way through some woods and out onto open farmland.

There were no sheep or cattle out in the fields that day so she let Tyson off the lead and ambled along happily, while he ran in mad circles through the long grass. Every few seconds Tyson's head would pop up above the level of the grass as he jumped up like a kangaroo to check where Kelly was.

It was a lovely warm sunny day. Kelly took off the denim shirt that she had on over her strappy T-shirt and tied it round her waist, as she and Tyson followed the footpath up the hill and along the edge of a wheat field. It wouldn't be long before the farmer would be out there harvesting. The wheat had already turned an even, pale gold colour, and Kelly could hear it popping and crackling in the heat.

In the corner of the field the path ran along the side of an overgrown copse, roughly fenced off with two strings of barbed wire suspended between wooden posts. Then it turned sharply on a ninety degree angle to follow the trees up towards a small gate into a meadow. It looked as though the ground inside the copse fell sharply downwards, forming a deep bowl in the earth, like a crater. As Kelly walked, she peered between the gaps in the vegetation, trying to make out what was on the other side of the fence line.

Just after she had passed through the gate into the meadow, she spotted a bigger gap in the bushes. A fence post had come loose in the ground and was leaning at an awkward angle, while the wire fence was bent down, as if someone had climbed over it. She glanced behind to check on Tyson and saw him happily sniffing around in the meadow. He had picked up a badger trail and was following it, nose to the ground like a bloodhound.

Kelly ducked under a low branch and stepped right up to the wire. She peered through the trees and bushes, trying to get a better view down into the crater. Suddenly, she flinched. There was something there. A shape, blocking out the light which otherwise filtered through the leaves. A deer perhaps? Then a sudden movement, and Kelly let out a little cry as she saw, peering back at her through the greenery, two blue eyes.

'Hello, Kelly.'

'Oh my God! It's you! I nearly died. What the hell are you doing in there?'

Ben stepped out from the trees, looking more than a little dishevelled and covered in dirt.

'I've been looking for rabbits. They love it down there. It's so sheltered and safe and the soil is much looser than up on the top, so it's a great place to dig a burrow. There's hundreds of the little devils. Hey, look who it is.'

Tyson had forgotten all about his badger trail. He'd raced over and was now happily licking Ben's hand.

'Why is there such a big hole in the ground anyway?' asked Kelly. 'I've been trying to work it out—why it's fenced off and everything.'

'It's one of the stone pits. Part of the quarry. There are four pits altogether but this one's the biggest. It seems to have become rather overgrown but some of the sides are still really steep and the loose soil over the top makes them pretty slippery. I suppose it's been fenced off to keep people out but it's a paradise for animals. Not just rabbits but badgers, foxes, even deer.'

'Ahh, a quarry. That's why the farm's called Stone Pit Farm.'

'Yup. No flies on you, eh?' Ben winked.

'Shut up!' giggled Kelly. 'I've never been up this far before. I didn't even know Wilmcote had a quarry.'

'Oh yes,' said Ben. 'The quarry was really important to the village when...well, in the nineteenth century. You know those rows of stone cottages on the main road down to the village green? The terraces?'

Kelly nodded.

'Well, they're quarry workers' cottages, and the main farm house is—I mean, *was* where the quarry owner lived.'

'Cor,' exclaimed Kelly. 'That's why it's quite grand for a farm house. It's great finding out about places, don't you think? You know, discovering why they're like they are now. What stone did they quarry here, then?'

'Limestone. Look, you can see chunks of it along the path.' Ben took Kelly further up the footpath, where some kind-hearted walker had used flat pieces of limestone to make stepping stones through a muddy patch.

'Cool,' said Kelly. 'Do you know what they used the stone for?'

'Well, those quarry workers' cottages in the village are built from stone from these pits. One of the pubs was too. That's why it's called the Mason's Arms, of course. But the stone's been used for churches, bridges, stately homes all over the place around here. Ragley Hall for one.'

'Wow!' said Kelly. 'You can see that place from up on the hill behind the Traveller site. It's huge. That's quite impressive.'

Ben nodded, smiling. 'That's not the most impressive thing about the quarry, either. Did you know that...?'

Kelly was already walking on around the perimeter of the quarry. 'But how did they get all the limestone out?' she shouted back to him. 'There aren't any roads up here.'

'By tram,' explained Ben, catching up with her. 'They loaded the stone onto trucks at the pit side, then it was pulled by horses along the tramway to the canal where they put it onto barges.' He paused, before mumbling, 'Oh, and then later they extended the tramlines to reach the railway.'

'Yes, of course. I guess the railway was really important to the quarry,' Kelly mused, putting a tired but happy Tyson back on his lead.

'Would you like me to walk back with you?' asked Ben. 'I can tell you some more along the way, if you like.'

Kelly smiled. She noticed that Ben had a row of freckles over the top of his nose. Sun kisses, her nana used to call them. 'Yes,' she said, rather breathlessly. 'I'd like that.'

The two friends walked around the edge of the quarry and followed the tramline back across the fields. At the bottom of the hill, at the side of the track, was a mound of compacted earth, set within a clump of small trees.

'I was thinking, on my way past here, that my brother could use that for a fantastic BMX jump,' observed Kelly. 'I must tell him about it when he gets back.'

'BMX?' enquired Ben.

'Yeah,' said Kelly, unsure what Ben wanted to know. 'The way the mud is so smooth, and the slope and the height of the mound and everything. It's a natural stunt ramp.'

'No it's not,' said Ben stiffly. 'I'll show you what it is. Look.'

He took Kelly's hand and led her off the path and round to the other side of the mound. There, out of sight from passing walkers, was what looked like a tiny cave, with loose soil and rubble piled up in its mouth.

'It looks like a dragon's lair!' squealed Kelly. 'What is it really?'

'It's one of the old lime kilns.'

Now it was Kelly's turn to look confused, so Ben explained how Wilmcote limestone had layers of darker, blue-grey rock, with more clay in it, sandwiched between the harder, pale brown layers. Rock with a high clay content made good lime and that was what the kiln was for.

It was like an oven. The men would fill it with lumps of stone from the quarry, add coal, then start a fire at the bottom. Once the fire was lit, they would wait for a few days, allowing the fire to build up and then die down again. When the kiln was cool, the men could rake out the lime that was left behind.

'But what was the lime used for?' asked Kelly, picking up one of the smaller rocks from the entrance to the kiln and rubbing it between her fingers.

'For building. To make mortar.'

'What, you mean, like cement?'

'Yes. Good Lord, geology isn't your best subject, is it?'

'No,' laughed Kelly, thinking how old-fashioned Ben could sound sometimes.

She sat herself down on a fallen log. 'I'm better at English, and history. Anything involving a good story. I just like imagining how places were in the past, and finding out their stories. Do you know what I mean?'

'I think so,' said Ben, sitting down next to her and stroking Tyson's head.

'Shut your eyes,' said Kelly. 'Go on. I'll do it too.'

Ben did as he was told, turning his face up to the sun.

'Now imagine you've gone back in time. It's...I don't know...1850 or something.'

She opened her right eye and peeped at Ben to see if he was playing along. He was, so she shut her eye again and carried on.

'The quarry is in full swing. You can hear the men chipping away in the stone pits. You can hear the rocks being loaded onto the carts. You can hear the horses snorting as they struggle to pull their heavy loads along the tramlines.'

'Can I smell the manure too?' sniggered Ben.

'If you like,' replied Kelly, refusing to be led off track. 'Go on. What else can you sense?'

'I can feel the heat from the kiln behind us,' said Ben. 'And I can hear the roaring of the fire, and the sound of the men's spades as they shovel in the limestone. I'm covered in dust. It's in my hair. Under my fingernails. I can smell bacon.'

For a moment Kelly thought Ben was pulling her leg again, but when she opened her eyes, ready to scold him, she saw he was miles away, his eyes screwed tightly shut. She remained silent and let him carry on.

'Umm, yes. They are frying bacon on their shovels, holding them in the mouth of the kiln.'

'Really?' interrupted Kelly, unable to contain her curiosity any longer. 'Did you make that up or did they really do that?'

Ben opened his eyes slowly and shook his head a little as if to clear the image from his mind. He seemed to be in a bit of a daze.

'Sorry. What did you say?'

'All that about frying bacon. Where did that come from?'

'Oh, I don't know. You told me to imagine I was back in time. I was just getting a bit carried away that's all.'

Kelly grinned. 'There's me thinking I was the daft romantic one. You're better at this than I am!'

The pair sat there for a while, chatting happily side by side on the tree trunk while Tyson chewed on a stick and rolled lazily in the grass. Then they made their way across the rest of the fields down to the canal. Ben showed Kelly where the tramway would have forked left and right, one route heading into a cutting where the quarry workers would have loaded their stone onto waiting canal barges, while the other route wound across a bridge—which had collapsed long ago—over the canal to the railway.

'Do you know when the railway was built?' asked Kelly, thinking that her dad might be interested to know that, too.

'Well, I don't know much about the railway, but I know it's been here since about 1860.'

'Hey!' Kelly exclaimed. 'Do you remember that old boot Tyson found? The one I told you about? Wouldn't it be amazing if it dated back that far? Imagine if it belonged to one of the quarry workers, or one of the men loading the stone onto the railway carriages, or even to someone who built the railway. Imagine that!'

Ben looked alarmed. 'Do you think it could have survived that long?'

'Buried in the ground like it was, I think it could have, yes.'

Ben went to lean over the side of the rickety old canal bridge. He stared into the water, his lips tight, forming a hard, thin line, while his forehead wrinkled into a frown.

Confused by his sudden change of mood, Kelly followed, dragging a now tired Tyson after her, and leaned on the bridge next to him. She stayed silent for a few moments. Then, without looking at him, she said quietly, 'I'm sorry. I went on a bit back there, didn't I? I know I can get a bit boring sometimes. It's just that, when I get my nose into a story, I can't stop asking questions. I don't like to let go. I'm a bit like Tyson. Like when he smelled that old boot stuck in the ground and kept on digging, oblivious to everything. I can't stop being curious.'

'It's fine,' grunted Ben. 'But perhaps we've both had enough history for one day. Let's talk about something else.'

Desperate not to upset her new friend, Kelly decided to ask about his mum and dad and where their cottage was. Ben still seemed a little quiet, almost cagey.

'I told you,' he said. 'It's called Stone Pit Cottage. It's down the track beyond the main farm house, which is the big house that belonged to the quarry owner. There's nothing down that track except our cottage. It's been in my family for years. My... now what would it be, my great-great-great-great grandad or something was the first one to live in it. He was a vicar. Then when he founded the church in the village he was given a vicarage alongside it. I think he gave the cottage to his daughter or something…or so my mother said.'

'Now who's talking history?' joked Kelly, impressed.

Ben laughed, but still looked a little unsettled. 'When I first met you, you said that your dad was working on the railway line.'

'Yes that's right. He's clearing the embankment.'

'Well, my father…my dad…he used to work on the railways, too.'

'Used to?' asked Kelly, tentatively.

'Yes. A long time ago.'

'And now?'

'Oh, now he just…he just looks after the farm land,' spluttered Ben, all the words coming out in a rush. 'That's why I can go anywhere I like round here. No one seems to mind me.'

'And your mum?'

'She keeps the house.'

'And teaches you,' added Kelly.

'Yes. That's right.'

'I'd like to meet them some time,' Kelly said. She saw that Ben looked less than enthusiastic, and tried a different tack. 'Well, I'm sure my parents would like to meet you, anyway. They always like to know who I'm friends with. Perhaps next time we hook up you could come to the campsite and say "Hi".'

'I'm… I'm not sure,' stammered Ben. 'I don't know if I could. I mean, I don't know how my parents would feel about it.'

Kelly bristled. 'Why's that? Because I'm a Traveller? You think they might not approve of me, is that it?'

When Ben didn't reply, Kelly took his silence as confirmation of her fears. 'Oh, don't worry about it!' she snapped. 'Listen, Tyson and I have got to go. We've been out a long time. My mum and dad'll be worried something bad has happened to me. Perhaps they'd be right!' She paused, to let her sarcasm have full effect. 'Thanks for the tour. It's been, oh, what do you people say?' She put on a posh accent. 'Most enlightening!'

And before Ben had the chance to say another word, she scooped Tyson up into her arms and ran off towards the railway, heading for home.

Chapter 12 – September 2012

Kelly didn't see Ben again for the rest of the summer holidays. It wasn't that she avoided him particularly—she had still been out walking with Tyson every day—she simply didn't make much of an effort to look for him. She suspected that she had over-reacted about his reluctance to meet her family, but she felt that it was up to him to seek her out and explain.

Meanwhile, she had been busy expanding her collection of treasure, tucked away in the box under her bed. She had added the stone which she had picked up at the lime kiln that day with Ben, and a piece of broken pottery she had found pressed into the mud in the footpath, with a faded but still beautiful blue bird painted on it. It looked like a stork and Kelly liked to think that it was from a once priceless Chinese vase.

Every time she slid the treasure chest out from under her bed to add her latest find, she would take out the old leather boot and examine it again, wishing that it would give her some clue about its owner or about how it had come to be buried in the stones and earth by the railway line. Was it just her, or did it look more shiny and in better shape each time she looked at it?

Before she knew it, the long summer days of August had given way to the first week of September, and Kelly found herself leaving a sad-looking Tyson behind with her mum as she headed off to catch her school bus.

She was no longer a 'newbie' and by the start of Year 8 she should have felt relaxed at school, part of the scene. But Kelly found herself feeling more on the sidelines than ever. All the talk in the tutor group that morning, while everyone waited for Mr Walker to come and take the register, was of overseas holidays on hot Spanish beaches, of trips to Disneyland or weeks at the beach in Cornwall or Wales. And all the girls except for her seemed to have spent the rest of the holidays together, and were recounting tales of sleepovers, days at the park, hanging out at the shopping centre and camp-outs in the garden.

Kelly took her usual seat at the back of the room and tried not to show that she was listening but, true to form, Charlotte spotted her and couldn't resist the chance to poke fun.

'Have you been on your *travels*, too, then, Kelly?' she sneered, emphasising the word 'travels' in case anyone had missed the joke. 'Where did you go?' Then before Kelly could answer, 'To a caravan park somewhere on the A36? Or did you go upmarket this year and stay on the M1? Lovely!'

'I stayed at home, Charlotte. And yes, I do have a home. Amazing, isn't it?' Kelly replied sarcastically. 'And you know, we have a car too. A real one with four wheels. No horse in sight. And no, I don't sell heather in my spare time, or read palms.'

Leanne, who was standing behind Charlotte and listening in, giggled. Charlotte shot her a look so frosty it could have cooled red-hot lava, and was desperately struggling to think of a clever come-back when Mr Walker walked into the room.

'Okay, okay, quiet everyone, please!' he commanded, raising his voice so it could be heard over the din. 'I know you are all thrilled to be back but you're going to have to control your excitement and settle down. I could hear you from the car park.'

Kelly sat stewing in furious silence at the back of the room while Mr Walker went through the register and began giving out the timetables for the year. Why had she let Charlotte get to her? She was normally so good at controlling her temper and letting stupid remarks like that wash over her. What was it about today? Why was she feeling so sensitive?

She tried to focus on the piece of paper Mr Walker had put in front of her. It mapped out the shape of her week for the coming term in rainbow colours—one for each subject. But her mind kept wandering. Did Ben have a timetable or did his mum just teach him whatever she felt like each day? Was he having lessons right now? Did he even have summer holidays, or did home education mean you carried on all year? She had never actually asked him. Why hadn't she asked him?

Then she realised what was making her so crotchety. It was that whole thing with Ben. She missed him. She had let the last two weeks of the summer holidays slip by, sulking at him for not coming to find her. Maybe she had been too hard on him. Even if she had been right, and his final comment to her when they were last together *had* been about her being a Traveller, was he being that unreasonable? There weren't many parents who would feel comfortable about letting their children visit a Traveller site. There was usually too much ignorance and nervousness on both sides for that to happen. And there was always the chance that Ben wasn't being prejudiced at all. Maybe the reason he didn't want her to meet his parents was that he was worried he would have to explain how they met, which would mean his parents would find out he'd been near the railway. He had told her he wasn't supposed to be there.

By the time the tutor group session was over and it was time to head off to her first lesson, Kelly had made up her mind. She was going to go and find Ben that evening, as soon as she got home. She had to tell him that she still wanted to be friends.

As if to confirm that she had made the right decision, something happened that afternoon that gave her even more of an incentive to find him.

Kelly had a double history lesson with Mr Walker, during which he set the class an extended history project. It was designed to develop their research skills, Mr Walker explained, and was an introduction to a new unit in their Year 8 history curriculum. He gave everyone a sheet headed, 'British history and the development of industrialisation and technology, and its impact on different people in Britain'.

'I want you to find out as much detail as you can about an event or an activity relevant to this topic,' he explained. 'It must have happened in your local area, somewhere near to where you live or within this part of the country. I want you to explain how industrialisation and technology changed people's lives. As always, I will need you to acknowledge your sources and the highest marks will be awarded for work which clearly shows detailed research using different kinds of sources. And I want to see your own interpretations of the facts.' He looked directly at Charlotte. 'So cutting and pasting chunks from Wikipedia won't get you an A.'

Charlotte pulled a face.

Mr Walker went on. 'Any questions, ask me. Otherwise I expect your work in during the last week before the half-term holiday. Oh, and you can present it in any format you like.'

This is a gift, reflected Kelly, thinking about the opening of the quarry and the impact of the railway when it came. Both of those things must have changed life in Wilmcote massively. It was perfect. All she needed to do was find out some more details. And she knew just the person to help her.

PART 3
Chapter 13 – Late Summer 1859

One of Alice's least favourite jobs at Stone Pit Farm house was cleaning the windows. The sheer amount of glass to polish was bad enough, but the frequency with which the windows needed cleaning was soul-destroying. In Wilmcote, the wind always seemed to blow in the same direction: across the quarry and over the open fields to the house, which meant that within a few days of being cleaned, the windows of Mr Greenslade's otherwise immaculate home were thick with dust once again. In the summer, when the sunlight seemed to show up every speck, the sight made Alice cringe.

How odd, she thought, *I can live with dirty windows in my own home but here, where I am the paid housekeeper, it feels unforgiveable.*

By leaning out as far as she could, Alice could clean all but the largest of the windows by herself without a ladder. And it was while cleaning one of the upstairs bedroom windows that she saw an unfamiliar carriage approaching. It pulled up in the courtyard at the front of the farm house and a small group of well-suited gentleman alighted, talking solemnly to one another. Alice recognised the tallest one among them as the Chairman of the Stratford-upon-Avon Railway Company, Reginald Adkins. He had visited the house before, but always alone. This looked altogether more serious.

Curious to discover what her husband's master had come to see her own employer about, she hurried downstairs to let the visitors in. After leading them to Mr Greenslade's study and offering them some refreshment, she left the door slightly ajar and hovered outside in the hall, from where she could just make out what was being said.

The gentlemen got down to business straight away. A low, gruff voice, which Alice recognised as belonging to Adkins, seemed to be doing most of the talking.

'We need to pull together on this, Greenslade,' Adkins stressed. 'Sir Charles Barry has threatened to withdraw his investment if the line isn't complete within the next twelve months.'

'But he can't do that!' exclaimed Greenslade.

'Apparently he can, and we cannot afford to upset him or any of our other shareholders. Some of them are powerful men who can help us to secure business elsewhere. So we are going to be throwing every resource we have at the Stratford-upon-Avon project. There is no way on earth that the railway company is going to miss that deadline. But we can only do so much. There are two crucial ingredients in this mix: our railway and your stone.'

'We have no problem with supply,' said Greenslade defensively. 'We have plenty of stone and plenty of hands to quarry it. Speed of transportation will only increase once the railway is here, so if everything is completed on time, we have no fear of missing our deadlines, either.'

'As I said. We are in this together,' Adkins continued, speaking more slowly now, 'because it is not just my business Sir Charles is threatening, it's yours.'

'What do you mean?' Alice could hear a tremble in Greenslade's voice.

'Sir Charles has asked me to inform you that if you do not deliver the full quantity of the stone promised under your original contract to London in time for the State Opening of Parliament next year, you will not receive the payment due to you at present, let alone for the remaining parts of the order.'

At that moment there was a movement on the other side of the door. Fearful that one of the visitors was about to discover her eavesdropping, Alice scurried off down the hall and darted through the kitchen doorway.

She was making such a rumpus, banging about pans in the kitchen in her efforts to sound busy, that she did not hear Mr Greenslade ringing the bell a short while later, summoning her to his study so that she could show his visitors out. He slammed the front door behind them with so much force, however, that Alice heard it above her own clattering, and stopped what she was doing in time to hear the carriage wheels crunching on the gravel as they carried the visitors out of the courtyard. Assuming that it was safe to return, she scurried back down the hallway and knocked lightly on Greenslade's office door.

'Yes?' he barked.

Alice peeped around the door. 'I'm sorry, Mr Greenslade, I didn't realise your guests were leaving so soon. Naturally I would have shown them out for you.'

'Yes, that would have been helpful, Alice!' Greenslade snapped sarcastically. 'I expect better of you. And you can tell that husband of yours that I shall be expecting better of him, too!'

'I'm sorry, sir. I don't understand.'

'My men have been breaking their backs quarrying the extra stone we need to send down to London. But if your husband and his workmates on that railway don't hurry up and finish the line soon, it will all be a waste of time. I shall be bankrupt, Alice. We won't get paid for half of the stone that has already been delivered, let alone the rest that is promised. And remember, this quarry employs most of the men in this village. It's not just me who stands to lose everything.'

Greenslade's words frightened Alice. It wasn't just what he said, it was the manner in which he uttered it. Her employer had never been anything but gentle and polite to her, so to speak to her so harshly was very out of character. This was a man under the greatest of pressure.

So, after work, Alice decided to do what she always did when she was upset: she rushed off to see her father.

She found him in the drawing room of the vicarage, where he was preparing for his Sunday service. His face lit up when Alice entered the room but his expression quickly changed to concern when he saw how anxious his daughter seemed. 'It's that good-for-nothing husband of yours, again, isn't it?' he exclaimed. 'What has he done now? If he's laid a finger on you, or Billy...'

Alice held up her hand to stop him. 'No, it's not William, Father. Not this time. It's more serious than that. This could affect everyone in Wilmcote.'

Alice sat down in the window seat next to her father and he held her hand while she recounted the conversation she had overheard between Richard Greenslade and the men from the railway company, and the uncharacteristically stern words he had directed at her.

'It seems so unfair,' she sighed. 'No one could be working harder, and yet if the railway doesn't get completed on time, everyone suffers. The quarry has to meet all its deadlines too, or Mr Greenslade won't get the payment he is owed for the stone. The men could lose their jobs. The railway company will be under threat. Families will suffer. Me, Billy…we have little enough to live on as it is. And the pressure on William and the others will be huge. Everyone will blame them if they can't finish the line on time. I don't know whether he will cope.'

Reverend Knott's face was grey. 'I have said it before, but if you hadn't been carrying that man's child, there is no way on God's blessed earth that I would have let you marry him.'

Alice opened her mouth to protest but her father put his finger to her lips to silence her. 'Let me finish,' he whispered. He took both her hands in his and looked into his daughter's eyes. 'Oh Alice my dear, I know you were young, and you thought you were in love with him, but be honest with me…if you knew then what you know now, would you really have chosen him?'

Alice looked down at the dry, cracked skin of her hands, worn sore from so much cleaning and scrubbing, as they lay in the soft, safe, upturned palms of her father, and bit her lip. Then she murmured, 'Well, I wouldn't have Billy, would I? William may be a lowly labourer but he gave me the most precious thing I have.'

The vicar let go of his daughter's hands and turned slightly away. 'Yes, there is that. But I feel as if I have let you down, allowing you to end up in a marriage where your welfare is so precarious. I always pictured you with a fine gentleman for a husband. By now you could have been living in a town house in Stratford-upon-Avon, not working your fingers to the bone as housekeeper and stuck in that tiny farm cottage. And even that meagre home was provided by me, your father, rather than the man you married.' The scalding chamber of resentment inside him was bubbling to the surface like lava, and he seemed unable to stem the flow. 'Thank God I put the cottage in your name and that swag-bellied fool doesn't have a claim to it. Otherwise I wouldn't put it past him to mortgage it from under you to pay for his next pint of ale!'

'Father, please!' Alice was torn between agreeing with her father and, out of sheer, stubborn pride, feeling that she ought to defend her husband. She felt partly to blame for William's troubles. She had stood by and let her father demean him far too often, and she knew how little self-confidence William had left. The more he was told that he was good for nothing, the less he seemed capable of.

But her loyalty to her husband aside, she worried even more for her son. She was determined that Billy would be allowed to carve a better future for himself—no matter what. And to do that she had to make sure that she could continue to feed and clothe him, and keep him in school long enough to complete his education. It was time to channel her father's anger into action.

'Whatever happens, Father, William cannot lose his job.' She stood and began to pace back and forth in front of her father, who was still perched on the chintz cushions in the window seat. 'And we know that he and the men are already stretched to their limits. So if Sir Charles and the railway company want to make sure that the branch line is completed in time, they will need to use more than threats. They will need to do their part. Now, that man Reginald Adkins, the Chairman of the railway company, he's in your congregation, am I correct?'

The vicar nodded.

'Then you must speak with him. Stress the impact on us all if the railway is not finished. Persuade him to hire more hands. He needs to understand that they are putting too much on the shoulders of men like William who are already working at full stretch and that they are asking the near impossible.'

The Reverend Frederick Knott was tired of digging his son-in-law out of hole after hole, but he found it impossible to refuse a heartfelt plea from his beloved daughter. Although he was not confident of success, he would at least try to give her what she wanted.

Chapter 14 – September 2012

Once Kelly had made her mind up about something, she wasted no time in making that thing happen. She had decided that she was ready to see Ben again, and she was desperate to tell him about the idea she had for her local history project. So as soon as she got home from school on that first day of term, she changed out of her school uniform and announced to her mum that she was taking Tyson for a walk.

She knew roughly where Ben's cottage must be, so she would head that way and keep on looking until she found it. If necessary, she would march right up to his front door and ask to see him. It didn't matter what his parents thought of her, or who she was. She was his friend and she had a right to see him. And if his parents asked her where she and Ben had met, she would just say 'Out on a walk,' or something vague like that. There was no need to mention the railway. She would prove to Ben that she could be trusted to keep his secrets.

After waiting at home all day for her, Tyson was delighted to be heading off towards the fields with Kelly once again. He pulled hard on the lead as they left the site, his stubby legs scrabbling at the ground and his breath rasping in his throat as he strained on his collar and did his best to drag Kelly along the track. They followed the footpath away from the caravan site and crossed the railway.

In between the railway and the canal, the footpath ran through an unused area of wooded land which was overgrown with a tangle of brambles and hawthorn trees. In places, Kelly had to duck down and walk while bent forwards, to avoid snagging her hair in the thorns and spiky branches overhead.

'This hasn't been cleared in years, has it, mate?' she said to Tyson, as he picked his way alongside her through the long grass and nettles. 'I'm glad I'm not wearing shorts.'

A little further along, they came into a clearing in front of an old tumbledown shed. Although substantial in size, the shed looked as if it hadn't been opened in ages. Kelly had to admit it looked a bit creepy. She wondered if it was something to do with the quarry or the railway, and made a mental note to ask Ben.

Feeling a little uncomfortable, Kelly hurried on. This time it was she who was tugging on the lead, trying to discourage Tyson from stopping to sniff the ground every few steps. She was relieved when, a little closer to the canal, the path started to widen again and they could move more quickly through the vegetation.

More relaxed, Kelly started to mentally rehearse what she would say to Ben when she saw him, until she and Tyson were brought to an abrupt halt by a loud flapping of feathers, erupting from the long grass next to the path. Kelly ducked and Tyson lurched sideways as a pheasant flew just inches above their heads, emitting an ugly, squawking noise that reminded Kelly of a screeching rusty gate hinge.

'Blimey! That made me jump out of my skin.' Kelly put one hand on her chest while she held tightly onto Tyson's lead with the other in case he tried to chase after it. 'Stupid bird. Why did it wait until we were right on top of it? If it had just stayed there in the grass, we would never have known it was there, would we? We would have walked right past it.'

Tyson, who had been just as surprised as Kelly, wagged his tail as if he agreed with her.

Kelly couldn't see where the pheasant had fled to, but as she looked into the long grass into which it had disappeared, a solid dark shape caught her eye. Something she hadn't noticed before when coming this way. It looked like the top of a circle of stones, almost completely covered in ivy, poking out above the waist-high weeds. Curious, she picked up Tyson and waded through the grass to take a closer look. It was an old well, its wooden lid now rotten and split with age.

'Wow! Look at this, Tyson,' she exclaimed. 'I wonder how long this has been here.'

She put Tyson down on the ground and told him to sit while she leaned over and peered down through the cracks in the wood. It took a few moments for her eyes to adjust but then she began to make out the moss-covered stones lining the shaft and then, way, way down at the bottom, what looked like the glint of a deep, dark pool, faintly illuminated by a thin shaft of sunlight beaming down through the broken wooden lid.

The air inside the well smelled musty, like rotting compost, and felt icy cool on Kelly's face. At first she was entranced by the way the flickering light danced about on the water down below, but then her blood ran cold. There was something else down there, she was sure of it. A flash of something solid. What on earth could it be? A water rat or something? A stick or plank of wood, perhaps, floating about? Was it still there? Had she imagined it? Without thinking, Kelly leaned further forwards until the tips of her toes were only just brushing the ground.

'Kelly!'

Startled by the voice crying out behind her, Kelly pushed down on the wooden lid with both hands to propel her body round. There was a sickening cracking noise as her left hand broke through one of the rotten planks, sending splinters of wood raining down into the black void beneath her. Her body span and her hip slammed hard against the rim of the well.

'Be careful!'

Gripping the cold stones with her right hand, Kelly pushed herself back up onto her feet. She blew out hard.

'What the hell were you doing, Kel?'

It was Ben, breathless, his nose only a few centimetres from hers, eyes wide in alarm.

'You called me Kel,' she said, so pleased to see him that she didn't think to answer his question. A broad smile spread across her face, breaking the tension, and Ben returned her grin.

The two of them held one another's gaze for a few moments, until Tyson shattered the silence by letting out three short little yaps to remind them that he was still there, keen to continue his walk.

'Thank you,' stammered Kelly, taking a step backwards. 'That probably wasn't very wise of me, was it?'

'No, not really,' said Ben. 'That whole lid could collapse at any moment. I thought you were going to fall in. But listen, about the last time we met. What I said. I didn't mean anything by it.'

'No, I know. I over-reacted.'

'Well, maybe just a little. I'm sure my parents would really like you. I'm sorry if I upset you.'

'I'm sorry too, for flying off the handle. It's just that I'm so used to people jumping to conclusions about me that I sometimes jump to the wrong conclusions about them. I don't give people a chance.'

'Friends again, then?' said Ben.

'Friends? Oh we're more than that now,' replied Kelly, 'We're partners *and* friends. Come on, let's find somewhere to sit down and talk. I've got lots to tell you.'

Ben led Kelly and Tyson along the rest of the path to the canal where the three of them flopped down on the grass at the side of the footbridge in the early evening sunshine. Kelly told him all about her history project and was delighted when he agreed to help her.

'We could make it a joint project,' she suggested. 'Do you think your mum would like that? It could be part of your history lessons, too?'

Ben nodded.

'Besides,' Kelly continued. 'I was thinking. Won't your parents know lots of other stuff about the history of this area, if they've lived here for so long? You said that the cottage had been in your family for years.'

'Yes, I imagine they would,' said Ben, sounding rather cautious. 'But they won't necessarily have *all* the answers. You'll just have to tell me what it is you need to know, and I'll do my best to remember. Remember to ask them, that is.'

Kelly smiled and watched her friend in silence as he gathered some tiny stones and started to throw them, one by one, into the water. She noticed how nerdy his shoes were and realised that he was sporting the same clothes as the previous times she had met him. She could still see traces of mud on his trousers, too, where Tyson had jumped up that first day on the railway bridge. Ben's family were clearly not very well off. It was probably a good thing that he didn't go to The Shakespeare Academy. People like Charlotte would eat him alive.

As much as she liked Ben, he was a little odd. At times he was so hesitant, so unsure of himself, as if in some way he needed help. *He must get lonely like me*, she thought, *being educated at home*. He certainly didn't seem to have any other real friends— at least, none that he had told her about. Perhaps this project would be good for both of them.

Chapter 15 – September 2012

Before the two friends parted that evening, Kelly outlined to Ben the brief she had been given for her history project, explaining that she had to include lots of evidence to back up everything she wrote.

'So you're going to have to take me to all the key historical sites around here—the quarry, the lime kiln, the tramway, that sort of thing. Can you do that?' Kelly asked, her eyes bright with enthusiasm. Hardly giving Ben time to nod, let alone reply, she went on, 'I'm fascinated by the stone pits and all the places where the stone ended up, so I think we should start our research there, don't you? The opening of the quarry must have triggered lots of changes here in Wilmcote. We just need to find out what they were.'

The pair agreed to meet up at the quarry the following Saturday morning. Their rendezvous point was the limestone stepping stones on the footpath near where Ben had emerged from the trees on that sunny day back in the summer holidays.

'I've brought my camera with me,' Kelly announced as she and Tyson ran up to Ben, who had arrived first. 'Mr Walker says we need to use as many different kinds of historical sources as we can. So photos are a good place to start, aren't they?'

'Er, I suppose so,' said Ben, looking dubiously at the camera. 'What kind of camera is it?'

'Oh, it's really lush. I had it for my birthday last year. It's digital. Takes high def video too, and I can link it up to Mum's laptop so it's easy to download the photos.'

'Oh, I see,' said Ben, who clearly didn't.

Kelly suddenly felt guilty. Perhaps Ben's mum and dad couldn't afford to buy things like digital cameras and laptops. She made a mental note to be a bit less flashy about her family's possessions in future. 'Anyway,' she hurried on, 'it doesn't matter what kind of camera it is as long as it takes photos. And the more photos the better, I say. The more pictures we have, the less room there will be for writing, eh?' She winked, and was relieved to see Ben laugh in response.

Ben led the way along the hedgerow until they came to the point where the barbed wire and the fence post were bent downwards.

'We can climb through here,' he instructed. 'But be very, very careful going down. Follow me and watch where I'm putting my feet. The slope's steep and the soil's pretty loose, so if you step in the wrong place you might start a landslide.'

He evidently saw Kelly's look of alarm. 'Look, Kel, it's a quarry. It's a dangerous place. But I know it well so just do what I do and you'll be fine.'

Ben climbed over the fence first and asked Kelly to pass Tyson over into his arms so he didn't get caught on the wire. Kelly followed and then took hold of Tyson's lead again, ready to edge her way down into the pit.

'There's enough of a gap in the trees here to get through, but you will need to keep your head low so you don't get caught on any spikes.'

Kelly watched closely as Ben took his first few tentative steps down over the edge of pit, feeling his footing as he went. Then she took a deep breath and started to follow, trying to place her feet where she had seen Ben putting his. Tyson, excited at the prospect of a new adventure, was straining at the lead and making it difficult for her to keep her balance.

'You're going to have to let him off,' Ben called, looking back up the slope to see how she was doing. 'He's going to pull you over. You'll both be safer on your own. And don't worry, he can't go far down here.'

Kelly was about to remind Ben of Tyson's lust for chasing rabbits and then thought better of it. Ben was right. She let the dog go and said a little silent prayer as he raced ahead down the quarry side, disappearing into the undergrowth.

After a few minutes of slow progress, Kelly and Ben finally made it down to the quarry floor. Left to its own devices for so long, the quarry had been transformed from a noisy, dusty, rock-strewn lunar landscape to a fertile green jungle, a secret garden hidden from the rest of the world by the abundant trees and hedges which had colonised its sides.

Down in the base of the pit, the bushes were lower and more sparse, so it was easier to move and look around and get an idea of the size and scale of the quarry. Tyson was in his element, running back and forth, his tail in the air, sniffing everything and anything he could find.

Kelly could see where the steepest rock faces must have been and where, to the far end, the ground sloped more gently, leading up to a narrow, funnel-shaped gap.

'Was that the main entrance into the pit, over there?' she asked Ben, pointing towards the shallower end of the pit.

'Yes. That was where they brought the carts in, so they could load them up with stone.'

Kelly made her way over to the base of one of the steeper sides of the old rock face where there was a pile of earth with some large pieces of limestone poking out. With her hand, she began to sweep off some of the loose soil to expose more of the rocks underneath. She wiggled one piece of rock back and forth until she was able to pull it free from the pile. Flat, smooth, and about the size of her palm, it was an almost perfect diamond shape, about five centimetres thick, ideal for scraping away soil and prising out more loose stones.

Using her new tool, Kelly carried on excavating for another twenty minutes. She found the repetition and the physicality of the work surprisingly relaxing—so much so that she let her imagination wander. For a moment she was back in Victorian times, chopping away at the stone face alongside dozens of other quarry workers. So when she removed another stone and exposed a piece of metal sticking out of the ground, at first she didn't react. But then she started to gently brush the soil away from around the object and her excitement grew as she realised that the protruding piece of metal was the handle of an old mug.

'Ben! Ben! Come over here! Look what I've found,' she shouted across to her friend, who had been poking about on the other side of the quarry, with Tyson at his heels. With Ben looking closely over her shoulder, Kelly carefully worked the mug free and held it up to the light. 'Do you think it belonged to one of the quarry workers?'

'No reason why not,' said Ben. The rusty old piece of metal, although flattened somewhat by the weight of the soil and rocks on top of it, had remained remarkably intact so that there was no doubt as to its original purpose.

'Tyson and I found something too.' Ben showed Kelly the remains of an old trowel. The handle had long since rotted away in the ground but the spike by which it had been attached, and the shape of the trowel itself, were clearly recognisable, despite being encrusted with rust-stained soil.

'Well, aren't we a couple of budding archaeologists!' said Kelly, with a smile. I think this deserves a celebratory photo, don't you? I can put it on Facebook. Our first find.'

Kelly proudly arranged the mug, the trowel and her diamond-shaped piece of limestone on a large rock nearby.

Then she turned back to Ben. 'Right. I need you to go over there and stand next to our finds. I want you in the photo too.'

'Why? Surely it's the artefacts that matter most.'

'Yes, but we need to give some idea of scale, so if you stand next to them people can see how big the objects are, and I can show how high that slope is behind you, too. Besides, it will be nice to have you in it.' Ben seemed reluctant to move. 'What? Don't tell me you're camera shy!' Kelly cried.

'No, I just think that it should be you in the picture, not me. Your teacher will want to know that you've done this yourself.'

'Okay, but he won't mind me having some help. I tell you what, I'll put it on self-timer. That way we can both be in it.'

Although still reluctant, Ben waited patiently while Kelly fiddled with the controls and made sure that the camera was positioned in just the right place to get them both in the frame.

By the time the little green light had flashed itself to a frenzy, and the shutter had finally clicked, minutes had passed. Kelly was just about to check the shot when Ben shouted, 'Hey Kel, where's Tyson?'

Clearly, the little dog had got bored of sniffing around in the same spot and had wandered off to find something more interesting to explore.

Kelly called his name, but there was no response. She tried again, and they strained their ears to see if they could hear him rustling about in the bushes.

'What was that?' whispered Kelly, reaching out to try to catch Ben's arm. 'Did you hear that tapping sound?'

There it was again. Tap, tap, tap. Quiet at first but gradually getting louder.

'It's coming from up there,' said Ben, pointing to the slope they had scrambled down. 'It must be Tyson. Tyson!' he shouted, cupping his hands around his mouth.

Silence. Then the tapping sound resumed. Kelly felt the hairs standing up on the back of her neck. Ben would probably laugh at her if she said it, but to her the noise sounded like someone chipping away at a piece of stone. If you let your imagination run away with you, she thought, it could very easily have been someone working in the quarry.

Ben took control. 'Come on,' he whispered. 'I think we had better get out of here. Whatever that noise is, it's not Tyson.'

He set off straight away, but Kelly, remembering her precious finds, ran back to load the stone, the old cup and trowel into her canvas shoulder bag. Not wanting to damage her camera, she pulled off her jacket and wrapped her camera in it, then placed that on top of the objects in the bag. She was moving as quickly as she could, but when she looked up Ben had disappeared from view and it dawned on her that she had no idea which way he had gone. Had he climbed back up the way they had come down, or had he gone another way, away from the source of the strange noise? She had no idea but, remembering Ben's warning about the quarry sides collapsing, she was too scared to take any other path than the one she had come down. She would just have to take her chances with the mystery quarryman.

She ran up the first part of the bank and then began to scramble up through the bushes. The higher she climbed, the steeper the bank grew, and she began to struggle to keep her footing, especially now that she had the added handicap of the heavy canvas bag, which kept swinging around her thighs, knocking her off balance.

She began to tremble, not knowing what she was more frightened of—falling back down, not being able to find Ben and Tyson, or running into a pick-wielding zombie. Her fear mounting, she was about to cry out when she looked up and saw a patch of blue sky above her. She was near to the top.

The thought of reaching ground level again spurred her on, and with one final effort, she launched herself up to catch hold of a low-hanging branch and used it to lever herself upwards to the lip of the quarry. That was when her eyes drew level with a pair of muddy old boots. Someone was towering over her. She froze, too terrified to look up to see who the boots belonged to.

Then a gruff voice. 'Grab my hand!'

Kelly glanced upwards, half expecting to see the ghostly figure of an old quarryman. But the whiskered face peering down at her belonged firmly in the twenty-first century. It was a local rambler—an angry one, his metal-tipped walking stick tapping furiously on the rocks at the pit edge. He pulled Kelly up to her feet beside him and almost dragged her through the bushes and back over the barbed wire fence. 'What on God's earth did you think you were doing down there young lady?' he growled. 'Did yer parents never tell you that disused quarries were not the best places to play? You could have got yerself killed.'

Kelly was about to reply when she noticed Tyson, tethered to the fence post. He was baring his teeth and letting out a low but persistent grumble. The man had used his belt as a makeshift lead and had looped it through Tyson's collar then over the post. Seeing Kelly, the furious little dog tried to shake himself free, and began biting at the belt.

'Oi, you little blighter. My wife bought me that belt!' He took a step towards Tyson.

'I'll stop him!' Kelly cried out, worried what the man was about to do. Taking his lead from her pocket, she dashed over to Tyson and swapped it for the belt.

'So, he's your mutt, is he?' the man snarled. 'I found him running free in the field up here. Having a whale of a time, he was, racing about, chasing the rabbits. You're just lucky that there weren't any sheep up here. A loose dog like that, running amok, could get himself shot. It was as much as I could do to catch hold of 'im.'

'I'm sorry,' Kelly said. 'But he's very protective towards me, so he doesn't like strangers handling him. I do usually keep him on the lead, but I knew there weren't any farm animals about.'

The man didn't soften. 'You still haven't told me what you were doing down there in the old quarry. You've no right to be there. You should stay on the footpath. If the farmer doesn't know you, he'll assume you're trespassing. And he can be a grumpy old so and so, can Tony. I can say that, cos he's a mate of mine. I live in the village.'

'Oh, it's okay,' replied Kelly, surreptitiously wiping the slobber off the man's belt on her jeans before handing it back. 'My friend, he's with me…' She looked around. 'Or at least, he was. He must have gone the other way. You spooked us a little and I got left behind. But wherever he is, his dad helps to look after the farm. He's allowed to play here. He comes here all the time.'

'Does he now?' remarked the rambler, raising his eyebrows. 'Well, allowed or not, that old quarry is dangerous. I'd find somewhere else to play, if I were you.'

Kelly really didn't like this pompous old man, with his designer walking gear and his fancy walking stick, which he pointed accusingly at her when he spoke. Normally she would have told him where to go, but not wanting to get Ben into trouble (where *was* he?) she bit her tongue, mumbled her thanks and hurried off to find Ben.

She found him sitting waiting for her on the tree trunk by the old lime kiln.

'I thought this would be a good place to wait for you. What happened?' he asked, giving her a lopsided smile.

'A man caught me climbing up the bank. That rambler. Didn't you see him?'

'Nope.' Ben shook his head. 'I must have gone a different way.'

'Well lucky old you!' said Kelly, a little annoyed, now, that Ben had gone off without making sure she was following. 'He wasn't very nice. He'd caught Tyson and had him tied to the post and was talking about how the farmer would shoot him. Oh, and he said he knew Tony.'

'Tony?'

'The farmer. The one your dad works for.'

'Oh, that Tony.' Ben looked anxious. 'Did he say anything else?'

'Only that we ought to find somewhere safer to hang out. Listen, are you sure we're okay to go into the quarry? The man was right, really. It *is* pretty dangerous.'

'Well, no one has stopped me before,' said Ben defensively.

That's not quite the same thing, thought Kelly to herself, but not wanting to get into an argument she let it go.

'I'm bushed,' she said, flopping down onto the tree trunk next to him. 'You know, if you don't mind, I might head home. I think Tyson and I have had enough excitement for one day and I don't want to bump into that man again.'

107

Ben shrugged, obviously far less shaken by the whole episode than Kelly.

'I think I'll take these into school on Monday, to see what Mr Walker makes of them,' Kelly said, patting the canvas by her side.

Ben offered to walk Kelly and Tyson back across the fields. When they reached the railway bridge, he announced that he had better turn back and head off in the direction of home.

'Okay,' agreed Kelly, grateful that he had stayed with her that far, in case they met up with the miserable rambler. 'Thanks for showing me the quarry today.'

Ben smiled. 'My pleasure. By the way, Kel. That boot you, well, Tyson found...'

'Yeah?'

'Can I see it?'

'Why?'

'I dunno. I just wondered if you might be right. If it *could* be a clue or a link to the past.'

'To what exactly?'

'To the people who built the railway.'

Kelly's face brightened. 'So you agree with me? It might be old?'

Ben gave a little shrug. 'Well, it's possible. Let's just say, I might have a way of finding out.'

'Now I'm curious.' Kelly laughed. 'Okay, I'll bring it next time we meet. Next Saturday maybe? On the canal bridge? Midday?'

'Sounds perfect,' said Ben.

Chapter 16 – September 2012

The Shakespeare Academy had a rule about not carrying bags around school. Every student was given a locker and encouraged to store their outdoor coats, bags and rucksacks there for the day, taking to lessons only the folders, books and pens and pencils they needed. The idea was introduced, said the school prospectus, to reduce the amount of lost property, and to protect students and staff from pupils who might otherwise smuggle unsuitable items into lessons. Whether a lump of rock, a jagged metal masonry tool and an old tin cup were the kind of items the headteacher had in mind when he introduced the new policy, Kelly wasn't sure, although she was pretty certain that he would consider them to be unsuitable.

So when she arrived at school on Monday morning, with her usual school bag slung over her right shoulder and her canvas bag slung over her left, she headed straight for her locker, planning on stowing away the artefacts until her history lesson after lunch.

Kelly's locker was at the end of the corridor along from her tutor room. Her morning bus always got her to school with plenty of time to spare, so it was usually quiet by the lockers when Kelly arrived. But not that morning. Leaning against the wall, one foot casually up behind her where it had already left a muddy smear on the fresh paintwork, was Charlotte, texting someone on her mobile phone. As always, Leanne was at her side.

'Well, look who it is!' Charlotte chanted, as she glanced up and saw Kelly approaching. 'If it isn't Miss Smart Arse who owns a real car with four wheels. That was what she said, wasn't it, Leanne?'

Leanne remained silent, looking away. Charlotte pulled herself upright and took a step closer to Kelly.

'So tell me, Traveller girl, how many *horse* power does your precious car have?'

'Oh, ha ha. Very funny,' said Kelly, rolling her eyes. She stepped sideways to make for her locker, but Charlotte shot out her hand and grabbed Kelly by the arm.

'What's in the bag?'

Kelly looked down at Charlotte's hand and then back up to meet the half-closed, sneering eyes.

'D'ya mind? I need to get to my locker.'

'Yeah, I do mind, actually. You didn't answer my question, *pikey*. I said, what's in the bag?'

'Nothing that you would be interested in, believe me.' Kelly shook her arm to escape Charlotte's grip. Charlotte loosened her fingers, but only so that she could grab the strap of the canvas bag instead.

'Let go!' muttered Kelly through gritted teeth, her nose just a few centimetres from Charlotte's.

'Or what?' sneered Charlotte, rocking her head from side to side in a taunting swagger. 'You'll put a Gypsy curse on me?'

Kelly felt the blood rush to her head. With both hands she shoved Charlotte backwards, sending her crashing into the lockers.

'You bitch!' screamed Charlotte, heaving her heavy body back up and launching herself at Kelly, grabbing a fistful of her hair as she did so.

'Argh!' Pain shot through Kelly's scalp. Desperate to break free, she bent over and span herself round, dragging Charlotte downwards with her. As she did so, her school bag slipped from her shoulder onto the floor with a thud, while the canvas bag on its long straps swung round her body like a pendulum and caught Charlotte on the side of the head. Charlotte slumped in a daze to the floor, and the bag fell to the ground, spewing its contents across the carpet towards Leanne who, unsure how to react, had remained frozen to the spot.

As Charlotte gave a piercing wail, Kelly scrambled across the floor on her hands and knees, desperate to return the spilled contents to the bag.

'Look what you've done!' she sobbed, as she discovered that the stone, which had been thrown against the skirting board, had split and that the cup was even more dented than before.

'Look what *I've* done?' screamed Charlotte. 'Look what *you've* done to my head!' Kelly looked up and was, despite her anger, shocked to see that blood was oozing between the fingers of the hand which Charlotte held clamped to the side of her forehead.

'What's going on here?' It was Mr Walker, who had heard the disturbance and had come rushing out of his room. 'Leanne, don't just stand there! Run and fetch Mrs Letterman. Tell her to bring the First Aid kit. Kelly, go and wait outside the head's office. And you can leave those things where they are,' he shouted, looking at the strange collection of items that Kelly had gathered into her lap and was madly trying to stuff into her bag.

Kelly was fighting back tears. She hadn't started anything, and she hadn't intended to hurt Charlotte, yet Mr Walker wasn't even giving her a chance to explain. Reluctantly, she got to her feet and sloped off down the corridor towards the stairs.

She had been sitting outside the head's office for a good fifteen minutes before Mr Walker appeared, carrying her school bag.

'Sir, I can explain,' stammered Kelly.

Mr Walker just held up his hand. 'Save it for the head. Come on, I'll take you in now.'

Kelly had never been inside the head's office before. It was much smaller than she expected, and smelled vaguely of over-ripe bananas. The headteacher, Mr Cole, gestured to a chair and told Kelly to sit down.

'Right, Miss Hearn,' he began. 'Mr Walker has already explained what happened, over the phone. There was a witness, I understand.'

Kelly nodded, a lump forming in her throat, making it impossible for her to speak.

'I accept that you may not have started this incident but we take any form of fighting very seriously here at The Shakespeare

Academy, and this particular fight has resulted in someone getting badly hurt. So I have no choice but to put you on a short-term suspension while we get to the bottom of it. That means I need to phone your parents and ask them to come into school to see me.'

Kelly found her voice and snorted, 'Good luck with that, sir!'

Mr Walker interjected, 'Kelly comes from a Traveller family, Mr Cole, and while her parents have agreed to her coming here, they're not too comfortable about coming into school themselves.'

'All right. Then I am more than happy to speak to your parents by telephone, Kelly. Will someone be there now, if I ring them?'

'Yes. My mum'll be there,' she mumbled, looking down at her lap.

Kelly listened while Mr Cole calmly explained to her mother who he was and what had happened. She knew how her mum would react—defensively. That was her style: refuse to accept any criticism of her offspring in public, then tear a strip off them in private. Kelly couldn't imagine that this phone call was going to do anything but make matters worse and she looked across to Mr Walker, with a hopeless, pleading expression. Mr Walker smiled lightly, trying to offer some silent encouragement.

It didn't start well. Even from the other side of the desk, Kelly could hear her mum's raised voice, ranting down the other end of the phone. But Mr Cole must have dealt with more than his fair share of angry parents, because he seemed to know just how to handle Mrs Candy Hearn. He let her have her say, and blow off some steam and then, to Kelly's surprise, began to sympathise with her. He understood, Mr Cole said, how difficult it was for Kelly. He knew that other students—and especially Charlotte Kennedy—had given her a hard time and he had received very positive reports about the way Kelly had handled herself throughout her first year. He assured Kelly's mum that Charlotte would face some serious sanctions for her bullying behaviour and for inciting this particular incident.

Kelly could hear that her mum had gone quiet. *Blimey*, she thought. *He's winning her over*. It was now her turn to give Mr Walker a little reassuring smile.

Then Mr Cole outlined his conclusion. 'It's out of my hands, Mrs Hearn,' he explained. 'Whether or not Kelly was to blame for the fight, she's caused physical injury and school policy states that I have to give her a fixed-term exclusion. That gives me time to speak with all the students and families involved, to let everyone have their say, and to ensure that we make a fair assessment on the cause of the incident.'

He explained that Kelly would need to be collected straight away and was to stay at home the next day, too. When she returned to school on Wednesday morning, she would be required to submit a five-hundred-word essay on how to resolve conflict without resorting to physicality.

Mum obviously agreed, because Mr Cole thanked her and hung up, then directed his attention towards Kelly again. 'Your mother is on her way. You can wait for her in reception. I'm sure I don't need to repeat what I told her. Are you clear about what's happening now?'

'Yes, sir.'

'Good. Now I don't expect to see you in my office again, Kelly Hearn. Not unless you're bringing me good news. And listen. If you experience any kind of bullying in future, we want you to tell a member of staff, okay? Mr Walker is here to help you. We all are. You don't need to handle it all by yourself.'

'Thank you,' whispered Kelly, finding herself having to fight back tears for the second time that morning.

Chapter 17 – September 2012

The good thing about being excluded for standing up to a bully is that your mum and dad go relatively easy on you. Kelly's mum had done her best to be stern in the car when she drove her home, and had tried to echo Mr Cole's mantra that violence was never the answer to conflict. But Kelly could tell that she was quietly pleased that Charlotte had finally been exposed and that the school was taking the bullying of her daughter seriously.

Dad didn't even try to pretend to be mad. He beamed at Kelly with pride. 'That girl wanted some sense knocking into her. Good on you, Kel. She won't bother you again.'

'I didn't mean to hurt her, though, Dad,' replied Kelly. 'And look where it's got me. An exclusion. That'll be on my school record. And I've got to write that stupid essay.'

Annoyed at herself, and still feeling that she had been punished unfairly, Kelly decided to write the essay that night, get it out of the way, and make the most of her day off. She would console herself with a long walk with Tyson and get some more research done for her history project.

She was particularly keen to go and take some more photographs. She was a bit disappointed with how the shots from the quarry had turned out. The close-ups of the artefacts were okay, but the photo she took on a self-timer, to show the site where they were found, was out of focus and she'd managed to cut Ben off altogether. So the next day she rose early and brought her camera and notebook with her to the breakfast table, ready to head out as soon as she had finished her cereal and toast.

It was a lovely morning, crisp, dry and sunny. Typical of that time of year when summer was just ending and autumn was just around the corner. Perfect for a hike up to the quarry.

'Hang on a minute,' said Mum, eyeing the camera. 'An exclusion is meant to be a punishment, you know, not an excuse to do as you please.'

'But this is for school work,' whined Kelly. 'For my history project.'

'Well okay. Maybe you can go out later, then. But not until you've done some jobs. I think you owe me some help in return for forcing me to speak to that headteacher of yours. I didn't know what to think when he first came on the phone. And I had to come out specially to pick you up. I was in the middle of icing a cake, too. The icing had gone rock hard by the time I got back. I had to throw it all away and start again.'

Kelly couldn't argue, so she whizzed through the list of jobs her mum gave her as fast as she could, looking out the window every few minutes to check that the weather was still fine.

It was after twelve by the time she finally stepped outside to pull on her walking boots, ready to head off.

She decided to start with the old lime kilns. To save time, she ate a sandwich on the way, stopping every now and then to feed tiny pieces to Tyson. She seemed to reach the site of the kilns in no time at all, and spent a good half hour photographing and sketching the one that Ben had first showed her.

Tyson found the stick he had been chewing when they were there last, and was blissfully happy, sitting by Kelly's side as she worked. He seemed to sense that this was a special treat, having Kelly home on a weekday, and was unusually well behaved. He hadn't even chased the hare that they had spotted bounding across the field as they approached the quarry. But he couldn't resist springing to his feet and racing up the path when he spied Ben approaching.

Startled, Kelly put down her sketch pad and stood up. 'What are you doing out here in the middle of the afternoon?' she asked, surprised to see him. 'Why aren't you having lessons? Your mum hasn't excluded you too, has she?'

'Excluded me?' asked Ben.

'Yes. I got into some trouble at school. They sent me home. Long story. More's the point, what are you up to? I didn't expect to see you.'

'Well, I don't think I'm in any trouble. My mother wouldn't let me out of the cottage if I was. When I'm being punished, my parents make me do all the horrible, smelly jobs, like cleaning the drains. Or I have to do the washing up for a week or wash everyone's underwear. Now that's bad!'

Kelly giggled. Ben sat down on the log and picked up her sketch pad.

Kelly looked at him expectantly. 'You still haven't said why you're here. You've got to admit, it's a bit weird. Talk about a coincidence. It's like you knew I'd be here.'

'Just lucky, I guess. And not so weird. I come here a lot. I don't have to do school work all day and my mum doesn't mind me coming out for some fresh air. Call it my physical education!'

Ben gave Kelly a lop-sided smile and a wink and she instantly forgot her next question. Ben patted the log next to him. 'Come on. Sit down. I'm dying to know what you did that was so bad they sent you home.'

Kelly recounted the fight with Charlotte and her trip to the headteacher's office. Ben sympathised and, like her mum and dad, seemed to think that Charlotte deserved everything that happened to her.

'I am glad it's all come to a head. It's quite a relief really. But I just can't help feeling mad at myself, for letting Charlotte get to me. She's probably laughing at me now, because she knows I've been excluded. And besides, I think I've lost our first bits of evidence, from the quarry. Mr Walker confiscated the bag of artefacts and my special stone got broken in the fight. It can't have done the other things any good either, being dropped on the floor.'

'Why on earth that does that matter?' asked Ben. 'There's plenty more rock in that quarry, and what's a few dents in an old tin mug?' He leaned towards Kelly as he spoke, moving his head closer to hers. Then, just as she was about to respond, he quickly withdrew again.

'Did you bring that boot with you?' he asked, rather hurriedly.

Kelly felt flustered. 'No. Well I didn't expect to see you, did I?'

'No, I suppose not.'

They fell silent. Kelly filled the awkwardness by finishing her sketch while Ben played tug-of-war with Tyson and his stick.

After a few minutes, Kelly looked at her watch and stood up. 'I'd better be heading back. Mum was keen to remind me that I'm not on a day's holiday. I shouldn't really push my luck and stay out too long.'

'Is it okay if I walk with you some of the way back?' asked Ben sheepishly.

'Yes, of course. I'd like that.'

* * *

The pair chatted happily as they walked back across the fields. Tyson was in his element, having someone new to throw sticks for him, and by the time they had crossed the canal, he was panting heavily.

Kelly headed for the small path that ran through the woods past the well and the old shed.

'There's a better path further on down here, you know,' said Ben. 'It's not so overgrown and it ends up by the same railway crossing.'

'I know,' Kelly said over her shoulder, as she ploughed on regardless. 'I came that way earlier, but I just fancy going back this way. I haven't done it since that day at the well.'

Ben reluctantly followed, but the closer they got to the old shed, the more he moaned about how overgrown the path was. 'This is the worst route, Kelly Hearn,' he grumbled. 'Can we please just turn back and go the other way?'

'You came this way the other day, and I didn't make you do it then!' snapped Kelly, increasingly irritated by his whining.

Ben pulled a face but, evidently seeing that Kelly was determined to continue, he shook his head and trudged on.

By the time they arrived at the clearing in front of the shed, the sun had gone in and a chilly wind had started to blow.

Kelly stopped, put Tyson on the lead, and turned to her friend. 'What do you think this old place used to be? Do you think it was a railway workers' hut? It's old enough and it's in the right place. It might have been put there when they first built the railway. If they used to transport some of the lime and limestone by train then there might be some clues inside. Something to connect it to the quarry.'

'There won't be any clues,' said Ben, looking most unhappy. 'Not any more at any rate.'

'Have you been inside it, then? You seem so sure.'

'No, but it's so ramshackle. I just don't think it's worth bothering with.'

'Aw, come on,' pleaded Kelly. 'It'll be an adventure. And I don't want to try and get inside on my own. It's creepy.'

'You're right, it's creepy, and it's probably unsafe, too. Come on, you said you had to get home.'

'Oh, Ben, it's hardly going to take long to look around a mouldy old shed. What on earth's the matter with you?'

'Well, if nothing else, I think it's going to rain and I don't want to get soaked walking back,' grumbled Ben. 'Look at those clouds.'

'Let's hurry up, then,' replied Kelly, more than a little annoyed by Ben's mood. He seemed to blow from hot to cold. One minute he was happy to help her with her research, the next he clammed up. 'Look, you promised you'd help me with this project. We're supposed to be partners. So the least you can do is give me a hand with these.'

There was a pile of old tiles in front of the shed door, placed there deliberately, it seemed, to stop the door from swinging open. There was no bolt on the door and it was skewed very precariously on its hinges.

Kelly let go of Tyson's lead and began to move the tiles, three or four at a time, to one side. Reluctantly, Ben followed suit, and as soon as the way was clear Kelly took hold of the rusty old door knob and pulled gently. Nothing.

'Be careful,' said Ben. 'The door frame's so rotten it looks like the whole thing might fall on top of you.'

Kelly didn't reply. Nothing Ben could say was going to stop her from getting inside. She poked the tip of her tongue out of the side of her mouth and frowned with concentration. She took hold of the door handle with both hands this time, and tugged again, but now she lifted as she pulled. There was a squeak of wood dragging across wood as the door budged a few centimetres. Two more pulls and jerks and the door was open just wide enough to squeeze through. A strong, musty aroma escaped out into the daylight and Kelly took a step backwards.

Ben stared into the utter darkness of the shed. 'I really don't like it. You can't see a thing in there.' His voice trembled.

'Chicken!' retorted Kelly. 'Your eyes'll get used to the dark once you're inside. Look, are you coming or not?' Ben hesitated. 'Well, I'm going in, with or without you.'

Ben sighed. 'Oh, hang on a minute. Just let me get Tyson. We don't want him to run off while we're inside.'

He walked over to Tyson, who was sitting patiently a few steps away, and picked up the lead which was trailing from the little dog's collar. 'Come on Tyson, you can protect us.'

But Tyson had other ideas. He wasn't going anywhere, even when Ben tugged so hard on his lead that his collar nearly slipped over his ears.

'Look, for heaven's sake, Kelly,' Ben cried. 'Tyson doesn't want to come in either! I really don't think we should...'

But Kelly had already slipped into the darkness.

'Tyson and I will have to stay here and stand guard,' Ben shouted after her. 'It's probably better if we don't both go in anyway, in case we get trapped. No one would ever find us in there.'

Once inside the shed, the foul smell intensified. That, combined with the inky darkness, forced Kelly to stop in her tracks as soon as she was on the other side of the door. She didn't want to breathe through her nose, but then she didn't particularly want to taste the air either, so she covered her mouth and nose with her hand and took shallow breaths through her fingers while she waited for her eyes to adjust.

She heard Ben's shouts and was not surprised that he wasn't following her in. *He had no intention of coming in here from the start*, she thought, and made a mental note to tease him endlessly when she got back outside.

There were, in fact, narrow chinks of light penetrating through cracks in the roof, and gradually Kelly started to make out eerie shapes all around her. 'Yup,' she whispered. 'It's creepy.'

Perhaps Ben was right to be cautious. What did Mum and Dad always say about not doing anything silly?

And what *was* that smell? It reminded Kelly of something. Was it stale beer or something? She wondered if some teenagers, or perhaps a homeless person, had been using the shed as a drinking den, but quickly dismissed the idea. No one had been in here for a very long time.

Kelly stood there for what seemed like an age, trying to build up the nerve to move forwards. She held her breath to silence the pounding in her ears. Only when she was certain that nothing was moving inside the shed did she inch a few steps deeper inside.

Her right foot hit something and she gasped, but it was just an old box, tipped on its side. She looked about her again and made out the outline of an old oil lamp on a table to the right. Ahead of her, on the floor, a few planks of wood lay in a pile, like giant pick-up sticks.

Kelly walked on towards the centre of the shed and blew out steadily, trying to calm herself down. Then she felt a rush of icy air on her face. She span round. Had Ben managed to force the door open some more? No. There were still only a few centimetres of light showing through the door frame. She caught a reassuring glimpse of leaves blowing in the wind outside.

'The wind must be picking up,' Kelly told herself, and turned back to face the far end of the shed once more. She wished she had a torch with her. And why was it so cold? It was summer, for God's sake.

Then the hairs stood up on the back of her neck. A noise. Inside the shed. A creaking sound. It reminded Kelly of the sound of rigging on an old sailing ship, rocking back and forth on the ocean. Or was it footsteps on creaky floorboards? Had Ben decided to join her? No. She knew the answer to that, and besides, Kelly was beginning to realise that the sound wasn't coming from behind her, but from above her head.

Then she remembered her camera. Accepting that she would have to inhale the bad smell, she removed her hand from her face and fumbled around in her jacket pocket until she found what she was looking for. Pointing the camera up into the darkness, her hands trembling, she quickly pressed the button.

Flash!

A movement.

Something above her head. Dangling from the ceiling.

Kelly screamed and dived towards the door, her back arched, fully expecting something to grab her before she got there. She threw all her weight against the creaking old wood and burst out into the light, just avoiding banging into Ben. Tyson jumped up at her legs, clearly sensing something was amiss.

'There...was...something in there,' panted Kelly, her eyes wide with fear. 'Hanging from the ceiling. I took a photo. I caught a glimpse but couldn't make it out.' She didn't dare look back.

'Don't worry,' Ben reassured her, standing back to inspect her for any sign of injury. 'It was probably just a bat. We see lots of them at night around here. That shed's a perfect roost for them. With all those holes in the roof, they can fly in and out, as easy as ABC.'

'But there was a noise,' said Kelly, trying to regain her composure. 'It didn't sound like bats to me.' She narrowed her eyes. 'You weren't trying to play a trick on me, were you? You know, to teach me a lesson for going in there?'

'Of course not!' said Ben. 'You don't really think I would do that, do you?'

Kelly shrugged, pushing her dishevelled hair back from her face.

Ben looked offended. 'I wouldn't. Ever. I wouldn't do that to you. But you're right, I didn't want you to go in there. I don't like this place. Nor does Tyson.'

'Well, you were right about one thing,' Kelly conceded. 'I didn't see any clues in there that would link this place to the quarry. And I'm not going back in for another look.'

* * *

When she had calmed down again and Tyson had stopped leaping about in excitement, Kelly took the dog's lead and followed Ben in silence along the path through the woods and back in the direction of the caravan site.

'Do you know what?' said Kelly, a few moments later. 'I think we need a map of this area. We need to find out exactly what all these buildings were used for, and we're clearly not going to be able to find out by just looking at them. Do you think your mum and dad would have old farm plans or local maps or something?'

'They might.' Ben sounded rather distracted.

'Well, it's worth asking, don't you think? If they don't have anything, perhaps we could ask Tony at the farm. We really want something that dates back to the nineteenth century. And any pictures of the place when the quarry was still open would be brilliant. Will you ask?'

'I will. But my father is very busy. I can't promise anything.'

'I know. Just see what you can do,' said Kelly. 'And I'll spend some more time on the internet. I can't stay online for long at home because it's my mum's laptop and she gets fed up when I'm on it for hours. But I can use the internet when I get back to school tomorrow. I'll see what I can find out about Wilmcote quarry and the railway.'

They reached the last stile where the footpath came out onto the lane near Kelly's site.

'I'd best get back now.' Ben handed Tyson over the stile to Kelly.

'Okay.' She felt a lot more settled now that home was in sight. 'How about we catch up after school tomorrow? You could come and meet me at the bus stop. I get off at the village green.'

'Sorry, I can't do that. I won't have time to come down there and get back in time for my supper.'

'What time do you eat?'

'Five o'clock sharp.'

'My bus gets in at four. That's plenty of time,' said Kelly.

'Well, not really. Not if we have any news to share about the quarry. We wouldn't have time to talk properly, or go and explore. How about I meet you at the canal bridge, at six o'clock, after I've had my supper? We'll still have a couple of hours before it gets really dark.'

'All right,' Kelly agreed, starting to walk off up the lane. 'I'll see you then. Sorry, I mean, *we'll* see you then.' She waved one of Tyson's front paws at Ben.

Ben smiled and waved back. 'Bye.' Then he called after her, 'Oh, and don't forget to bring that old boot with you. I still want to have a look at it.'

PART 4

Chapter 18 – Christmas 1859

The winter of 1859 was harsh for the people of Wilmcote. Snow came well before Christmas, fell deep, and lasted for fourteen days, wrapping the village in a thick white blanket which the children adored but the adults loathed. Work in the quarry, which was dangerous at the best of times, became utterly treacherous.

For the first few days of the snow, Richard Greenslade forced his men to keep digging, terrified that production would otherwise fall too far behind schedule. But eventually, with the loaded trams struggling on frozen tracks, and the ponies repeatedly getting stuck in snow drifts, he was forced to reduce his workforce to a skeleton crew, who could work only the shallowest and least dangerous rock face. With a heavy heart, he sent the rest of his labourers home until further notice.

Without work to go to, the men gathered in the ale house, complaining about their lack of pay, while those lucky enough to still be earning a wage huddled around the lime kilns, complaining about frostbitten fingers and toes, and rocks so slippery that they spent more time on their backsides in the wet snow than on their feet.

Work on the railway was badly affected too. Only the last section of track between Wilmcote and Stratford-upon-Avon remained incomplete, and the men had been spurred on by the thought that the end was in sight. But now the frozen ground slowed their progress to a snail's pace. Working hours were slashed and dozens of Steamheads found themselves joining their Pithead friends, drowning their sorrows in the Mason's Arms, praying for a thaw.

* * *

The atmosphere in the Dentons' cottage kitchen on one of those snowy mid-December mornings, as the family sat around their kitchen table, was as icy as the wind whistling through the cracks around the door.

'You won't get much in your Christmas stocking this year, my boy,' William said to Billy. 'In fact, think yourself lucky if you get a stocking at all. I get paid by the day so if this snow keeps up much longer, we're done for.'

'Grandpa will see us right,' said Alice, ruffling her son's fluffy blond hair. Her only wish was to shield her son from their struggles, but the second the words came out of her mouth, Alice realised how foolish they were. She had unwittingly lit a touch paper and her husband's temper flared.

'No, he bleedin' well won't,' William shouted, slamming his mug down so hard that hot tea sloshed across the table. 'We're not giving that old goat an excuse to interfere in our affairs again. No wages, no matter. I'll make sure we have a bird on this table on Christmas Day, even if I have to go out and kill it myself. And there'll be presents in the boy's stocking, too.'

'I don't want anything, Father,' Billy said quietly. 'It's fine.'

'No, it's not fine,' spat William, rising from his chair. 'It's not fine when your wife doesn't have any faith left in you.'

'William!' exclaimed Alice, who had mopped up the spilled tea and was now putting the kettle back on the stove. 'You know that's not what I meant.' *Not again, please*, she thought. *Don't let's go through all this again.*

William met her gaze over the top of Billy's head and she could see, almost feel, the pain in his eyes. 'I can't do this any more, Alice,' he murmured. 'No matter what I do, I just...' Alice took a step towards him but he rose to his feet and turned away. She and Billy watched him leave the room, his head bowed. Then they heard a rustle as he put on his coat and cap, a gentle thud, thud as he pulled on his boots, and the click of the front door as he left.

'Where's he going?' Billy asked his mother. 'I thought there was no work today.'

'I expect he'll go and see the foreman, see if there is anything he can do. If not, I expect he'll be waiting outside the Mason's Arms when it opens.'

Alice flopped down dejectedly into the seat next to Billy and watched him eat the rest of his porridge.

'Is it true what they are saying at school?' Billy asked, as he scraped the bowl clean with his spoon. 'That the quarry won't receive another penny unless the last batch of stone is delivered on time?'

'I'm afraid so.'

'But that's not fair!' exclaimed Billy. 'Father and the others can't possibly work any faster, and they couldn't have stopped the snow from falling, could they?'

Alice smiled at her son. No matter what, he always tried to see the best in his father. 'Don't you worry,' she said, giving him a kiss on the cheek. 'I'm sure it will all be fine in the end.'

Chapter 19 – September 2012

On Wednesday morning, when Kelly walked back into her tutor group room, there was no sign of Charlotte. Leanne was sitting on her own, looking a little lost with the empty space beside her. As Kelly slipped by to take her usual seat at the back of the classroom, Leanne dropped her eyes.

Charlotte still hadn't come by the time Mr Walker arrived and he made no mention of her as he ran through the register, missing out her name from the list.

Registration at The Shakespeare Academy was also a chance for students to ask their tutor questions, or share anything that was worrying them. Kelly was itching to ask about Charlotte, but didn't want to talk about the fight in front of her tutor group. The sooner everyone forgot about that, the better.

But she wasn't kept wondering for long. When it was time for the first lesson, Mr Walker dismissed the form but asked Kelly and Leanne to stay back. He waited until the three of them were alone, then began, 'I expect you are both wondering where Charlotte is.'

Both girls nodded.

'Well, I'm afraid she won't be coming back to this school.'

Kelly blinked and swallowed hard. Leanne didn't react.

'Charlotte's parents have decided to move her to another school. And before you say anything—' He looked at Kelly. '—This wasn't just about what happened on Monday. We informed Charlotte's parents about all the previous incidents of bullying which she's been involved in, too. I know you were at the receiving end of a lot of those, Kelly, and I'm genuinely sorry about that. But we needed someone to speak up before we could act.' Mr Walker looked over at Leanne. 'Thankfully, someone was brave enough to do just that.'

It took a few seconds for her teacher's meaning to sink in. When it finally did, Kelly turned to Leanne, who met her gaze with a nervous smile. Mr Walker continued, 'Charlotte's parents have found her a place at a school which can offer her some additional support. Plus, we all agreed that a fresh start somewhere else might be just what she needs.'

Kelly's stomach leapt, delight bubbling up inside her. Not only had The Shakespeare Academy suddenly become a happier place, but for the first time ever, one of her classmates had actually stood up for her. More than that. Leanne had gone out on a limb for her.

'So are you both all right?' Mr Walker asked. 'Do you have any questions? Anything you want to say?'

Kelly and Leanne exchanged glances then both shook their heads. 'No, sir.'

'Good!' said Mr Walker, rubbing his hands together. 'Then we'd all better get off to lessons.'

The girls started to head for the door.

'Oh, and Kelly. If you want to come and see me at break time, I will give you your bag back.' Kelly couldn't believe she had forgotten about that. 'And I want to talk to you about the objects you dropped. I found them rather fascinating.'

Kelly could hardly concentrate after that. During her first two lessons, she kept thinking how brilliant school was going to be without Charlotte around. She wondered what had made Leanne finally rat on her friend. Had she ever really liked Charlotte? Maybe she'd just been too afraid of her to tell her what she really thought.

And on top of all that, she couldn't wait to hear what Mr Walker had found so fascinating about the contents of her canvas bag.

When finally the bell rang for break, she rushed down the corridor to the tutor group room and knocked on the door. Mr Walker was already there, her three treasured artefacts spread out on the desk in front of him.

'So do you want to tell me what you were doing with a rock and two rusty bits of old metal in your bag, Miss Hearn?' he asked, with a wry smile.

Kelly reminded him about her choice of topic for the history project and how she and her friend had found the items in the abandoned quarry in Wilmcote. Then she told him all about the various sites they had identified so far—the stone pits, the lime kilns and the tramlines.

'But there are still some old buildings we can't identify, and we really need to get a better sense of the whole site and how the quarry linked to the railway. My friend's trying to get hold of a map or a plan, from the time when the quarry was working. I know we need to pin down some more accurate dates.'

Mr Walker scratched his chin and nodded. He seemed impressed by what Kelly had told him so far. 'Well, if there is evidence of tramlines leading from the quarry to the canal and to the railway, then you're probably talking about the mid-nineteenth century onwards, in the middle of Queen Victoria's reign. Certainly most of the railway network in England was more or less in place by the 1850s.'

Kelly remembered something Ben had said on one of their first walks around the old quarry site. 'I think my friend said that Wilmcote station opened around 1860. So that would be about right, wouldn't it, for a small branch line?'

'Definitely,' agreed Mr Walker. 'And your quarry would have been in its heyday around that time.'

Kelly sat down and rummaged in her school bag for her notebook. 'So what do you think about these things we found, sir?' she asked. 'Could they date back to the 1850s?'

'The mug, yes, that looks like it could easily be Victorian to me. And if you found it in the quarry it probably belonged to one of the masons. They would have needed a hot mug of tea or two to wet their whistles working in all that dust, and to warm them up during the winter, too. It would have been hard labour, you know, in those days. In fact, I remember reading something...hold on a minute.' Kelly watched as her teacher went over to his bookshelf, traced along the various spines with his finger, and then pulled out a tatty, well-thumbed volume.

'*How the Industrial Revolution Changed the World*,' he read out. 'Borrow this, if you like. It will be perfect for your project.'

'Thank you, sir,' said Kelly, pleased.

Mr Walker was flicking through the pages. 'Yes. Here it is. I knew I had read this somewhere. It's in a chapter talking about manual work. And it's a limestone quarry, too, like the one in Wilmcote. Listen to this.' He read: 'The quarrymen brought tea, bread, cheese and fat bacon for their midday meal. The bacon would be fried on shovels at the kilns and the men would then pour the liquid fat into their mugs of tea.'

He looked up from the page. Kelly stared at him, mouth open.

'It's a great image, isn't it?' he said.

Kelly found herself unable to speak. A great image. Yes. A picture of Ben, sitting next to her on a log, dreaming of bacon cooking.

Mr Walker picked up the other piece of mangled metal. 'This looks like an old trowel or small shovel.' He held it to his nose and sniffed. 'I wonder if anyone ever fried any bacon on this. What do you reckon, Kelly?' He broke into such a broad, infectious smile that Kelly burst out laughing. She pushed the image of Ben to the back of her mind and picked up the two broken pieces of stone.

'This stone is limestone, I know that,' she said. 'But I'd like to know a bit more about what it was used for and who Wilmcote quarry's biggest customers were.'

'Well, it was definitely a popular building material at the time. And I took the liberty of showing it to Mrs Arnold, the Head of Geography. She said it's called lias stone.'

'It's lovely and smooth,' said Kelly. 'And it was a perfect diamond shape until it got broken.'

'But look *how* it's broken.' Mr Walker took the two pieces from her and fitted them back together. 'Look how cleanly it has split. That's what made it especially good for paving and flooring, Mrs Arnold said. It splits so easily into sheets.'

'My friend told me that they built parts of Ragley Hall from Wilmcote stone. I wonder if that's what they used it for there, for the floors.'

'Well that would be quite an important contract for the quarry to win,' said Mr Walker, 'but not as impressive as the thing I found out next. After I spoke to Mrs Arnold, I did a little bit of research myself and looked up your quarry at Wilmcote on the internet.'

'And...?'

'If I asked you to name one of the most famous buildings in the country, one which was really important in our history, what do you think you would say?'

Kelly thought for a minute, shaking her head and looking up to the ceiling for inspiration. 'Gosh, I don't know. Warwick Castle? That's not far away. No, somewhere more important. Westminster Abbey? Buckingham Palace?'

'You're getting closer. And it was a palace, yes, but not one that a king or queen lived in.'

'In London?'

'Yes.'

Kelly was stumped. 'I can't think,' she said, frustrated but enjoying the game.

Mr Walker leaned towards her and lowered his voice conspiratorially. 'Well, did you know that the Houses of Parliament are also known as the Palace of Westminster?'

Kelly sat back in her chair, not knowing what to say.

Mr Walker filled her stunned silence. He held up one of the pieces of limestone. 'Could this be the perfect paving stone for the most important building in the world? Walked upon by dozens of prime ministers, secretaries of state, hundreds of MPs, and even kings and queens. Queen Victoria, Edward VII, King George V, our Queen today...'

'Wow! It could!' cried Kelly, interrupting his flow. 'That would have been a pretty important contract!'

'You're right there,' said Mr Walker, looking at his watch. 'Look, we've run out of time, but I suggest you find out what building work was going on at the Houses of Parliament in the nineteenth century and how that might tally with Wilmcote history.'

'I will,' replied Kelly, hurriedly gathering up her things and placing the artefacts carefully back inside the canvas bag. 'Thank you so much, sir. This is all so cool.'

Once again, Kelly found herself watching the clock all through her lessons, wishing the time away until lunch. Not thinking for one second about food, she raced down the hallway towards the LRC. She didn't see Leanne coming out of the toilets and walking towards her until she was nearly on top of her.

'Oh, it's you!' she said abruptly, 'Sorry, I didn't see you.'

'Have you had your lunch yet?' Leanne enquired, timidly. 'Cos I was wondering if I could buy you a sandwich.'

'Er, no. I'm skipping lunch today. I have something to do.' Then, realising how unfriendly she must sound, she added, 'But thanks for asking.'

Leanne touched Kelly's arm to stop her moving off, clearly needing to say her piece. 'Look, I just wanted to say I'm sorry. Charlotte was wrong to treat you like she did.'

Kelly pulled her arm away and tucked her hair behind her ear. 'So why didn't you stop her? Why didn't you say anything?'

'Sometimes I tried to. But I guess she bullied me, too, really. She made it pretty clear that I had to go along with it. She said that if I didn't stick with her, she would tell everyone about my dad. He's left my mum, you see.'

Kelly moved to the side of the corridor and beckoned Leanne to come closer. 'Look, I'm really sorry, Leanne. That's rough. But why did you let Charlotte hold that over you? Nearly everyone's parents are splitting up these days. It's not that unusual.'

'It *is*, when your dad leaves your mum for a man.'

'For a... Oh, I see!' Kelly's eyes widened as the penny dropped. 'But Leanne, that's not something to be ashamed of.'

'Don't you think so?'

'Well, it's different. And I happen to like different.'

Leanne grinned and looked down at her feet, before asking, 'So, how about that lunch?'

'Nah, sorry. I really *do* have something to do on the computer. But maybe tomorrow?'

Leanne's face lit up. 'You're on.'

Chapter 20 – Christmas 1859

Sir Charles Barry spent the Christmas of 1859 at home with his family. The heavy snow had made the celebrations all the more magical for his children and Barry was determined not to dampen their spirits. But in truth, he had found it difficult to push his troubles to the back of his mind. So when his friend Sir Francis Throckmorton joined them for Boxing Day lunch, the conversation soon turned to less festive matters.

The cook, the housekeeper and the maid had been given the day off and sent home with a box of leftovers to share with their own families, so Sarah had laid out a cold buffet. While she was busy clearing it away, the two gentleman went to sit by the fire with a glass of malt whisky each.

'So what's troubling you, my friend?' said Sir Francis, leaning forwards in his chair, as soon as Sarah had left the room. 'You're hardly bursting with Christmas cheer.'

'Where do I begin?' replied Barry, raising in hands in exasperation. 'The Westminster project is going to be the death of me. The Chambers may be finished and in use, but we still have a long way to go.'

'How long do you think? Since your original estimate was, oh what was it, six years?' Sir Francis smirked.

Barry glared at him. 'Yes, and it will be twenty years this coming May. You don't think I know that? And I shall soon be turning sixty-five. Good God, man, I shall go to my grave regretting the day I ever mentioned that six-year figure.'

'I apologise, Sir Charles. I was jesting. I'm not apportioning any blame. I know you were pressured into providing an unrealistic date. On a project of this scale it's almost impossible to foresee all the problems that might crop up.'

'Exactly,' agreed Barry, staring into the fire. 'All this snow is a perfect example. It's so cold that the mortar won't dry, the water supplies are all frozen, and the delays we have had with deliveries are crippling us. The stone supply from Wilmcote dwindled to almost nothing in the approach to Christmas.'

Sir Francis swirled his glass, the golden whisky glowing warmly in the firelight. 'But the bulk of the construction is now complete, which is marvellous, isn't it?'

'Certainly. Most of the work now is interior finishing. But that's no easy task. I have my late friend Pugin to thank for that, with his sumptuous designs. Carvings, gilt work, panelling, furniture, even door knobs and spill trays—the standard of workmanship required is beyond anything I have seen before. It will be stunning, I can assure you of that, but I can't allow the work to run a day over the twenty years mark and I must have the whole thing signed off by the State Opening of Parliament in November. If we are not finished by then, I may as well throw myself off the clock tower. My reputation will be in tatters.'

He rose sharply to his feet, unable to sit still any longer, and crossed the room to collect a crystal decanter from its silver tray on the intricately carved walnut sideboard. He was speaking more rapidly now, not waiting for Throckmorton to make comment.

'Oh and we must not forget Prince Albert's latest request—a mosaic in the central lobby. That will be time-consuming if we are to get it just right. And there are yards and yards of limestone paving slabs still to be laid.'

Barry reached up to his collar and slipped his fingers inside to try to loosen its grip. His face felt puffy and hot, and when he came closer to top up his tumbler with another generous shot of whisky, his pouring hand trembled.

'Perhaps I can help relieve you of one of your worries,' Throckmorton offered, gesturing to his host to retake his seat opposite him. 'I know you are worrying about the supply of limestone from Wilmcote, so getting that new Stratford-upon-Avon railway line finished would be a huge weight off your shoulders, would it not?'

'It would indeed,' sighed Barry.

Throckmorton tapped his nose with his index finger. 'Well, I have heard that the Stratford-upon-Avon Railway Company have approached Parliament about another branch line, south of the town. Perhaps I can convince them that if they can finish the Stratford-upon-Avon to Hatton branch by the end of September, then their other application might pass through Parliament more swiftly—perhaps even at a lower cost. That might put them on their toes and make them think it's worth throwing more manpower at the problem.'

'You would do that?' asked Barry, hopefully.

'For you, my friend, yes.' He smiled and raised his glass at Barry.

'I would be forever in your debt.'

Sir Francis chuckled. 'Oh, I'm sure there will be something you can do for me in return.'

Barry wasn't surprised. Sir Francis was his friend, but Barry was a desperate man, in dire financial straits, and Sir Francis had not reached his position of power without taking advantage of a few desperate men along the way.

Barry was about to respond when Sarah entered the room.

Seeing her, Sir Francis cleared his throat and said loudly, 'Anyway, enough about Westminster. It's Christmas.'

Sarah shot her husband a sharp look. 'I knew if I left you two alone together for five minutes that you would be discussing business. You are quite right, Sir Francis. That's enough about Westminster. My husband needs a rest from that matter.'

'Sarah!' Barry looked anxiously from his wife to his friend. 'You will offend our guest.'

Barry sensed that his relationship with Sir Francis Throckmorton had just changed. He hoped that the MP was doing nothing more than helping him out, as a friend. But somehow, being beholden to a man so cut-throat in business matters was unsettling.

Chapter 21 – September 2012

Kelly was the first to get off the school bus when it pulled up at the village green, so excited was she about meeting up with Ben later that evening. She couldn't wait to tell him everything she had found out, and especially the part about the Houses of Parliament.

While on the school computers that lunchtime, she had followed Mr Walker's advice and done some more research. Sure enough, work on Sir Charles Barry's new building was still ongoing in September 1860 when the Stratford-upon-Avon railway line opened. Kelly was certain that this was linked to Wilmcote quarry's contract to supply stone.

'Oh, why couldn't Ben have met me off the bus?' Kelly moaned to herself as she walked home up the lane. 'I could have told him all this by now.'

Willing six o'clock to come faster than normal, she broke into a run and got back home in record time.

'You've got home fast today,' Mum said.

Kelly pecked her on the cheek and slipped past her straight into her bedroom.

'I know. I ran,' she called back. 'I'm meeting Ben later, at six. I've got stuff to do before I go.'

Kelly began to change out of her school uniform, while her mum continued the conversation from the kitchen, where she was preparing some vegetables for dinner.

'You're spending a lot of time with that boy,' she said. 'Your dad and I are a bit concerned, to be honest. We haven't even met him.'

'He's really nice, Mum. Very sensible.' Kelly emphasised the word 'sensible', mimicking how Mum would say it.

'Sensible or not, we don't know him from Adam and we're not too happy about you staying out so late on these school nights. It's getting dark earlier and earlier.'

'But I can't meet Ben until six, after he's had his supper. And it's all arranged.'

'Well, this will have to be the last time, Kelly.' Mum's voice took on a firm note. 'After tonight you either see Ben straight after school or at the weekend. And I want you to promise me you will be home by seven tonight.'

'I will,' sang Kelly.

'And if Ben's so sensible, he won't mind walking you home. Perhaps he can introduce himself to us at the same time.' Kelly didn't reply. 'And Tyson goes with you, of course.'

'Okay, okay,' Kelly assured her, closing her bedroom door.

She leaned against the back of the door and sighed. She didn't really mind Mum laying down the law. She got where she was coming from. In fact, Kelly was quite surprised that her parents hadn't insisted on meeting Ben before. They didn't usually like her mixing with anyone outside their own community. But perhaps her going to high school had softened them. They had seen that she hadn't changed. She was still the same old Kel.

Satisfied that her mum wasn't going to come in and continue the conversation, Kelly knelt down and pulled her treasure box out from under her bed. She lifted the lid and took out the boot. 'Is it just me or does the leather look brighter?' she mused. It felt softer, more supple, too.

'I wonder who you belonged to,' she whispered. Then she chuckled. She had had a good day finding things out so far. She had discovered all kinds of surprises. So who knew? Maybe she would trace the history of the old boot, too.

She found an old T-shirt and wrapped it around the boot before slipping it into her canvas bag. Then she grabbed her camera and notebook and popped them into the bag as well. She was all set.

By the time Kelly had eaten her tea and helped Mum to dry the dishes, she and Tyson were late leaving the site. She didn't reach the canal until after six, even though they ran all the way. But to her relief, Kelly could see Ben waiting patiently on the bridge as she and Tyson approached. He was standing right on the apex of the small bridge, one foot either side of the narrow gap which ran down the middle of it, staring down through the crack into the olive-green water beneath.

'They used to drop the towing line down here,' he said without looking up. 'When the boats were drawn by horses.'

'Uh?' Kelly grunted, trying to catch her breath. 'What do you mean?'

'Without this gap they would have had to make the bridge much wider to allow the towpath to continue under it. That was expensive. But if they left a gap in the top of the bridge like this, they could thread the tow line through it as they sailed under, and they didn't have to unhitch the horse up on the towpath. Narrow bridge. Cheaper to build. Clever, hey?'

'Ingenious,' said Kelly, laughing. She was starting to regain her composure. 'Look, sorry I'm a bit late.'

'It's fine,' replied Ben, smiling. 'I knew you were coming.'

'Yeah but it means we've got less than an hour.'

'Then you'd better take a look at this right away.' Ben pulled a narrow, sepia-coloured envelope from his shirt pocket and waved it enticingly in front of Kelly's face. 'No, Tyson, it's not for you,' he added, as the excited little dog jumped up, convinced he was getting a treat. 'This is for Kelly. A map of the quarry. Showing everything that was here in the 1850s, before the railway was built.'

'Wow!' exclaimed Kelly, taking the envelope from him and gently extracting the contents. 'This looks a bit delicate.'

'It is. It's very old now.'

'Where did you find it?'

'Oh,' said Ben, scratching his head. 'I remembered that there was one in the attic.'

Kelly tied Tyson's lead to the rail where he wasn't in any danger of spoiling the old document, and she and Ben went to sit on the grassy slope next to the bridge. Kelly carefully unfolded the map and began examining it closely, checking off all the sites she and Ben had visited. Ben was right about the route of the tramway from the main quarry pit. A dotted line showed it winding its way down the hill past the lime kilns, which were marked with a series of ink lines, like tally marks, pointing inwards in a tiny circle. The tramline led to a series of buildings by the side of the canal labelled Blue Lias Lime and Cement Works.

'We haven't seen any sign of those, have we?' asked Kelly.

'No. They're long gone. Although the ground is very bumpy over there. Perhaps that's the foundations, under the soil.'

'What about that hut in the wood, near the well?' Kelly traced the map with her finger. 'Look. The well is marked on, but not the shed. That means it must have been put there later. I still think it had something to do with the railway. If this map is definitely dated 1850, and we know the railway opened in 1860, the shed could have been put there sometime in between. Perhaps it was a workmen's hut, or a storage hut.'

'Or it could be nothing to do with the railway at all,' said Ben. 'What else can we see on the map? Look, here's my cottage.'

Kelly wasn't listening. She couldn't shake the feeling that the shed was connected, somehow, to the railway. Then she remembered something. She jumped to her feet and went over to her bag, which Tyson was happily curled up against as he lay on the grass.

'Sorry, Tyson,' she mumbled, as she delved inside.

'What are you looking for?' asked Ben.

'My camera. I took a photo, didn't I? Inside the shed.'

'Yes, but it was pitch black in there,' said Ben. 'What could the camera possibly see?'

'It's got a flash.'

'What flash? You never said anything about seeing a flash.'

'No, silly! I'm talking about the camera's flash.'

Kelly sat down next to Ben and began scanning through all the photos she had taken. 'Look. There's the lime kiln. It was after that,' she said, tilting the view finder so Ben could see too. 'Here. There's the shed. Before I went in.'

She flicked through two more shots. One a close up of the old door handle, the next completely black.

'There. I told you. It was too dark,' crowed Ben, sounding almost relieved.

But then Kelly pressed the scroll button once more, and they both gasped. Lit up perfectly by her flash, hanging down from a roof beam, was a rope. A rope tied into the shape of a hangman's noose.

'What the hell...?' cried Kelly, almost dropping the camera.

Wide-eyed, she looked up at Ben, who had turned a ghostly shade of white.

Kelly felt a little dizzy. The memory of the creaking noise she had heard in the shed was all too clear. 'I'm a bit creeped out,' she said quietly. 'Why on earth would there be a noose in there?'

She saw Ben swallow hard. He was clearly contemplating the possibilities. After a few seconds, he said, 'You know, it's most likely some part of a pulley system. If the shed was used to store equipment for the railway—sleepers maybe—they probably needed some way of lifting things. Some of that stuff was incredibly heavy, you know.'

Kelly wasn't convinced, but she couldn't think of any other

practical reason for the noose being there, and her nana had always told her not to pick holes in someone's argument unless you could think of something better.

'Perhaps you're right. I did see some old pieces of timber in there.' Kelly switched off her camera and slipped it into her pocket. She nodded at the map. 'What else can you see on there?'

Ben began explaining what he knew about some of the other features that were marked, including an old barn further along the canal which was a sawmill. 'That was where they cut the stone. They did that near to the canal because they needed water to pour over the stones as they were cut. They used sand too.'

'But what did the masons cut the stone with? That must have been tough.' Kelly tried to sound interested, but she couldn't get the picture of the rope out of her head.

'Well they had engines by then, for power. It wasn't done by hand.'

'Would there be anything left inside the barn, do you think? An old engine?'

'I doubt it,' laughed Ben. 'The tinkers will have robbed all the metal long ago—' He stopped short, realising what he had just said.

Kelly's mouth closed into a small pout. She marched over to Tyson and began fumbling with his lead, untying him as quickly as she could.

'What are you doing?' asked Ben, tentatively.

Kelly shook her head, frustrated by the tears which spilled so easily down her cheeks. 'I thought you were different,' she sobbed, 'but you're just as prejudiced as the rest of them! We're not all thieves, you know!'

Ben looked appalled. 'No. Wait. Kelly, I didn't mean...'

Kelly wasn't listening. She grabbed her bag and began to drag Tyson towards the footpath. 'I had some great news to tell you but you can forget it. I'm going to finish this project on my own. I don't need help from someone like you!'

'But what about the map?' Ben called after her.

'You can keep it!' she barked back, over her shoulder.

Chapter 22 – September 2012

Kelly woke up the next morning feeling as wretched as the weather. She could hear the rain splattering against the window above her pillow and when she reached out to hit the snooze button on her alarm clock, the chill in her room created instant goosebumps on her arm. Groaning, she pulled her duvet up tight around her neck and snuggled back down into the warmth. But the precious extra few minutes of sleep that Kelly hoped for eluded her. The angry words that she had directed at Ben the night before buzzed around her brain, and when she closed her eyes, one image after the other flickered on the back of her eyelids like a gruesome slide show—Ben using that horrible T word; the old map, handwritten labels and black lines merging into one; menacing dark water rippling at the end of a slimy green well shaft; the cobweb-strewn shed; and that sickening, twisted, knotted loop of rope.

Kelly knew it was no good. She was not going to get back to sleep now. She might as well get up. She threw back the duvet and reached for her school uniform, shivering as she pulled on her skirt and fumbled with cold fingers at the buttons on her blouse. She kept replaying her conversation with Ben in her head and it made her angry and frustrated at the same time.

She had been so excited about sharing her news about the Houses of Parliament with Ben, yet with the discovery of that photo, and the old map, she hadn't even got round to telling him. And then he had made that stupid remark about tinkers. She felt so let down. Ben might have pretended to be cool about Travellers, but under the surface he was as prejudiced as everyone else.

Kelly's mood was not helped by her parents' comments over breakfast. When Kelly had burst into the caravan the night before, hoping to retreat straight to her room, her mum had demanded to know where Ben was and why he hadn't walked her home, as agreed. 'We had a fight, okay?' Kelly had blurted out, wiping away her tears with the back of her hand. 'I wouldn't have let him walk me home even if he'd paid me.'

Mum had let the matter lie at that point, but she had obviously been talking about it with Kelly's dad afterwards, because over breakfast they both seemed keen to press Kelly further.

'There was no need to snap at me when you came in last night,' commented Mum as she poured herself a coffee. 'I'm only looking out for you. And having you wandering about the countryside all evening with a boy we've never met isn't exactly ideal.'

'I was gone less than an hour, Mum!' Kelly mumbled, through a mouthful of Rice Krispies. 'And it won't be a problem from now on it, will it? I won't be seeing Ben any more.'

'Look, Kelly, we're sorry you and your friend have fallen out,' Dad said. 'But it's like we always say, mixing with outsiders ain't easy. Better to stick to your own kind.'

'He seemed so nice though.' Kelly put her spoon down. She didn't feel like eating any more. 'I thought he was different.'

Apparently reassured, Kelly's dad waved an olive branch in the form of a lift to the bus stop. Hearing the rain still pouring outside, Kelly enthusiastically accepted and dashed off to her room to fetch her coat and her school bag.

She kissed her mum goodbye, pulled the hood of her coat down low over her head, jumped down from the caravan, waved to Tyson who was peering miserably out at her from the door of his kennel, and raced down the path towards her dad's Nissan. At the gate, Dad pulled up and glanced over at Kelly with a lop-sided grin.

'Oh do I have to?' Kelly whined, realising that he wanted her to get out and open the gate. 'I thought the whole point of this lift was to keep me dry!'

Dad just nodded, giving her a cheeky wink.

Reluctantly, Kelly climbed out, her shoes squelching on the wet grass. She dragged the gate open, held it while Dad drove through, and was about to close it again when she noticed an envelope sticking out of their post box, which stood in a row of boxes at the entrance to the site, each bearing a family name. Dropping the latch on the gate, she ran over to the box and grabbed the envelope, shielding it with her body from the worst of the rain as she raced to get back inside the car.

'What you got there, love?' asked Dad, tipping his head in the direction of the envelope.

'I don't know.' Kelly turned the envelope over to see her name written in large letters on the front. It was a large, old-fashioned style envelope, sealed at what was now a rather soggy end, not with glue but by a thin piece of red string wrapped around a red cardboard disc. Kelly unwound the string, opened the flap and tipped the contents out onto her lap.

'It's from Ben,' she announced, as the car bumped along the lane.

'Peace offering?' enquired Dad.

'Maybe,' she mumbled, recognising the map from the night before. Along with it was a note, written in the same ink and the same, surprisingly elaborate handwriting as the envelope.

I'M SORRY! I did not wish to offend you. You have taught me so much yet I still have so much to learn. I hope you can forgive me and we can still be friends. But whatever happens, I want you to have this. Don't give up!

Ben

One side of Kelly's mouth curled into a smile. Without saying anything, she began to slip the note and the map back inside the envelope but as she did so, she noticed another document tucked in between the folds of the map. It was a tiny, yellowed, newspaper cutting.

The movement of the car and the small type size made it difficult to read at first, and Kelly had to hold the clipping up in front of her face to bring it into focus. It was headed *The Stratford-upon-Avon Times* and the date at the top read 15th March, 1861. But it was the headline that caused Kelly to take a sharp intake of breath:

'Accidental Death' verdict
in Bishopton Hill Railway Tragedy

A coroner's inquest into the loss of four lives at Bishopton Hill on the Stratford-upon-Avon to Hatton railway line in September last year has resulted in a verdict of accidental death. The owners of the line, the Stratford-upon-Avon Railway Company, were found not guilty of any negligence or mis-management. It was established that nothing could have been done to prevent this freak yet tragic accident which happened just outside the village of Wilmcote.

'Oh my God!' Kelly shrieked, covering her open mouth with her hand.

'What? What?' cried Dad, rapidly looking about him to see what he was about to hit, and stamping so hard on the brakes that his tyres locked. The car slid to a halt a few metres short of the bus stop.

'Sorry, Dad. Sorry. It's nothing. Well, I mean, not nothing. Just something Ben has found. It's about the railway.' She waved the newspaper clipping, as if trying to fan the expression of alarm off her father's face.

'Jeez, Kelly! I thought I was about to hit something.'

'No. You're fine, Dad. But there *was* an accident here. Four people were killed!'

'You're joking? Anyone we know?'

'No.' Kelly laughed. 'I don't know who it was. And it was a hundred and fifty years ago, Dad.'

'Oh well, that's all right then.'

'Well, not really.'

'No, you know what I mean. A hundred-and-fifty-year-old accident? What's that got to do with you? With us? Now?'

'It means I have a whole new chapter for my history project, that's for sure!' Kelly put the clipping safely inside the envelope. 'It's not just history now, Dad, it's a mystery, too. I've got to find out who the victims were.'

Dad playfully nudged her upper arm with his fist. 'I don't know, Kel. You're one on your own, you are. You're a clever girl, that's for sure. Perhaps you *were* right about staying on at school.'

Kelly smiled broadly. 'Thanks, Dad.' She leaned over to plant a big kiss on his cheek.

'Any time.' Dad watched Kelly in silence as she gathered her things and prepared to put up her umbrella as she stepped out of the car. She met his eyes as she popped her head back inside to say goodbye.

'I'm guessing this means you'll be wanting to see that boy again, though?' Dad asked, his smile turning to a slight grimace.

'I think I have to,' said Kelly quietly. 'Besides, he has apologised, in the note. Is that okay with you if I see him again? Can you back me up with Mum?'

Dad sighed. 'I guess so. But if he upsets you like that again, he'll have me to answer to. And your mum and I meant what we said about wanting to meet him.'

'Sure. Thanks, Dad,' said Kelly once more. She closed the door, stepped back and gave a little wave with her brolly.

As Kelly watched Dad's car pull away along the wet road, she noticed the postman walking towards her. He was a sprightly, friendly-faced, middle-aged chap with a bushy brown beard, and Kelly had bumped into him many times while out on her walks with Tyson. He waved to Kelly who, after checking her watch, dashed over to him.

She spoke quickly. 'I haven't got much time. My bus is coming any second. But could you possibly do something for me on your round today?'

The postman grinned. 'Depends on what it is. Anything to do with heavy boxes or angry guard dogs and you can count me out.'

'No, nothing like that,' laughed Kelly. 'I just wondered if you could put a note through someone's door for me.'

'Well... I'm not supposed to, really, love.'

'Pleeeease?' begged Kelly, putting her hands together as if in prayer. 'It's for my friend. I've got to get a message to him and I don't know his phone number. It's really important.'

The postman relented. 'Oh, go on then. But just this once.'

Kelly handed her umbrella to the postman who, to his own surprise, took it without question and held it over her while she rummaged for a notebook and began scribbling a note.

Ben
Apology accepted.
Meet 6pm tonight (Thursday). Campsite gate. Urgent!
Love Kelly

Kelly folded the note three times then wrote *Ben, Stone Pit Cottage* on the outside. Taking her umbrella back, she pressed the note into the postman's hand. Over his shoulder she could see her bus approaching.

'Do you know the cottage at the end of the lane beyond Stone Pit Farm? Stone Pit Cottage?'

'Er, yes,' said the postman. 'Well, I mean, I know where it is but I never go any further than the gate. They never get any parcels. Rarely get any letters either. Mostly just a bit of junk mail and I always stick that in the postbox at the end of the track. I'll put your note in there, if you like.'

'I guess that'll be okay,' said Kelly, walking backwards away from him, ready to jump on her bus when it pulled up. 'But I need to be sure my friend'll see the note today. You couldn't go up to the cottage for me, could you? Pop it through the door?' She gave him one of her nicest smiles.

'Look, love, that's a long, shabby old lane and it's full of pot-holes, and I'm already doing you a favour,' the postman shouted back. 'Besides, are you *sure* you've got the right address 'cause...'

The end of his sentence was washed away as a stressed parent on the school run zoomed by in her people carrier and decanted the contents of a giant puddle over the pavement. Kelly, who narrowly escaped a drenching, was unsure whether or not to run back and grab her note from the postman, but she couldn't think of any better way of getting the note to Ben. Instead, she gave him a cheerful wave and mouthed 'Thank you,' as she stepped onto her bus.

PART 5

Chapter 23 – September 1860

Therefore, my dear brothers and sisters, stand firm. Let nothing move you. Always give yourselves fully to the work of the Lord, because you know nothing you do in the Lord's service is in vain.'

Billy reached the end of his reading and gently closed his Bible before stepping out from behind the lectern and returning to his seat in the front row pew beside his mother. She smiled at him and patted the empty place as he approached. Alice always looked forward to her father's Sunday morning service. It was an hour of peace and tranquillity, when she felt safe and sheltered from life's challenges. She particularly enjoyed the services when Billy read. He spoke so well, his voice so clear and confident, that she was left bursting with pride, and she knew that her father, looking on from his seat beside the lectern, shared her emotion.

Furthermore, this week Billy had chosen the reading himself from the list in the Lectionary—a fact her father had made clear to his congregation when he invited his grandson to come and stand before them. *1 Corinthians 15:51-58*, a passage about the resurrection of Jesus Christ, revealing the 'secret truth' about the glorious after-life open to those who chose a life of hard work and good deeds. Billy had selected it for his father, to give him and the men like him, who were so exhausted from months of hard labour on the railway, the encouragement and strength of mind to reach their goal which, like the coming autumn, was now close enough to almost reach out and touch.

Alice felt humbled by her son's ability to see the best in his father. In spite of all the tension which William caused in their home, his constant nagging at Billy to leave school, and—they had to admit it—his increasing reliance on alcohol to boost his morale, Billy never gave up on him. He always believed that his father would come good. He had even made excuses for him that morning, when it was time to leave for Church and he was still unconscious in his bed. 'He's exhausted, Mother,' Billy had said. 'God will understand.'

Alice hoped that Billy was right and she prayed that God would also understand why she was no longer finding it easy to be so generous in spirit.

Billy and Alice held back as the congregation filed out of the church at the end of the service, each person stopping in the doorway to shake hands with Reverend Knott and offer him their thanks. When, finally, the last of them had gone, Alice and Billy stepped outside into the crisp September air.

'You *are* still coming to the vicarage for lunch?' asked the vicar, greeting his daughter with a kiss on the cheek.

'Of course,' Alice replied, patting her father on the arm.

'Without William? He is missing lunch as well as the service?'

Alice looked down and spoke to her feet. 'William is not well, Father. He has to rest.'

The vicar glanced at his grandson, raising his eyebrows in disbelief, but Billy backed up his mother's statement with a swift nod of his head. In an effort to divert his grandfather from the topic, he began walking towards the rectory.

'The colours of the leaves are simply gorgeous this time of year, aren't they, Father?' asked Alice, with the same intention as Billy.

But her father was not going to allow himself be led off track. 'Is he so in need of rest that he is unable to give his thanks to God? Surely he could rest after lunch. And besides, why *is* he in need of all this rest? I heard that all the line was now laid.'

'That's right, Father, it is,' replied Alice, hurrying along between the gravestones. 'But there's still an awful lot to do to prepare for the official opening. That's just two weeks away and everything has to be working smoothly before the first train runs.'

Billy joined in. 'Most of the workforce has been laid off now, Grandpa. The few that are left are all local men, like Father. Father says the foreman has them running back and forth all the time. Everything has to look spick and span and there are still last-minute adjustments to be made to the line.'

'Well I do appreciate that there must be a lot of pressure on them,' the vicar conceded. 'Richard Greenslade is certainly desperate to get his stone down to London more quickly. I'm surprised he hasn't insisted that they start sending goods trains down the line already. He's got a stake in the railway, I believe, so he ought to have a say in what goes on, too.'

They reached the vicarage and went inside. The vicar touched his grandson on the shoulder. 'Billy, be a good boy and go to the kitchen to tell Cook that we're back. That roast beef smells more than ready to me.'

As soon as the boy was out of earshot, Alice's father returned to the topic of his son-in-law. 'If it really *was* an exhausting workload that kept that husband of yours in his crib, I might forgive him, but I know that's not the case. He might be suffering, all right, but not from illness. I know it's the demon drink! I saw him with my own eyes, staggering homewards up the lane last night, hanging off the shoulders of those friends of his.'

Alice went pale. Tired of constantly covering for her husband, she collapsed into a chair and put her head in her hands.

Her father continued his rant. 'William should be ashamed of himself, leaving his wife and son at home of an evening with barely a loaf of bread on the table while he spends all the money he earns on ale.'

'He deserves to let off some steam. I'm not exaggerating the pressure he is under,' said Alice, blowing her nose into her handkerchief.

'Maybe not, but *you* deserve a husband who is well-mannered and doesn't bring you shame. And I'll wager he doesn't treat you well when he gets home full of ale. If he ever gives me reason to suspect that he's laid a finger on you...'

'My father would never do that!' Billy was standing in the doorway, glaring, his fists clenched at his sides. 'He loves my mother. He's trying so hard to please everyone—his foreman, Mother, me...and you! He knows he can never please you.'

'You're right there, my lad. He'll never please me as long as he keeps climbing into a cask of ale to drown out his problems.' The vicar was now in full flow, unable to stop the venomous words spilling from his lips. 'It's shameful. After all I've done to welcome God into this community. Those quarrymen may have brought wealth to the village but they've taken us to the depths of debauchery at the same time, and your father's at the heart of it. Oh yes. He may have left the quarry face, but he's still a—what do they call it? A Stonehead at heart.'

'Shut your mouth!' Billy, stiff with rage, had taken a step towards his grandfather.

'Stop it!' screamed Alice. 'Both of you. Apologise to your grandfather, Billy, now!'

'Why me?' Billy hissed at her through gritted teeth. 'You heard what he said.'

'Because he's your grandfather. He only says it because he loves you, Billy.' Billy, still fuming, said nothing. 'Then do it for me,' pleaded Alice, crossing the room to stand between her son and her father.

Billy's shoulders dropped. He looked past his mother directly into his grandfather's eyes. 'I'm sorry, Grandpa,' he croaked. 'But you're wrong about Father. He'll see us right. If the line opens on time, he'll get two extra months' pay. We'll be fine.'

The vicar turned to his daughter. 'At least let me give you some money until then, Alice. I know how bad things are. You need not tell William.'

Alice wanted to accept, but when she saw the look in Billy's eye she changed her mind. 'Thank you, Father, but no. Billy's right. William is due some extra wages, and he'd be so angry if he knew I had accepted your money. We are already taking your charity by living in your cottage. We must leave the man with some pride.'

'You mean he still has some of that?' scoffed the vicar.

'Father, please!' cried Alice, exasperated.

'I'm sorry, my dear, it's just… Well, you know how I feel.'

The three of them fell into silence; all reluctant participants in an awkward, three-way stand-off, no one wanting or willing to back down. Then they heard Cook's footsteps approaching in the hallway and the smell of their lunch filled their nostrils once more.

'That smells wonderful!' exclaimed the vicar, forcing cheer into his voice. 'Alice, Billy, we should eat. Oh, and you can take one setting away, thank you, Cook. Unfortunately, there will be only three of us eating, not four, as it should be.'

* * *

Ignoring this last barbed comment, Billy dropped reluctantly into his chair. He had lost his appetite both for lunch and for the fight with his grandfather. It was a battle he knew he could he never win. Nor could he ever completely sympathise with either side. Billy knew that his grandfather's words, no matter how harsh, sprang from a loving place. He was right to worry about his son-in-law's drinking, but he misunderstood the reasons for it and would certainly never accept that *he* was one of those reasons. Billy loved his father. It was as simple as that. If he didn't stand up for him, no one would.

Chapter 24 – September 2012

At six o'clock sharp, the Hearns' caravan door opened and Kelly emerged, wrapped up warm against the chilly evening and clutching Ben's envelope in her hand.

'Come on, Tyson,' she said. 'Mum and Dad say I need you as my minder again.'

She had had to sweet-talk her parents into letting her keep her appointment with Ben. After the previous night's episode they were less than enthusiastic about her giving Ben another chance. But after she had rattled on all through dinner about the newspaper cutting, how she hadn't even told Ben yet about Wilmcote's connection to the Houses of Parliament, and how she was sure the building of the railway was linked, they relented.

'We were serious about wanting to meet Ben, though, Kelly,' Mum reminded her, as she cleared away the plates.

'Well, he's coming here tonight, isn't he?'

'I thought you were meeting him out on the lane,' said Dad.

'Well, yes. I didn't think it was fair to ask him to come through the gate. It's a bit daunting, coming onto the site, if you're not one of us. You know that.'

'Maybe, but you should bring him in to say hello before he goes,' Mum insisted. 'And don't forget, we want you back by seven again. And no getting up to any mischief.'

'Like what?'

'Well, you obviously like this boy, and your dad and I are putting a lot of trust in you, letting you go off with him on your own. So you just behave yourself. You know what I mean.'

Kelly squirmed in her seat. 'Mum! He's just a friend.'

She couldn't believe Mum had said that. Clearly, she and Dad had been talking about it when Kelly was not there, and they were obviously keen to get a glimpse of Ben because she was sure the caravan curtains twitched as she walked away. She was doubly pleased she had told Ben to meet her outside the campsite gate where he would be out of their line of sight. She only hoped that he had got her message and would turn up.

As she led Tyson round the corner, Kelly let out a sigh of relief. He was there, waiting patiently, kicking stones off the grass verge into the lane. Tyson barked and pulled her towards him.

'You got my note,' she cried out. 'I was worried you wouldn't see it in time.'

Ben looked a little surprised. 'Note? Oh, yes. Of course. I knew you wanted to see me.'

Kelly glanced back over her shoulder. 'I'm not the only one,' she muttered under her breath.

'What was that?' asked Ben.

'Oh nothing. It's just my mum and dad. They want to meet you. I think they think that we're...you know...more than just...'

168

'More than just what?' Ben looked baffled.

'Well, more than just friends.' Kelly giggled, her face turning red.

'Oh, I think I see what you mean.' Ben giggled back.

'Thanks for coming, though, Ben. And thanks for the apology.' She held up the envelope.

Ben smiled. 'I wasn't talking about you, when I said that thing about tinkers. I didn't mean it about anyone, really. It's just something my grandfather says sometimes.'

'Your grandfather? You've never mentioned him before. Is he still alive?'

'No. No, he's not,' said Ben quietly.

He looked sad, so Kelly switched the conversation back onto the envelope. 'Giving me the map was a good enough apology, but that newspaper cutting! That swung it. I knew I had to see you when I read that.'

'What cutting?' asked Ben, looking perplexed.

'The one in the envelope with the map.'

Ben shook his head. 'I found that envelope in the same place as the map. I thought it was empty. I just used it to keep the map dry. A cutting from a newspaper, you say?'

'Yes. It's about an accident, on the railway line, here in Wilmcote, in September 1860. Four people were killed.'

Ben staggered slightly. Noticing, Kelly sat down on the grass, ignoring the fact that it was still slightly damp, and gestured to Ben to join her. Tyson instantly leapt onto Ben's lap and began licking his face. Ben pushed his muzzle away. 'I don't know what to say,' he stammered.

'Yeah, I know. It's weird, huh? It must have happened around the time when the railway line first opened. But listen, do you know what else was going on in 1860?'

Ben swallowed, drew Tyson towards him again and shook his head.

'The Houses of Parliament were being rebuilt, down in London. There had been a massive fire. And can you guess one of the materials they used to build it?'

They answered in unison: 'Wilmcote stone.'

Kelly felt on fire with excitement. She knew that her history project was going to be the best she had ever done. She had such a great story to tell. It had local interest, involved big business deals and one of the country's most famous buildings—and now, apparently, a tragedy.

'What else does it say in the news story?' asked Ben.

Kelly read out the entire contents of the clipping.

'A freak, tragic accident,' Ben repeated, staring out into space.

'I know. What do you think that means? Who do you think got killed? Passengers? The railway line can't have been open for long in September1860, so if it was passengers, they must have been some of the first ones.'

Ben nudged Tyson off his lap and rubbed his face with his hands. 'If it was passengers then the news story would say something about a crash, surely. Something bad would have happened to the engine or the carriages. And you would expect there to be some mention of other people being injured as well.'

'Good thinking, Sherlock,' said Kelly.

'Who?'

'Sherlock Holmes, you idiot,' sniggered Kelly. Ben didn't laugh. Kelly got to her feet, wiped the wet blades of grass off the seat of her jeans, and began pacing up and down. 'If the victims weren't passengers, then they had to have been workers. Maybe something went wrong. Maybe they were hurt while they were working on the line.'

'I think that's what happened,' he agreed. 'And if the railway company was accused of...what did they say?' He looked at the clipping. '...*negligence and mismanagement*, then someone obviously thought they were to blame.'

Kelly stopped pacing. She had remembered something that she read on the internet at school.

'The building work on the Houses of Parliament was overrunning by miles,' she announced, expecting everything to make sense to Ben. He shook his head, obviously at a loss to understand where she was going with her logic.

'The architect—Charles Barry, he was called—he said the new Parliament buildings would only take him six years to complete, but he was still working on them in 1860. That was twenty years after they laid the first foundation stone. Now that's what I call a man under pressure.' Kelly felt decidedly pleased with herself. She could have been a lawyer, laying out her case in court. She pointed at Ben, like a witness in the witness box. 'And what causes more hold-ups than anything on a building project?'

'Er…' Ben looked blank.

'Oh come on, don't you ever watch *Grand Designs*? Suppliers, that's what! Suppliers who let you down, who are late with their deliveries. Suppliers like Wilmcote quarry! My guess is that the new railway line was crucial to Wilmcote quarry. Having a train track right next to the quarry must have meant they could move their stone about faster than they ever could before by canal.'

'They were desperate to get the line finished,' added Ben, picking up on Kelly's line of thought. 'So they were rushing it.'

'Exactly!' replied Kelly, triumphantly, retaking her place next to Ben on the grass, satisfied that her case was closed.

'But the newspaper story does say that the railway company was found not guilty,' Ben reminded her.

'I know. But it wouldn't be the first time that a powerful company with deep pockets managed to wriggle off the hook. I think there's more to it. That cutting comes from *The Stratford-upon-Avon Times*, for heaven's sake. It was a local paper. Surely they ought to have made more of a story about four local people being killed. I mean, that's such a short piece, and they don't even name the victims. And look.' She took the piece of paper from Ben and pointed to the edges. 'It looks like the story was tucked away in the bottom corner of the page. Call me cynical, but it's almost like they were trying to bury it.'

The pair sat in silence for a few moments, mulling everything over, with Tyson stretched out between them, enjoying some fuss.

'What do you reckon, Tyson?' Kelly cooed at the little dog as she tickled him behind the ear. 'Perhaps I should take you for another walk by the railway. Maybe you could dig up some clues. You're good at digging, aren't you?'

Ben recoiled, as if someone had slapped him round the face.

'Are you okay, Ben?' Kelly enquired. 'You've gone awfully white. You look like you're about to throw up.'

'I'm fine,' replied Ben quickly. 'But that boot. Can I see it?'

'Yes, of course,' said Kelly, getting straight to her feet. 'I forgot. You didn't actually see it last time, did you? It's back in a box in my room. Why don't you come and get it with me? You can meet Mum and Dad at the same time. That'll keep them happy.'

'Er, do you mind if I don't?' stammered Ben. 'It's not that I don't want to meet them. It's just…well, I do feel a bit sick after all. I think I'd better just wait here, for now, if that's all right.'

Kelly didn't argue. Spewing all over the caravan would not get Ben off to a good start with Mum and Dad. Leaving Tyson with him, she ran back and began to scramble over the gate. She heard Ben calling after her.

'You know you said your dad was clearing the embankment? Does that mean he would have a map of this stretch of the line?'

'Bound to,' shouted Kelly. 'I'll ask.'

Mum and Dad were curled up on the sofa watching TV when Kelly appeared in the doorway. They looked expectantly at her.

'I'm not coming back in yet,' she announced breathlessly. 'I just need to get something.'

Before Mum and Dad could argue she disappeared into her room, emerging less than thirty seconds later, clutching the old leather boot in her hand.

'Everything okay?' asked Mum, looking puzzled.

'Yes, fine thanks,' Kelly replied. 'I'm just going to show this to Ben. Oh, and Dad?'

'Yeees?' he replied, not taking his eyes off the TV.

'Do you have a map of the railway line? Where you are working?'

173

'Yep, sure do. Tells us where the signals are and all that.'

'Can I borrow it? Just for ten minutes. Ben and I need to check something.'

When he saw Kelly returning, his favourite toy in her hand, Tyson started to yap. Ben stood up, and the little dog bounded towards Kelly, who gave him the boot and pointed towards Ben.

'Go on, Tyson, give it to Ben!'

Off he raced and, to Kelly's surprise, did exactly as he was told, dropping the boot politely at Ben's feet.

'Thadda boy,' crooned Kelly, as she caught up with him and gave him lots of fuss. Then she looked up at Ben. He had picked up the boot and was standing still, staring at it intently.

'What do you think?' she asked. 'Have a look inside, see if you can make out any old markings.'

'No need.' Ben still looked rather pale. 'I can see you're right. It *does* look old.' He thrust the boot back to her and quickly changed the subject. 'Did you get the map?'

Kelly nodded, put the boot down on the ground and unfolded the map her dad had given her. 'What are we looking for?'

'Well, the newspaper article called it the Bishopton Hill accident. Where is that exactly in relation to the line?'

Kelly traced the black line representing the railway with her finger, moving slowly out from Stratford-upon-Avon. Sure enough, before the footbridge and Wilmcote station, there was a series of contours marking the position of a small hill, right on a bend in the track. The hill was labelled Bishopton.

'That's it, all right,' confirmed Ben. 'That was where it happened.'

'And not only that,' said Kelly excitedly, 'that's where Tyson found the boot!'

For a split second, Kelly thought Ben's eyes turned misty. Then he shook his head and they seemed to come back into focus. 'It's getting late,' he said. 'You have to get back. I don't want to get you in any trouble.'

He leaned towards her and Kelly's heart gave a little leap. Then she felt a touch on her arm, light as a feather, and looked down to see the newspaper clipping tucked into her jacket pocket. When she looked up again, Ben was moving away.

'But wait,' she said, her voice suddenly tight. 'Mum and Dad wanted to meet you.'

'I can't, Kel, not now. I'm really sorry. It's nearly seven and my parents said I couldn't stay out too long tonight either. I've really got to go. Maybe next time?'

'Okay,' replied Kelly trying to sound cool. Truthfully she had hoped he would come in with her and perhaps stay a while, but instead she said, 'It would probably all be a bit embarrassing anyway. Like I said, I think Mum and Dad are convinced we're an item.'

'An item?'

'You know, boyfriend and girlfriend. Crazy, hey?'

Ben chuckled as he crossed over the lane.

'Listen,' Kelly called after him. 'I don't know about you, but I'm curious to know who died in that accident.'

Ben stopped and turned round. 'How can we do that?'

'Well there are birth and death records...but we might not need to go that far. If they were local people, there might be some clues in the churchyard. The victims could be buried there. Fancy a trip to the cemetery?'

'Er, maybe. When?'

'How about tomorrow, before school? If we met there at seven-thirty, I'd still have half an hour or so before my bus.'

'Seven-thirty? I guess that's all right,' said Ben, looking a little unsure. 'It will be empty then, won't it? I mean, we can explore without being disturbed, can't we?' Kelly nodded. 'Fine. I'll see you then. Can you apologise to your parents for me, for not coming to introduce myself?'

'Will do.'

Kelly watched Ben climb up onto the stile at the start of the footpath. She didn't expect him to look back again, but just before he jumped down the other side he paused and his eyes met hers across the lane.

'Would it be that crazy then?' he called, smiling cheekily at her.

'What?' asked Kelly, bemused.

'If you and I *were*, what did you call it? An item?'

'I guess not,' she laughed nervously, 'but I wouldn't rate the chances of it lasting.'

'Why not?'

'A farm boy whose family has lived in the same cottage for centuries and a Traveller girl with roaming in her blood? Come on!'

Ben laughed and waved her goodbye.

Kelly stood and held her breath as Ben moved away along the path. She watched him until she had to strain her eyes to make out his shape, getting smaller and smaller in the distance. Only when he had completely disappeared from view did she finally let out a little whistle and summon Tyson to her side.

She looked down and smiled. 'Are you going to carry that for me? Good lad. Just don't chew it. I think that boot might be rather special after all.'

Chapter 25 – September 1860

Most of the building work on the Palace of Westminster was now complete, and Sir Charles Barry's monthly inspection should have been a positive one. But he was so tired of the whole project, and so stressed by years of overcoming one problem or delay after the next, that he was unable to enjoy the fruits of his labours or appreciate the building's magnificence. He felt anxious and irritable, and in every room, hall or chamber he entered, he could see only more and more items for the snag list.

At Sir Charles' side as he paced about the palace was his son, Edward. Now thirty-seven and a tall, slim, fine-looking gentleman, Edward had followed his father into architecture, and had become his right-hand man in the practice. He had come to know the building almost as intimately as his father.

'This project is now twenty years old,' Sir Charles moaned, coming to a halt in the entrance to the Royal Gallery. 'Twenty years since your dear mother laid that first foundation stone! And I boasted that it would take me six. If I am unable to sign off the project before the State Opening of Parliament in

November, it will be beyond a joke. I will be a joke. But who am I trying to fool? I am a joke already!'

Edward looked sympathetically at his father, red-faced, breathless and perspiring after their ascent of the Royal Staircase which led up to the first floor from the base of Victoria Tower. 'You could never be that, Father. Come, let's rest a moment while you catch your breath.'

Sir Charles stopped to pull a handkerchief from his top pocket and dab at his forehead, but he refused to sit down. Hurrying along the length of the Royal Gallery, he led his son into the Prince's Chamber. 'There are some extraordinarily expensive carpets to be fitted in this part of the building next month. This place needs to be completely clean and dust free before then. Look at this!' Sir Charles wiped his finger across the knee of the enthroned statue that dominated the room. 'Whatever would Her Majesty say if she saw herself covered in a layer of dust!'

'Father, calm yourself. All this will be taken care of,' Edward said. 'It's not all your responsibility. You shouldn't be worrying about a bit of dust here and there. Besides, Richard Greenslade at Wilmcote has promised faithfully that we will have delivery of the last batch of flooring stone next week. I understand it's all ready to be loaded onto the wagons, and he's promised to send a team of his best stonemasons to help finish off the job on site.'

'Promised faithfully, has he? Well, he's more of a gambling man than I. He's relying on that new track being fully operational in, what, the next three days? Talk about a close shave! If he lets me down, I'll wring his neck.'

'Steady on,' said Edward. 'Look, why don't you send Greenslade a telegram? Tell him to sit on that railway company's back from dawn till dusk until that first train leaves the station.'

'Good idea,' said Sir Charles, patting his son's shoulder approvingly. 'I shall tell him in no uncertain terms, that if my stone is not here in London by the beginning of next week, he'll be reimbursing me for my share in the line. We had a deal and I don't want to learn that my financial investment was a waste of time.'

Chapter 26 – September 1860

It was into Alice's trembling hand that the telegram was placed. She knew as soon as she saw the London office stamp in the corner that it was from Sir Charles Barry, and she doubted that it would be good news. But, conscious that the message must be urgent, she hurried down the hall to Greenslade's study right away.

'Sorry to disturb you, Mr Greenslade,' she said quietly, after knocking on the door and entering the room, 'but there's a telegram for you. I think it's from London.'

She handed the paper over and took a silent step back, hoping that her employer wouldn't dismiss her before he read it. She wanted to see his reaction. Perhaps he would tell her what it said.

She was in luck. He was obviously as anxious as she to know what Sir Charles had to say, for he seized the telegram and scanned it rapidly, moving his lips as he read each word, while a deep furrow formed in his brow. 'Good Lord! As if I wasn't under enough pressure,' he mumbled, throwing the telegram down onto his desk.

'Oh dear. Is it bad news? Can I help, Mr Greenslade?'

'I wish you could, Alice! But there's nothing you can do. Although your husband can, and his workmates. They need to put in as much extra effort as they can and make sure my stone is making its way down that railway line by next week.'

Greenslade picked up the telegram and began reading it through again.

'But there are only three days to go until the official opening,' Alice reminded him. 'They're already working so hard, Mr Greenslade, I know they are.'

'I'm not criticising your husband, or any of his workmates. They've worked their tails off in the past few weeks. And I know that the railway company has already driven a test engine up and down the line between Stratford-upon-Avon and Hatton junction. But I heard this morning that the driver reported some vibration on the bend in the track near Bishopton Hill. So there are still some running repairs to do.'

'Will that mean they will have put back the official opening?'

'Oh no, no, no. They can't afford to do that.' Greenslade got to his feet and put on his coat. 'They just need to get the engineers to pack some extra ballast around the track at that point. I'm sure they can do that without bringing everything to a halt.'

Alice nodded, not moving from the spot as he walked past her, heading for the door. She decided to risk asking one last question.

'Was that what the telegram was about, sir? The railway?'

Greenslade paused, his hand on the door knob, and for a split second Alice thought he was going to reprimand her for speaking out of turn. Then he said, 'In a nutshell, yes. Let's just say it's given me one more reason to make sure that my delivery is on that train and arriving in London by the start of next week.'

Seeing the worry on his face, Alice felt she had to offer something. 'It's not much, I know, but I can ask William to spread the word among the men. Ask them to give it one last push.'

Greenslade smiled. 'Thank you, Alice. Hopefully, if we all play our part, we will all be on that station platform on Saturday with something to celebrate. And if we are, I promise you that there will be a bonus in everyone's pay packet, including yours!'

Now it was Alice's turn to smile.

Greenslade glanced at the old carriage clock on the mantelpiece above the fire. 'Heavens! It's nearly noon already. I must be off. Can you tell my wife that I have gone into town on an urgent matter, please? I have to pay Reginald Adkins a visit at the Stratford-upon-Avon Railway Company offices.'

Chapter 27 – September 2012

For Kelly, Friday morning usually meant a hurried slice of toast and a last-minute rush down to the bus stop. She was never good at getting out of bed on school days, and as she grew more and more tired throughout the week, leaving behind the comfort of her warm duvet became an increasingly big challenge. This wasn't helped by the fact that she allowed herself one extra snooze each day, so that by the time Friday came around, she got up a whole fifteen minutes later.

But Kelly's approach to getting up on this particular Friday was quite different. So excited was she about meeting Ben at the churchyard that she had set her alarm a whole hour earlier and, when it went off, jumped straight out of bed. By seven o'clock, she was already sitting at the breakfast table, dipping a banana into her pineapple yoghurt.

She heard a door click and saw her dad staggering out of her parents' bedroom, rubbing his eyes and still dressed in his pyjamas.

'Am I still dreaming or is that my daughter up and dressed before I am?'

'No dream. It's really me,' said Kelly, swallowing a mouthful of banana.

'Why so early?' enquired Dad, filling the kettle from the tap.

'I'm meeting Ben at the churchyard in half an hour.'

Dad put the kettle down on the draining board and turned to face Kelly. 'Isn't this getting a bit ridiculous, all this sneaking off and meeting boys all the time?'

'I'm not sneaking anywhere, and it's only one boy!'

'Well, all right, but when were you going to tell me and your mum where you were going? I don't remember you mentioning it. And it might only be one boy but we don't know him from Adam. You didn't bring him in to meet us, last night, did you?'

'No, I know. I'm sorry. He had to dash off. His parents had given him a curfew too. But he did ask me to apologise to you.' Kelly scraped the bottom of her yoghurt pot with her spoon. 'And I didn't say anything about meeting Ben this morning because I didn't think it would be a big deal. The churchyard is just down the road from the bus stop so all I'm doing is leaving half an hour early. I'm going straight from there to the bus stop. I didn't think you'd mind.'

Dad shrugged then turned to continue making his pot of tea. 'So why the churchyard? Why go at the crack of dawn?' He ducked his head to look out of the window above the sink. 'Have you seen outside? It's a misty old morning. Looks freezing to me. It's hardly the morning for a trip to a spooky old graveyard—even if your boyfriend's going to be there.'

'Dad!' cried Kelly. 'I've told you. Ben's just a friend! And that's not why we're meeting, anyway. It's to do with our history

185

project. We're wondering if the people who were killed in that railway accident—you know, the one in that newspaper cutting? We wondered if they might be buried in the churchyard. There might be some clues there as to who they were.'

Dad sat down next to her. 'Don't you think you're going into a bit too much detail on this project of yours? How long do your teachers expect you to spend on it? It seems to be turning into an epic.'

'Well, it kind of is,' conceded Kelly, 'but only because it's so fascinating. It's like a real mystery, Dad. I'm desperate to know what happened in the accident. I mean, just think! It happened pretty much on the very spot where you're working now. And where Tyson found that old boot.'

Dad nodded. He seemed to understand

'Anyway, the project's not due in till half term. So I've still got plenty of time.'

'And what about this Ben lad?' asked Dad. 'What does he want to get out of it?'

Kelly thought for a moment. 'Well, he's doing it as a history project too. And Wilmcote is where he's grown up. His family have lived here for centuries. I don't know really, but it's like he believes this place has a story to tell, and he wants to piece it together.'

There was a click as the boiling kettle switched itself off. Dad rose from the seat. 'Well, Kel, just be careful, love. If you're looking at gravestones, you're not only dealing with a story from history, you're dealing with real people's lives. There might still be relatives about. Be sensitive, yeah?'

Kelly smiled and nodded. 'I will. You know I will.' Then she glanced at her watch and gasped. 'Ah! I've got to go. It's nearly ten past. I'll have to run.'

There was no doubt about it: autumn was closing in. And Dad was right. It was really cold outside and the dampness of the heavy mist clawed its way through Kelly's blazer as she lifted the latch on the gate and entered the churchyard. Even the mad dash that had brought her there had not warmed her up. She turned up her blazer collar to stop the cold air from creeping down her back, and checked her watch. Seven thirty-three. She had made good time.

Starting up the gravel path, Kelly glanced left and right, reading the inscriptions on two tall memorials which marked the first two graves at the front of the church. One was a tall, narrow obelisk with a cross perched on the top; the other was a weeping angel, which reminded Kelly of a terrifying episode of *Doctor Who*. Her brother had deliberately recorded it so he could play it over and over again and laugh as Kelly dived behind the nearest cushion.

Avoiding the angel's gaze, Kelly read the inscription on the plinth beneath her feet. *'At Rest. Oh! Twill be sweet to meet on that blest shore. All sorrow passed, all pains fore'er o'er.'* It was a memorial to someone called John Howard, who had died in 1925. 'That's far too late,' said Kelly out loud.

Meanwhile the obelisk appeared to be marking the site of a family grave. The Lawrences. Four generations. Kelly deduced that the Lawrences must have been a very wealthy family if they could afford such an imposing gravestone. It commanded pride of place in the churchyard, too. It would be hard to pass by without noticing it and remembering who lay beneath.

Kelly knew that most of the graves were located further away from the road, behind the church, so she followed the narrow path around past the main church door. On her right, out of the corner of her eye, she detected a movement. Assuming it was Ben, Kelly called out his name into the mist but received no response. The churchyard remained eerily silent. Kelly reassured herself that it was just a bird swooping by or maybe a squirrel in the hedge.

Refusing to be put off, she focused on the task in hand and began checking all the tombstones, working her way along each row from left to right, so she didn't miss any. By the end of the second row, she was starting to feel rather melancholy. Each stone was a snapshot of loss. 'Beloved' mothers, 'kind and true' husbands, 'tender' sisters, brothers 'gone but not forgotten', children 'sleeping peacefully': so many departed relatives 'held in loving memory'.

Kelly was crouched down trying to decipher the faded inscription on one particularly old stone which was almost completely covered in scaly, yellow lichen, when something dark and heavy whistled past her ear, brushing the hair off her shoulder, hitting the gravestone and bouncing off to one side. Kelly screamed and ducked down, covering her face with her hands, hardly daring to imagine what it was.

'Oh Kelly, I'm so sorry. I wasn't aiming it at you, honestly!'

Kelly breathed out and let her hands fall from her face, relief mixing with rage. 'What the hell?' she screeched, rounding on her friend. 'That was not funny! I was jumpy enough. It's really spooky here in this mist. And you're late!'

Ben grimaced. 'I didn't mean to frighten you. I'm sorry.' He tried a smile.

Inside, Kelly softened, but she was determined not to let Ben know that he was forgiven just yet. 'What did you throw at me, anyway?' she snapped. Ben nodded towards the patch of damp grass where the missile had landed.

Kelly followed his gaze then let out another little scream, this time in disbelief. 'That's Tyson's boot. But how did you....? Where did you...? It can't be. I put it back in my treasure chest last night.'

She looked back at Ben, who was smiling more broadly now. The damp, early morning mist had darkened his usually bouncy blond fringe and plastered it flat to his forehead. He looked quite different.

Without saying anything, Ben reached over, picked up the old boot and handed it to Kelly.

She still wanted an explanation. 'How come you've got my boot?'

'Blimey, I thought you were good at examining clues!' Ben tutted and took the boot back from her, holding it up. 'Look. Your boot is for a right foot, this one's for the left.'

Kelly's mouth dropped open. 'What? You think they're a matching pair? No! That's too good to be true!'

'Well, they look the same, don't they? When you brought me your boot last night, I knew straight away that I had one just like it.'

'You what?' asked Kelly, incredulous.

'What I mean to say is, I saw one just like it. When I was looking through old family stuff up in the attic. You remember, when I found the map? That's why I kept asking after the one you had. I didn't really believe that the two would match, but when you showed me your boot I could see it was the same.'

Kelly got to her feet, realising that her school tights were soaking wet from the grass. She didn't care. Her mind was working at a rate of knots, trying to figure out what this meant. She didn't know what to say.

Ben spoke for her. 'You've been wondering if the boot belonged to someone involved in the accident, haven't you?'

Kelly nodded then walked towards him and looked up into his eyes. 'But do you know what this means?' Her breath made its own mist in the narrow space between them as she whispered. 'If the boots *are* a matching pair, and one was in your attic, we could be looking for the grave of one of your relatives. Are you ready for that?'

Ben blinked and looked away.

'Because if you want to stop, we can. It's just a history project, after all.' Kelly reached out to touch Ben's face but he took a step backwards.

'No, it's all right,' he muttered, almost to himself. 'I want to find out.'

Worried that Ben might change his mind and decide they should leave, Kelly told him which gravestones she had already checked and set him to work, looking at the inscriptions on the gravestones along the rows from the far end.

'That way we will meet in the middle and know we haven't missed any,' she explained. 'And don't forget, we're really looking for four graves. The news clipping said there were four victims.'

Kelly and Ben worked their way along the gravestones. As she discounted one after the next, Kelly began to get frustrated. The minutes were ticking away and soon she would have to go and join the queue for the school bus. She lifted her gaze and squinted through the mist, trying to see how far Ben had got. As she did so, a break in the usual pattern of the headstones caught her eye. About half way between her and Ben, she could see a spot where, rather than the usual single headstones equally spaced, there was one slightly taller headstone with a gap at either side and four little stones in a row at the foot of the grave.

She held her breath and tiptoed across, praying that the inscriptions would be clear enough to read.

'Oh my God, Ben! Come and look at this!' she spluttered, when the engraving came into focus. Ben ran over to her side.

'Look at the date!' whispered Kelly, her fingers brushing away the dirt.

Ben read: 'Died, 28th September, 1860.'

The two friends glanced at one another, eyes wide.

Ben continued to read, taking each phrase slowly, one at a time:

A bitter cup, a shock severe;

To part with ones we loved so dear.'

He paused and swallowed hard. His voice cracked with emotion as he completed the verse:

'Our loss is great, we will not complain.

But trust in Christ to meet again. RIP.'

'That's so sad,' said Kelly. '28th September, 1860. It's the right date, but it doesn't say anything about a railway accident. That's a bit strange, don't you think? I've seen inscriptions here which talk about people having been killed at war, and there was one which said a woman had drowned. There's a recent one for a local fire-fighter, too. It said he was killed while on service. So why not mention something as major as a railway accident? Four people dying at once in tiny old Wilmcote must have made an impact, surely! Wouldn't they want people to remember it?'

Ben remained silent. Kelly stepped back to get a better view of the four footstones, poking out of the grass like a row of tiny baby teeth.

'Ooh, these are harder to read,' she complained, parting the blades of grass that were obscuring the letters carved into the stone. One by one, she made out the initials and ages of the deceased:

'E. R. S. Age 36.

'L. T. W. Age 27.

'G. G. B. Age 43.'

Kelly crouched down to wipe away the moss from the fourth footstone. Her lips parted as she prepared to read out the final set of initials, but it was Ben who spoke, his voice thin and wobbly in the cold air:

'W. T. D. Age 35.'

'That's right!' exclaimed Kelly. 'Had you seen it already?'

When Ben didn't reply, she straightened up, staring quizzically at him. Ben met her gaze, his face ashen. 'That last one— W. T. D. It stands for William Thomas Denton.'

Kelly was shocked. 'How do you know that?'

'I don't know…' He staggered backwards, his eyes filling with tears.

Thinking Ben was about to fall, Kelly took a step towards him, but he backed away from her, dropping the boot at his feet.

'I've got to go, Kel,' he muttered, moving further away between the gravestones. 'I can't be here. Just let me go.' He turned and began to run away across the churchyard.

'Ben!' Kelly called after him. 'Ben!'

She snatched the boot up from the grass and considered running after him, but something told her to do as Ben had asked, and let him go. Anxious and confused, she watched her friend disappear into the mist. She wasn't surprised to feel tears prickling her own eyes, too. Kelly had no idea what to say or do, or why he had reacted so badly, but her dad's words of advice over breakfast came back to her.

When she was sure that Ben was not coming back. Kelly rummaged in her school bag for her notebook and pen. Quickly, she copied out the inscriptions on all five stones. At the bottom of the page, in capital letters, she wrote WILLIAM THOMAS DENTON, and next to the name, a giant question mark. Then, deep in thought, she made her way back to the path and headed for the bus stop.

Chapter 28 – September 2012

Even after double English, normally one of her favourite lessons of the week, Kelly was still feeling unsettled by her early morning adventure in the churchyard. She was certain that the grave she and Ben had found was the one they were after. The date, four victims, and that epitaph: A shock severe. These were tragic, unexpected deaths, that was for sure. But she couldn't understand why there were no names, only the four sets of initials and ages on the footstones. And why no mention of how these four people died? It was as if no one wanted the world to know what had happened to them.

Kelly needed some advice, so at break-time, rather than heading to the canteen for her usual apple juice and flapjack slice, she climbed the stairs to the history department on the top floor, hoping that Mr Walker would be in his room. Thankfully, she found him there, cleaning his whiteboard and humming the opening bars of an old AC/DC tune.

'Sir?' she said tentatively, knocking quietly on the door.

'Kelly!' The teacher broke into a grin. 'Everything all right?'

Kelly told Mr Walker everything, bringing him up to date

about the map, the newspaper cutting and what she had discovered that morning. She could see that he was intrigued.

'I've just got to find out some more about this William Denton, but I don't want to upset my friend.'

'No, well, that's understandable.' Mr Walker folded his arms across his chest as he perched on the edge of his desk. 'Perhaps you should work on this on your own for a while. Give your friend some time. He'll let you know when he's ready to open up some more—or maybe to find out more.'

'That's what I thought,' agreed Kelly. 'But I don't know where to go next, to be honest.'

Mr Walker explained that if she had a name, and the date of death, Kelly might stand a good chance of tracking down a death certificate. 'They started making official civil records of births, marriages and deaths in 1837, so you're well after that. Death records for this area aren't online yet, so you have to write to the Records Office, or go there in person and apply for copies. That would probably be the quickest thing to do. The office is easy to get to. It's right next to the Town Hall. And the staff are usually really helpful. I went there a lot last summer when I was working on that book about our local First World War heroes. They open every weekday until four I think.'

'What would I need to do?' asked Kelly, getting out her notebook.

'Just give them the details of the person you want them to search for. First and last name, the date they died, and where. They will check to see if they hold the death certificate you want and if they do, you can apply for a copy.'

'Would they be able to trace someone from just the initials and the date and place of death?' asked Kelly.

Mr Walker pulled a face. 'Hmm, that might be tricky. I think a full name is easier. I'm not sure you'll be able to trace all four of your victims. Anyway, that'd be a bit expensive for you. It costs a tenner for each death certificate.'

Kelly groaned. 'I might have to stick to William, then, for now.'

She thanked Mr Walker and virtually skipped off to her next lesson in the maths block. Her spirits had lifted. She was back on the trail.

For the rest of the morning, and especially during a particularly dull algebra exercise, William Thomas Denton kept popping into Kelly's head. Could she really find out who he was? Would she discover why this man was significant to Ben? She hoped so—and she hoped that Ben would understand why she had to keep digging.

Then her heart sank. Mr Walker had said the Records Office closed at four. Even if she went straight there after school, realistically she would only have a few minutes before they closed. That would be no use at all. And tomorrow was Saturday. They wouldn't be open.

The need to know some answers about the mysterious W. T. D. was like an itch she had to scratch. She would have to bunk off school and go to the records office that afternoon. There was nothing else she could do.

Kelly checked her pocket. She had enough money. No surprise really. She'd been so busy meeting up with Ben lately that she hadn't had time to go to the shop, where she usually spent most of her allowance.

She sat through the rest of her maths lesson biting her nails, secretly planning her escape from school while her maths teacher's monotonous voice droned on and on in the background about what x and n were equal to. For once, Kelly didn't care. Her stomach was doing somersaults as she weighed up all the risks of playing truant.

When the bell finally rang for lunch, she was first out of the classroom. She shot down the corridor to her locker and took out her bag and coat. Then she nervously waited for Leanne to appear.

As she approached, Leanne smiled and waved. Friday was fish and chip day in the canteen and the pair of them had planned to eat together. Her face fell when she saw Kelly holding her coat.

'You going somewhere?'

'Ssssh,' hissed Kelly. 'I need you to cover for me. I've got to sneak out for an hour or two. I'll definitely be back in time for the bus but I'm not going to be here for afternoon registration. Can you cover for me?'

Leanne grinned conspiratorially. 'Course I can. Does a bear shi—'

'All right, all right!' Kelly cut in, pulling her friend closer and out of ear-shot from a group of Year 11 boys who were mucking about by the lockers behind them. 'Can you tell Mr Walker that I'm doing an errand or something? I don't know. Say I'm putting out chairs for afternoon assembly. Anything so he doesn't mark me down as absent.'

Leanne nodded. 'Sure. But just be careful. You'll have to sign out, so make sure you time it so that there are no teachers about when you do it. Charlotte used to tell Reception she had a dental appointment or something. They never checked.'

'Thanks, Leanne,' whispered Kelly. 'I owe you one.'

'No, you don't,' said Leanne, giving Kelly a wink. 'I still owe you plenty.'

* * *

The lady at the Records Office was really helpful. Kelly explained that she was working on a history project for school and the lady seemed to accept that as a reason for her to be there during school time. That was a relief. Sneaking out had made Kelly feel sick with nerves. The fact that she was missing lunch and her stomach was empty didn't help.

The lady entered the details that Kelly had for William Denton into her computer and then asked Kelly to take a seat, while she went off to see what records they had in their archive.

Alone in the waiting area, Kelly sucked on an old humbug she had found in her blazer pocket. It had been there so long that bits of the wrapper had stuck to the sweet, but Kelly didn't care.

The lady seemed to be gone a long time. There was nothing to do or read to keep Kelly occupied, apart from a dull-looking poster on the wall about using online census records to trace your family history. The stuffy warmth of the room, combined with fatigue after her early start to the day and a slump in energy after the adrenaline rush of sneaking out of school, all began to make Kelly feel decidedly drowsy. When the back office door suddenly opened, Kelly jumped and shot to her feet as if she had been electrified.

Pleased to be bringing good news to such an eager customer, the lady trotted triumphantly back to her desk and gestured to Kelly to sit down in the chair opposite her. 'I've found your William Denton,' she chirped, 'so we can definitely provide you with a copy of his death records.'

'Brilliant.' Kelly beamed.

The lady peered over the top of her glasses at her. 'But you will need to pay a fee of £10. Are you able to do that, my dear?'

'Sure.' Kelly felt around in her pocket and produced a crumpled ten-pound note.

'Lovely,' said the lady rather primly, taking the tatty note from Kelly with her fingertips as if afraid she would catch something, and dropping it into her cash box. 'Now, I just need you to complete your details on this form. I will give you a copy of the form and that will act as your receipt. All right?'

Kelly nodded, accepting the lady's offer of the use of her pen.

'How long will it take? The certificate I mean.'

'Oh, we will post it out to you. Should be with you by this time next week, at the latest.'

Kelly left the Records Office feeling a little deflated. She had thought that she would be able to bring the certificate away with her. Still, at least there was a death record for William Denton. It could have been worse.

By the time she got back to school, it was well after two o'clock. Her last lesson on a Friday was French, and started at twenty past, so she only had ten minutes or so to stay out of trouble before the corridors would be full of students moving from one classroom to the next. She decided to drop off her bag at her locker and head to the toilets. But as she was hurriedly signing back in at Reception, she heard a familiar voice barking her name. Her heart sank.

'Kelly Hearn. Where do you think you've been?' It was Mr Walker, this time without the usual friendly smile on his face.

'Er... I had to go the dentist, sir,' Kelly stammered.

'Was that after you had to put out the chairs in the hall, or before?'

'After?' Kelly said hopefully.

'So your parents have phoned in, have they, to explain that they were taking you out? Or sent a letter perhaps?'

Kelly's shoulders dropped. 'Sorry, sir. They haven't. I think they must have forgotten.'

'Kelly, you aren't lying to me are you? I would be very disappointed if you were.'

Kelly couldn't look her tutor in the eye. She knew that he had put two and two together. She felt guilt oozing out of every pore. 'I've been to the Records Office, Mr Walker,' she mumbled.

'What was that?'

'I've been to the Records Office,' she said a little louder, sneaking a look up at her teacher through her fringe. 'I'm so sorry. I was just so curious. I couldn't wait. I knew I wouldn't have time after school. Please don't be mad.'

'Kelly, as much as I admire your enthusiasm and your dedication to your homework, playing truant is a very serious matter. You know I can't let it slide.'

Kelly nodded. Her face burned red with embarrassment and her eyes welled up with tears. She knew what was coming next.

'Detention. Monday after school. And I shall be telephoning your parents.'

Kelly bit her bottom lip.

'Now where *should* you be right now?'

'French, sir.'

'Then you'd better get moving, before you get into any more trouble.'

That evening, Kelly had to endure another grilling from her parents. Sure enough, Mr Walker had phoned them and explained that Kelly had left the school premises without authorisation, and that she had missed a lesson. Kelly was pretty sure that her mum and dad were more angry about her wandering off into Stratford-upon-Avon on her own than they were about her missing classes, but either way they were furious, and she was sent to her room straight after dinner.

Lying on her bed, staring up at the ceiling, Kelly wondered what Ben was doing, and if he was okay. She wished she could phone him, but she had no idea what his number was. Perhaps she should just go round to his cottage tomorrow. Surely he must have told his parents about her by now. They wouldn't mind, would they?

She leaned down over the side of the bed, pulled out her treasure chest and slid off the lid. The old boot was right on the top, and considering its age, and the fact that Tyson had been carrying it around the night before, it looked as good as new. She picked up the matching boot that Ben had left behind that morning, and held the two up alongside one another. Yes, they were a perfect pair.

Suddenly, she heard a movement outside her door, so she quickly dropped the boots into the box, replaced the lid and kicked the chest back under the bed.

'Whatcha up to, Trouble?' asked Mum as she opened the door.

'Nothing.' Kelly shuffled across the bed to make space for Mum to sit down.

'I would have hoped you'd been using the time to think about what your dad and I spoke to you about over dinner. Why playing hooky isn't on, that is.'

'I have,' Kelly assured her. 'And I know you'll say I'm being cheeky, but don't you think that you guys have changed your tune a bit? You didn't even want me to go to secondary school, and now you're hopping mad at me for missing a lesson.'

'It's the lying and the sneaking about that bothers us, Kelly. Your dad and I are worried about you. Ever since you met Ben, you've hardly been here. You're always off to meet him here, there and everywhere and all you focus on is that flippin' history project.'

'Well, it's important to me. So's Ben.'

'I know. And I know we should be proud of you, really, for taking your school work so seriously. Lord knows it's something I never had the chance to do. But we don't want you to forget everything else, you know...forget your roots. You know what I'm trying to say, Kel?'

'I won't, Mum. I love the life you and Dad have given me.'

Mum rubbed Kelly's arm fondly.

Kelly hadn't finished. 'And this quarry story. The mystery about what happened in that accident on the railway. I know I've been spending a lot of time on it, Mum, but there's something keeps drawing me back to it. I think it's because the answers are so hard to find. It's like a challenge. Apart from that tiny news clipping, there's nothing else written down anywhere— certainly not on the internet. That's why I risked going to the Records Office.'

'I get you. But stories don't always need to be written down to be remembered, Kelly. You should know that. Storytelling's part of our culture. Perhaps that's what you need to find for your Wilmcote mystery, a local storyteller. If any facts have been passed down over the years, they'll know about it.'

It was a long shot, thought Kelly, but Mum might be on to something. 'Thanks, Mum. I'll do some asking about. Ben might know if there's anyone around here like that.'

'Well, okay, but promise you will tell us what you are up to, from now on, young lady. And no more sneaking off from school, all right?'

PART 6

Chapter 29 – 28th September 1860

It had only just got light when there was a knock on the door of Stone Pit Cottage. Billy stirred, yawned and rubbed his eyes, but remained quietly in his bed, hoping to hear one of his parents heading downstairs. His room was cold and he had no desire to get up earlier than was necessary. But when no one in the cottage stirred, the knocking came again, louder and more insistent this time. Sighing, Billy threw back his blankets, sat up and fumbled around in the gloom for his dressing gown. The wooden floor was chilly under his feet as he padded across the room and out onto the landing. He paused briefly at the top of the stairs then, convinced that he was the only one who had heard the knocking, hurried down and pulled open the front door.

Standing there sheltering in the porch from the rain, blowing on his cold hands, was one of his father's workmates, George Banks. He looked surprised to see Billy.

'Oh, it's you, Billy. Sorry if I woke you. Where's your father?'

Billy shook his head, confused. George looked agitated. 'I told him I'd be waiting at the end of the lane at quarter to six sharp. There's some more ballast needs packing in the track on the

Bishopton Hill bend. We've got to get it done by lunchtime. The foreman warned us last night and we promised we'd meet up with him at first light at the station. If we're a minute after six we can wave goodbye to that bonus—to our jobs, even.'

'Father must have overslept,' croaked Billy, worry creeping into the pit of his stomach. 'Wait just one minute, please!'

Billy ran upstairs and opened the door into his parents' room, knowing even before he looked that his father's side of the bed would be empty. He had heard the front door slamming late the previous night, and had tried to block out the sound of cursing as his father staggered drunkenly up the stairs. Clearly he had been banished to the boxroom again.

Alice stirred when she heard the bedroom door opening. 'Everything all right, Billy?' she mumbled.

'It's fine, Mother, don't worry. It's just George calling for Dad. They have to go to work early. I'll get him. You stay there. Go back to sleep for a bit.'

Alice nodded and turned over, pulling her blanket up over her head.

Billy closed the door gently then crossed the landing to reach the boxroom. His heart sank as he pushed the door open. The rank smell of stale beer and sweat filled his nostrils and a deep, rattling snore rose from his father's unconscious form. He was sprawled diagonally across the small bed, on top of the covers and still dressed in yesterday's clothes.

Billy tried to rouse him, shaking him by the shoulder and tugging at his shirt sleeve. 'You've got to get up, Father. You've got to go to work. George is here.'

William groaned and tried to swat his son away.

This was not going to be easy. Billy wanted to shout at his father to pull himself together and get up, but he didn't want his mother to wake and see him in such a state.

He ran back down the stairs as quietly as he could. George was pacing back and forth outside. 'He's overslept but he's awake now. He's getting dressed,' Billy lied. 'He said you were to go on ahead. No point you all risking being late. He'll meet you there. Can you tell the foreman he's on his way?'

George readily agreed, looking relieved. As soon as he was gone, Billy dashed back upstairs and tried again to rouse his father.

'Father, please. You've got to wake up. It's nearly six.'

'Leave me alone,' William slurred. 'Lemme just stop 'ere.'

'Just think about that bonus you've been promised, Father,' Billy coaxed. 'Just imagine the smile that'll put on Mother's face when you get it.'

'Mmmm, Alice. My Alice...'

For a moment Billy thought he had got through to him. But when his father turned and he saw the clownish grin on his face, the half open, unfocused eyes, he realised William was still inebriated.

His pleas became more desperate. 'Come on, Father. Can't you see? You're going to lose your job. Then everything Grandpa's been saying about you will be true. All you're doing is proving him right. You've got to get up.'

Harnessing all the strength he could muster, Billy dragged his father into a sitting position, pulling his legs over the side of the bed and heaving him upright by his arms.

William groaned. 'Urgh! I don't feel so good, Billy.'

Billy let go of his hands. His father slumped forwards and his chest heaved. He dropped his head between his knees and vomited uncontrollably onto the rug.

Billy stepped back in horror. All traces of sympathy turned to red hot anger. 'Father, how could you? You're disgusting! Why do I keep defending you?'

William groaned and collapsed sideways, wiping his mouth with the back of his hand. 'Sorry, son,' he mumbled.

Billy shook his head in despair, and snatched up his father's work jacket from the chair beside him. 'Don't think for one minute that what I'm going to do is for you!' he spat, turning on his heel.

He stormed out of the room and back into his own bedroom where he pulled on some old overalls and shoved his arms into the sleeves of his father's jacket. Then he ran downstairs and out into the back porch where he stepped into his brown work boots. As he tied the laces, he gritted his teeth and cursed his father's drinking. He knew what he had to do, and he knew that it was the only way to save the family from ruin and protect his mother's pride. Finally, he reached for his cap, which hung on the coat rack next to his father's, and pulled it down low over his eyes. Then he closed the door quietly behind him and ran off up the damp, muddy lane.

Chapter 30 – September 2012

Just as the kind lady in the Records Office had promised, an envelope with Kelly's name on it was waiting in the Hearns' post box on Friday morning.

'That document you were waiting for has come, love,' called Mum from the caravan as Kelly made her usual fuss of Tyson when she got home from school.

'This is it, Tyson,' Kelly whispered to the little dog as she scratched behind his left ear. 'Hopefully I'll get some of the answers I've been looking for.'

She skipped into the caravan and plonked herself down at the table where the envelope lay. Savouring the excitement, Kelly gazed down at it while she took off her coat and made herself comfortable. She picked it up carefully and ran her thumb under the flap.

Her initial reaction was surprise at the quality of the document that had been photocopied for her. Somehow she hadn't anticipated the certificate being quite so neat and efficient looking. But there it was—a certified copy of an entry of death for the Stratford-upon-Avon Registration District.

Handwritten at the top, in a beautifully formed script, was the date 1860, and columns two and three of the form confirmed that the deceased was male, aged 35, and that his full name was William Thomas Denton. The memory of Ben saying that name in the graveyard came back to her, and, once again, Kelly wondered how he knew what those initials on the gravestone stood for.

Kelly's eye was then drawn to the column headed 'When and where died'. Under the date of 28th September 1860, the location was given simply as Wilmcote. Kelly let out a little sigh of disappointment. But then, as she tracked across the sheet with her index finger, her heart leapt. William's occupation was listed as Railway Labourer. This was it. She was certain that what she was about to read next would confirm exactly how William had died.

But the cause of death was recorded in just three words: 'Killed on railroad'.

'Any use?' asked Mum, sliding into the bench seat next to her.

'I'm not really sure.' Kelly turned the sheet over in the vain hope that there would be more information on the other side. 'It's pretty clear that this William Denton is the man buried in the churchyard, and he definitely worked and was killed on the railway. And the month and year of his death is the same as the accident mentioned in that newspaper clipping.'

'Well, that's good then, yes?' asked Mum.

'Yes, kind of. But this doesn't tell me *how* he died. Don't you think that's a bit suspicious? Wouldn't you expect the death certificate to say more than just *killed on the railway*?'

Mum shrugged. 'I don't know, love. I don't think it necessarily would.'

Kelly pursed her lips and blew out, disappointed. 'I kind of hoped this might tell me where William lived, too, but there's no home address for him.'

She sat in silence for a few seconds, staring at the certificate, then her eyes widened.

'What is it?' Mum asked. 'Spotted something else?'

'No, but I've just *thought* of something else. Census records. There was a poster about tracing your family history in the Records Office. It said something about doing it online. I might have enough information about William Denton to track him down that way. But I need to borrow your laptop. Can I, Mum? I'll need the internet.'

'Sure, love. Just don't mess anything up. You know how confused I get if you move things about on there.'

Kelly giggled. Mum was useless with computers. She only used her laptop to look at photos and play music and games. But at least she let Kelly borrow it now and again.

As soon as she had opened up the browser, Kelly searched for *Census* and clicked on the National Archives website. 'Yay!' she cried, clapping her hands. 'It says that census records for England and Wales are available online for the years between 1841 and 1911.'

She scrolled down and clicked on the records for England, 1851. 'No good looking at 1861, he was dead by then,' she said out loud. She entered all the information that she had about William Thomas Denton hit search and held her breath.

A list of all the William Dentons recorded in England in that year appeared on the screen, but only one name had the right county next to it. His year of birth was given as 1825, which was spot on for the man Kelly was looking for. With excitement bubbling up inside her, she clicked on his name.

'Oh damn!' she exclaimed. 'I can't see the record without signing up for a free trial. And I have to give credit card details.'

Mum peered over her daughter's shoulder. 'Well, I don't mind you putting in my details, if it's just a free trial. Don't forget to cancel it afterwards though.'

Her mum was as curious as Kelly to find out how far they could follow William's trail. They activated the free trial and before she knew it, Kelly found herself looking at the family details of William Thomas Denton, age twenty-six, quarryman and head of the household at Stone Pit Cottage.

'Oh my God!' shrieked Kelly. 'Stone Pit Cottage. That's Ben's house. Ben said the cottage had been in his family for years. William really is his relative! I knew it!'

'I wonder what kind of relative,' said Mum. 'A great-great-grandad or uncle or something maybe? Does it say whether he was married or had any kids?'

Kelly scrolled down the record to the list of Household Members. 'Yes. Here. It says Alice Denton, age 21. She's listed as his wife. And there's a son, Billy Denton, age four. Wow!'

'So that means Alice was seventeen when she had him.'

'She was quite young, then.'

'I reckon it would depend on your circumstances. I'll bet people lower down in society had kids much younger than the toffs.'

'The census says that William was working in the quarry in 1851. That's pretty low down in society, I guess. I wonder if moving on to being a railway labourer was seen as a step up?'

'Maybe. I certainly think *I'd* prefer it. But then again, it didn't bring poor William and his family much luck did it, if he ended up getting killed?'

Kelly shook her head. She was lost in thought. This family were just names on an old census record, hidden away in some huge, faceless database, but it felt like she knew them, and she was surprised how sad she felt, especially when she tried to visualise little four-year-old Billy, whose father would be dead by the time he reached his teens.

Kelly was glad that the next day was a Saturday. She hadn't seen Ben for a week, since that misty morning in the churchyard. She had wanted to give him time to sort out whatever it was that was bothering him. But she had hoped he would make the first move and get in contact with her. So far, nothing. Even so, Kelly might have left things a little longer to calm down had she not managed to lay her hands on these documents. News of a death certificate *and* a census record was too much to hold in. She had to share it with Ben.

The next morning, as soon as all her jobs were done, Kelly set off for Ben's cottage, with Tyson in tow and her notebook and copies of the records in her bag. It was a beautiful morning— clear sunny skies and crisp underfoot. The unexpected sunshine filled Kelly with positive energy. She couldn't wait to see Ben.

And she didn't have to wait long. She saw him the moment she started along the footpath into the woods, walking towards her. He was wearing the same old trousers he always did and, Kelly noticed, in spite of the chill in the air, he had no jacket on top of his favourite green checked shirt. Although Ben looked quite relaxed and happy, Kelly felt a strange sense of disquiet. It seemed so odd that after a whole week of silence, there he should be, walking towards the campsite, as if he knew she needed to see him. She wondered if Ben had come this way at other times during the last seven days, waiting for her to go for a walk with Tyson. Or was it just a happy coincidence that they had decided to find one another at exactly the same time?

Tyson began to yap and pulled at his leash. Kelly tried to rein him in, embarrassed that a little dog could drag her along in such an ungainly fashion, but her feet were slipping on the fallen leaves so she had no choice but to break into a jog.

'Hello there,' said Ben, looking a bit sheepish, as Kelly got closer. Kelly presumed that he felt bad about the way their last meeting had ended. To show that there were no hard feelings, she stepped up to him, murmured 'S'good to see you,' and went to give him a kiss on the cheek. As she did it, she realised that this was the first time she and Ben had been quite so close. Ben must have realised that too, because he pulled back before she could touch him, a look of surprise on his face.

Kelly felt the need to explain. 'I've been worried about you, Ben Denton.' She curled Tyson's lead around her fingers. 'That's your surname, isn't it? Denton. You never told me.'

Ben looked shocked. When he responded, he spoke slowly. 'Yes. Denton's my family name. I knew there had to be a connection the moment I saw those initials on the gravestone.'

'But you knew what W. T. D. stood for.'

'Not really. I mean, I think I just saw the D and thought of my own name. D for Denton.'

'But you said the whole name.'

'When?'

'In the churchyard. Last Friday. You said William Thomas Denton.'

Ben reached down and picked up a stick. 'Why don't you let Tyson off?' He waved the stick at the little dog, 'You want to play fetch, don't you, boy?'

'Ben?' Kelly didn't understand.

'There you go,' said Ben, still ignoring her and unclipping Tyson's lead. 'Good lad. Fetch the stick!'

Kelly watched as Ben threw the stick into the trees and Tyson shot off after it, his little legs pumping furiously, propelling him at top speed through the grass. Should she press Ben further? Remembering her father's advice, she decided to try a different angle. 'Well, since I saw you last, I've been to the Records Office.'

Ben didn't respond, but she carried on. 'I managed to get hold of a copy of William Denton's death certificate. The age and dates match those on the grave, and it looks like he *was* killed working on the railway. And if he is in a shared grave with three others, we've got to be talking about the same accident that's described in that newspaper article.'

Ben was looking at her again, but she found it difficult to read his expression. Something between intrigued and anxious. Choosing her words carefully, she continued. 'I found William in the Census records too, for 1851. He lived in your cottage, Ben, didn't he? And he had a wife and a son.'

Ben swallowed hard. 'It said that?'

'Yes, it lists everyone in the household on that date. They're your relatives, aren't they?'

'Apparently,' muttered Ben, turning away.

For a few minutes the pair walked in silence along the footpath, side by side, into the wood. Eventually, Ben asked tentatively, 'What else did it say?'

'Not a lot, but one thing *was* interesting. It listed William's occupation as a quarryman. Imagine that! He must have worked in Wilmcote quarry before he went to work on the railway.' Kelly paused, before asking, in a small voice, 'Do you know anything else about your relatives, then, Ben?'

'Not really.'

Kelly wanted to get everything clear in her head. 'Well, what *do* we know?' she said, climbing up to perch on the top of a stile. 'We know that the railway was opened on 29th September 1860, and we know that Wilmcote quarry was supplying stone for the Houses of Parliament. For a job as big as that, as far away as London, the new railway line must have been a real bonus. It would have been by far the quickest way to move the stone. Far better than moving it by canal. Yes?'

Ben nodded, climbing up to sit alongside her. Tyson sniffed about beneath their dangling feet.

Kelly carried on. 'And *now* we know that on the day before the railway officially opened, four men died—and at least one of them was a railway labourer. So chances are they all were, if they were buried together. They were certainly all local. They could even have been friends.'

'Yes I think they were,' said Ben, looking at his hands.

'Yet there is hardly any information about the accident that we've been able to find. There was no detail on William's death certificate, no mention on the internet—just that newspaper clipping you found. And there was nothing obvious on the men's gravestones, not even their full names. How weird is that?'

'Very,' said Ben. 'You would think the victims deserved to be named at least.'

'Exactly!' said Kelly, delighted that at last Ben seemed to be on the same page as her. 'But why? It's like someone was trying to gloss over it. Make as little fuss as possible, or deliberately make the details hard for people to trace. Who could have something to hide, do you think?'

'Someone with the power and influence to cover up four deaths.'

Kelly shivered. 'Ooh, that's quite a scary thought. Almost as disturbing as that hangman's noose in the old shed!'

Ben sprang off the stile as if an electric current had passed through it. Tyson gave a yelp of protest.

'Hey, watch out!' cried Kelly. 'You trod on his tail!'

Ben spun round. 'Why do you have to keep going on about that noose? I told you it gives me the creeps. Besides, what can it possibly have to do with anything?'

'*Sorry.*' Kelly's apology dripped with sarcasm as she climbed down to scoop Tyson up into her arms. 'I forgot you were such a baby about that.'

Ben didn't look amused, so Kelly decided to let it drop.

'Whatever,' she resumed. 'There must have been plenty of people in Wilmcote who knew what went on. An accident like that couldn't have been swept under the carpet completely. People talk in small communities, don't they?' She plopped Tyson into Ben's arms, forcing him to give the dog a conciliatory cuddle. 'Mum suggested asking somebody local. Someone who might have a good knowledge of history round here—a storyteller or a local historian or someone like that. But I don't really know anyone in the village, apart from you.'

'Nor do I,' said Ben.

'But you've lived here all your life!'

'I know, but I don't have any school friends, and my parents... well, they're always busy on the farm. They don't socialise much.'

The two friends fell silent, contemplating their next move.

'I've got an idea,' announced Kelly. 'I think we should go to the pub!'

'What?' asked Ben, placing Tyson back on the ground. 'Why?'

'Because if you're looking for locals—I mean, old folk who have lived here a long time, people who might have relatives who told them stories about this place—it's not a bad place to start. The landlord is bound to know who's who in the village. He might be able to suggest someone we could talk to. Come on!'

Kelly patted her leg to summon Tyson to her side and began to walk off in the direction of the village. Ben hung back. 'I can't go into a pub.'

'Why not?'

'Well, my mother will kill me for starters. She hates those places. Besides, children aren't allowed in, are they?'

'I'm thirteen next month,' laughed Kelly. 'Hardly a child, and neither are you. Anyway, we aren't buying drinks. We just want to ask a few questions, see who's in there. Surely we can do that.'

She waited for Ben to reply, but could see that he wasn't convinced.

'Oh, you can wait outside, then!' she said impatiently. 'At least I'm going to try.'

Wilmcote had two pubs. The biggest and usually the busiest was the Mary Arden Inn, which was popular with tourists. Kelly aimed for the smaller pub, the Mason's Arms, which was more popular with the locals. She had been in there with Mum and Dad and her brother for a Sunday lunch a couple of times. They did the biggest Yorkshire puddings Kelly had ever seen.

There was a public footpath across the fields which came out into the centre of the village along the back of the Mason's Arms garden, and a gap in the hedge where you could get through. It took a good half hour for the two friends to get there, and by the time they reached the gap in the hedge, Ben had fallen quite a way back. Kelly waited for him to catch up.

'What's wrong with you?' she scoffed, when he slouched through the hedge and flopped down on a bench tucked away at the end of the pub garden. 'You can't be that tired, surely?'

'I walked nearly all the way to yours. Anyway, you might as well have gone ahead and gone inside. I'm not coming in.'

'Oh, Ben! Your mum doesn't need to know. You really can be a baby sometimes.'

Ben simply shrugged.

Kelly rolled her eyes. 'Oh well, it looks like it's Kelly Hearn or nothing. If you're staying here, you might as well make yourself useful. Look after the dog.' She tied Tyson's lead to the leg of the bench and, without another word, strode round the corner and up the path towards the rear entrance of the pub.

Inside, the Mason's Arms was dimly lit but welcomingly warm. A log fire crackled in the grate on the far side of the room and huddled around it were a few old local chaps enjoying a pint. Besides them there were two couples having a pub lunch, but apart from that it was fairly quiet.

Nervously, Kelly approached the bar. She recognised the landlord, put on her best smile and nodded a greeting to him.

'Can I help you, young lady?' he asked, his expression not matching the welcoming ambience of his pub.

'I'm not sure,' Kelly stammered.

'Then maybe you'd better come back with your parents, hey? I can't serve kids, you know. And I'm not giving out any free glasses of water either.'

'No, I mean, I don't want to buy anything. I'm looking for someone. I was hoping you might be able to help.'

'Oh aye,' remarked the landlord, dubiously.

'I'm working on a school project, about the history of Wilmcote, and I need to find some local people who have lived here a long time. Ideally, people with relatives who have lived here since the Victorian times. When the quarry was open.'

'Look, love, we might be called the Mason's Arms, but that doesn't make me an expert on the quarry.'

'I know. But I thought perhaps you would know someone who might be.'

The landlord sighed and rolled his eyes. *Grumpy old fart*, thought Kelly, convinced he was about to send her packing. But then he gestured to an old man sitting in the corner, in the alcove next to the fire, nursing his pint.

'I suppose you could ask old Jim. His family have been here for ever. I think his great granddad used to work the quarry. But you'll need to be quick. And you'll have to speak up. He's as deaf as a post.'

'Perfect!' exclaimed Kelly. 'I don't mean perfect that he's deaf.'

The landlord smirked.

'Oh, you know what I mean. Thank you. I'm really grateful.'

Kelly crossed the bar, feeling very uncomfortable. She felt as though everyone was staring at her. She wished Ben had come too.

Jim had a friendly, white-whiskery face. He smiled at Kelly, with glassy blue-grey eyes, and smacked his lips as he placed his pint glass down on a beer mat.

'Hello,' said Kelly, speaking as loudly as she dared. 'Do you mind if I sit down? The landlord said you might be able to help me with some questions I have about Wilmcote history.'

Old Jim raised his eyebrows and smiled, relishing the opportunity to be useful to someone. 'I can certainly try, my dear. Please...' He gestured to Kelly to pull up a chair.

Slowly, she told the old man all about her school project and asked if he knew anything, in particular about the history of the quarry and the railway.

'Yes, yes,' Jim replied, folding his arms and chuckling. 'My grandfather used to work in the quarry. But it's all a long time ago. I don't remember much. I'm ninety-six, you know.'

'Wow,' said Kelly, 'that's not bad going.'

'No, indeed. Not bad at all.' He picked up his glass and winked. 'I put it down to a drop of the old ale. A pint a day keeps the doctor away. Isn't that what they say?'

'Something like that,' Kelly chuckled. She liked Jim already.

'My grandfather used to come here to the Mason's too. This was his seat. I always sit here. I see it as carrying on a family tradition. And I'm ninety-six now, you know.'

'Yes, you said.' Kelly glanced over at the bar and, seeing the landlord eyeing her, decided to get old Jim back on track. She was about to ask a question when he picked up his thread.

'Oh yes, this place was full of quarrymen in my grandfather's day, and labourers from the railway. He used to tell me a thing or two about what they got up to in here.'

'Did your grandfather ever mention any names? A William Denton perhaps? He worked in the quarry and on the railway.'

'Denton, did you say?'

Kelly nodded.

The old man screwed up his eyes and scratched his beard. 'I don't know. It's a long time ago. I was only about your age when my grandfather died.'

He took a slug of his beer, and Kelly watched as he licked the froth from his moustache. Then she saw a flicker in his eyes.

'Nah, I don't remember any names, love, but I'll never forget the story of those chaps who got killed.'

221

'On the railway?' prompted Kelly.

'Aye, that's right. On the railway. Four of 'em wiped out at the same time. Terrible it was. Not many people know about that.'

'I do,' announced Kelly, inching forwards onto the edge of her chair, 'and I'm trying to find out what happened. Oh, please tell me you know some details.'

Old Jim lent towards her, and lowered his voice to a whisper, clearly relishing the chance to impart some of his knowledge. 'They said it was just an accident. But it wasn't. It was downright negligence.'

Kelly's eyes were wide with anticipation. 'Go on,' she whispered back.

'They shouldn't have been running trains on that track at all that day. There were still repairs to do. Some folk tried to blame the driver, but the poor bugger didn't have any warning. He had no idea there were men on the track. If he had he'd have blown his whistle, wouldn't he?'

Kelly's hand had gone to her mouth. 'So what are you saying? The men were working on the track and got hit by a train?'

Old Jim grimaced and nodded. 'Completely splattered by it, they were. Bits everywhere. Couldn't even tell who was who.'

'Oh my God!' Kelly exclaimed, her heart thumping. 'So who *was* to blame?'

'There was talk that it was the railway company's fault. It was a new line and they'd been rushing to get it finished in time for an official opening. Lots of VIPs were coming, and all that jazz. Cutting corners they were. Running trains along the line before it was ready.'

Kelly exhaled. It was too horrible to imagine.

Old Jim went on. 'And I don't think the labourers had a look-out either.'

'A look-out?'

'Yes. Someone posted further up the track, to look out for trains coming. To tell the workers to step aside.'

'So what happened?' asked Kelly. 'How come the rail company didn't get into trouble?'

'Oooh, I don't know, my dear. It was a long time ago. Things were different then. They didn't have all this health and safety nonsense. These companies could get away with murder.'

'Literally,' agreed Kelly.

'I think there was an inquest or something, but I don't know what happened with that.'

'I do. They decided it was just an accident. I've got an old newspaper cutting about it. There was an inquest but no one was considered to be at fault. The verdict was accidental death.'

Jim snorted. 'Hmm. That'd be right. The big boys always manage to get away with it, don't they? No one cares about the poor working folk. Ah well. It's all water under the bridge now.'

'Maybe,' pondered Kelly.

Behind her, someone turned up the volume on the television. The horse racing was about to start at Newmarket. Jim's attention immediately switched from her face to the large plasma screen on the wall over her shoulder. Kelly could tell she was not going to get any more from him today. Besides, he had turned out to be amazingly useful, ninety-six or not.

'I'll leave you to it, Jim,' she shouted, getting up from her chair. 'Thank you so much. You don't know how much you have helped.'

Old Jim held out a liver-spotted hand across the table to shake Kelly's. 'My pleasure, my dear. Any time...but don't leave it too long, I'm ninety-six, you know.'

When she got back outside, Kelly found Ben and Tyson waiting patiently in the autumn sunshine. Ben was still perched on the bench, stroking Tyson who was on the wooden seat alongside him.

As Kelly approached, Ben looked up apologetically and shrugged his shoulders. 'I'm sorry, Kel. I'm not much help to you, am I?'

'It's okay,' she replied, giving Tyson a biscuit from her pocket. 'It was fine. More than fine, actually.'

'You were gone a long time. I guessed you had found someone to talk to.'

'I did. A lovely man called Old Jim.' She giggled. 'He was ninety-six, you know.'

'And?'

'We've definitely got ourselves a cover-up. The four men were run over by a train, Ben. That's how they died. It was awful. Old Jim said the railway line wasn't even officially opened yet. They were still working on the line. And the railway company was either cutting corners because they had a deadline to meet, or hiding the fact that they had started to use the track before it was ready—or, who knows, it could have been both. I'm sure what Old Jim said wasn't just gossip. I believe him. And the more I think about it, there has to be a reason why there's no mention of how those men died on their gravestones, not even their full names. It's like someone wanted to bury the truth along with them.'

'But there was the inquest,' Ben said.

'Yes, but how on earth did they reach that accidental death verdict? From what Old Jim says, there were some serious questions about why those men got killed. I think I'm going to have another look on the internet. Perhaps I've missed something. There's *got* to be some more details somewhere.' Kelly picked up Tyson and placed him back on the ground. 'Come on, I'll tell you everything Old Jim said while we walk back.'

By the time they were approaching the campsite, Kelly had pretty much repeated her conversation with Old Jim word for word and the two of them had each come up with several theories as to how the railway company managed to come out of the whole thing so squeaky clean.

'Kel,' Ben said, stopping to look directly into her eyes. 'Why are you doing all this? It happened so many years ago. What does it matter to you?'

'Well, it's for our history project.'

'Yes, I know, but it's become more than that. I can tell.'

Kelly looked down and shuffled her feet. 'I dunno. I'm inquisitive, I guess. I like a good story, and this certainly has everything that I like in a story…death, a bit of mystery, a cover-up. Perhaps I will write it one day. Get it published.'

Ben grinned. 'Now that would be good.'

'Yeah,' laughed Kelly. 'But you know, I feel like this story found me. It all began when Tyson dug up that boot. It's like the truth wants to be dug up too.'

Ben nodded. 'You know, I think you've pretty much got all the answers to this mystery already. You just need to piece them together.'

Kelly agreed, wondering if Mr Walker might be able to help her. 'Shall we meet Monday evening? You could come and say hello to my mum and dad at last.'

'I was thinking that you could come to my cottage,' said Ben. 'After school. For supper. It's time for you to see where I live.'

Kelly didn't argue. She was thrilled to bits. 'That would be lovely. I can meet your family.'

Ben nodded and smiled back at his friend. 'See you, Kel.'

'See you, Ben.'

Ben started to walk away, then suddenly he turned, ran back to her, and kissed her on the cheek. His kiss was so light that Kelly touched her face, not even sure if she had really felt his lips at all.

'What was that for?' she squeaked, taken aback.

'I just wanted to say thank you,' said Ben. 'For being inquisitive. For being you.'

Chapter 31 – 28th September 1860

Billy's trousers were wet and filthy by the time he sprinted onto the brand new platform at Wilmcote Station. He had run all the way down the muddy track from the cottage, trying to leap the deepest, grittiest puddles, desperate to catch up with George and the others. They were already there on the platform, gathered around their foreman, as Billy appeared round the corner and slowed to a walk. In spite of the cold, Billy was in a bath of perspiration inside his jacket, and he was breathing so hard he wouldn't have been able to speak, even if he'd wanted to.

'You're cutting it fine, William Denton,' remarked the foreman, checking his pocket watch.

Billy bent over, catching his breath, and held up his hand by way of an apology. Before straightening up, he pulled his cap down even lower over his eyes and turned up his jacket collar to obscure as much of his face as he could. He was glad for the excuse of the wind and the rain. Even so, as he glanced to his side, he spotted Ted, his father's closest friend, squinting at him from a few yards away. Ted's eyes widened in recognition, but to Billy's relief, he remained silent and switched his attention back to the foreman, who was now giving the men his instructions for the morning.

'The test runs threw up some vibration on the Bishopton bend on the northbound line,' the foreman announced in a loud voice. 'The ballast must have been laid too thin. Ain't no surprise, really, the speed we've been made to lay this track at. But if we don't pack it deeper now, the soil underneath will sink. So set to it. I want it done by lunchtime.'

The four labourers all nodded and turned to head off in the direction of the Bishopton bend.

'One more thing,' said the foreman, calling them back, a note of nervousness in his voice. 'You'll need to listen out for trains.'

'What?' asked George, squinting at his boss through the rain, the angle of his eyebrows conveying his confusion.

'They said they might be running a couple of test trains today.'

'On the southbound side, though, yes? Not much point running a test on the northbound side till we're finished.'

The foreman looked embarrassed. 'To be honest, I'm not sure. It was all a bit vague. Best keep your wits about you, just in case.'

George shook his head in resignation, and signalled to the others to start making their way down the track.

As soon as they were out of the foreman's earshot, Ted sidled up to Billy and caught his arm.

'What the hell do you think you're doing, son?' he muttered under his breath.

Billy's eyes darted over his shoulder to George and Lewis, who were a few paces behind. They hadn't heard. Billy lowered his voice to a whisper. 'Dad's not well. I think you probably know why. I'm here to take his place and earn his wage and make sure my mother sees that bonus. I'm old enough.'

'If the foreman finds out...'

Billy cut in. 'My father needs to keep his job, Ted. And you need me. If this job doesn't get done this morning, no one gets that bonus, including you.'

Ted smiled wryly. 'Then you'd better get to work Billy lad. Just do as I tell you, and no slacking. I'll clear it with George and Lewis.'

Billy went on ahead down the track while Ted dropped back to have a word with the other two men. Glancing back, he saw them nodding their heads in understanding and felt the relief wash over him. All he had to do was keep his head down and help them finish packing the ballast, and they were in the clear.

By now, the clouds had dropped so low that, as Billy looked into the distance, it was hard to see where the ground finished and the sky began. He wiped away the driving rain from his face and tried to focus on the dark lines that were the railway tracks. Less than thirty yards ahead, they too were swallowed up in the grey blanket of mist, as they disappeared around the Bishopton bend.

'Here we are, lads,' bellowed Ted, as they reached two huge piles of crushed stone, heaped up on the embankment. 'Let's get stuck in.'

'That father of yours doesn't know how lucky he is,' said George as he passed by Billy and slapped him on the back. 'You've got gumption, lad, I'll give you that.'

Ted threw him a shovel. 'Here you go, Billy. You can use that.'

The four labourers set to their task, packing the ballast under and in between the rails and sleepers. Always backbreaking work, the job was made even harder by the conditions. The clay soil along the side of the track was saturated and sucked at their feet as they trudged back and forth to the ballast pile, coating their boots in heavy clods. The handles of their shovels were made slippery by the rain, and Billy lost his grip more times than he could count.

'Don't forget to listen out for trains, Billy,' yelled Lewis, the youngest of the three men. 'There mustn't be enough spare hands today to give us a look-out.'

Ted noticed the worried expression on Billy's face. 'Don't worry, lad,' he laughed. 'You'll feel the rails rumbling before you hear anything. And if you do, shout. Just don't wait until you hear the engine whistle. Don't rely on the driver seeing you first!'

Billy nodded, but his father's friend's advice didn't ease his anxiety. He had been so sure of himself when he left the cottage. He would protect his mother, prove that even though he had stayed on at school, he wasn't afraid of manual labour when it was needed, and shame his father into turning his life around. But now Billy's confidence was beginning to slide and he felt nervous and disoriented. Instructions were being barked at him from every direction and his senses were being invaded. The wind roared in his ears. The driving rain stung his face. His nose fizzed with the pungent aroma of creosote from the sleepers beneath his feet, and the sweat was turning his skin cold inside his clothes.

Think of Mother, he repeated to himself, over and over again. *Just keep thinking of Mother.*

By eleven o'clock, Billy's hands were raw and he had blisters on every finger. He hadn't thought to pick up his father's gloves and none of the others had a spare pair. But they were starting to make some progress and that helped to take his mind off the pain.

Meanwhile, the wind had picked up and was now lashing the rain down onto the track. At first, when Billy felt the rail beneath him starting to tremble, he thought it was just the wind, whistling over the metal. But then he realised that the trembling had a steady rhythm.

'I think there's a train coming!' he called out to George, who was the closest to him.

George stopped shovelling and listened. 'It's all right,' he shouted back. 'It's on the other track, on the southbound side. But we'd best hold fire just in case.'

George shouted up the line to Ted and Lewis and all four men stopped shovelling and strained their ears to listen. Sure enough, they heard a whistle coming from the Wilmcote direction.

'Carry on!' yelled Ted. 'It's southbound.'

The men resumed work, the noise of the approaching train growing louder and louder, echoing off the low cloud. His eyelashes heavy with raindrops, Billy saw the engine coming into sight, bearing down on them through the mist. Unused to the noise and the proximity of the massive engine as it tore past, just feet away from him, Billy was terrified. He dropped his shovel to the ground and covered his ears as, one after the next, the empty goods carts roared by and flew round the bend towards Stratford-upon-Avon.

It felt like every inch of the earth beneath his feet was shaking and the rush of air from the passing train whipped his cap off his head and threw it into the dirt at the side of the line. Billy span round to see where it had gone, and his mouth fell open. But the blood-curdling scream that might have sent a warning to the others was lost amid the wind and the rain and the thunderous rattling of the southbound train.

Billy was the only one of the four men to see the second, northbound train hurtling at them, before it hit them.

* * *

In the driving rain, and with his line of sight obscured by the passing southbound train coming round the bend ahead of him, the engine driver had no idea of the devastation he was about to cause. With no advance notice given to him about workmen on the line, his hand never strayed to the whistle which might have given the men the notice they needed to step aside.

But he did feel the bump beneath his wheels: enough of a bump to cause him to pull on the brakes. Knowing how long it took his train, its wagons fully loaded with stone as they were, to come to a complete halt, the engine driver was prepared for a long trudge back up the track to check out the source of the problem. But nothing could have prepared him for the sight that lay scattered before him as he approached the Bishopton bend.

Chapter 32 – September 2012

When Kelly arrived at school on Monday morning, she went straight to her tutor group room rather than going to the canteen to catch up with Leanne. She wanted to tell Mr Walker what she had found out over the weekend. In a way, she also wanted to prove to him that something positive had come out of her secret trip to the Records Office. It wasn't as if Mr Walker had been unpleasant with Kelly since her detention, but clearly he was disappointed with her for being dishonest, and it gnawed away at her. She wanted to make him understand why it had all been so important to her—even important enough to play truant.

And it seemed to be working. Mr Walker listened intently while Kelly told him all the information she had gleaned on William Denton, and said more than once how impressed he was with her research skills.

'You really are going the extra mile with this project, Kelly. It's fantastic,' he gushed, taking a sip from his 'Keep calm, I'm a history teacher' coffee mug. 'I wish all the students put as much effort in.'

'Thanks, sir.' Kelly grinned. 'I'm really enjoying it, but it's kind of frustrating too. I keep running into so many dead ends.'

'Like what?' Mr Walker asked.

'Like what happened at the inquest into the rail accident. I had another look on the internet yesterday on Mum's laptop, but I can't find any mention of it. All I have is this tiny newspaper cutting.' She held up the yellowed piece of paper.

'We could try searching the British Newspaper Archive,' suggested Mr Walker. 'The school has a subscription to that. It's online.' He checked his watch. 'Come on, there's still ten minutes or so until registration. Let's have a quick look now.'

'Wow, thanks, sir!' Mr Walker really was the best teacher ever.

He opened up the website on his computer screen and Kelly gave him the date of the inquest.

'The fifteenth of March, 1861, Stratford-upon-Avon railway,' the teacher said out loud, as he typed the letters into the search box.

A long list of possible newspaper articles popped up, but as they scrolled down, none of them seemed quite right.

'Hang on, let's try something slightly different,' said Mr Walker, peering at the newspaper clipping. He deleted the words Stratford-upon-Avon railway from the search box and replaced them with Bishopton Hill Railway Disaster. Once again a list of results appeared.

Kelly spotted it straight away. 'There!' she shrieked. 'There's something from the Birmingham Daily Post.'

Mr Walker clicked on the entry and opened up a full-screen view of a page from the paper.

'Blimey!' exclaimed Kelly, shocked by how tiny all the type was. There were no photographs or big, bold headlines, like in modern newspapers. Just lines and lines of text, with all the stories squashed together and a handful of dull-looking adverts in a column on the left.

'Here it is,' said Mr Walker, pointing to a heading which read: Stratford-upon-Avon Rail Disaster—Verdict Reached. He zoomed in and read out the whole report. The inquest had been held over two days, during which time the engine driver, the doctor who was called to the scene, a foreman and the Chairman of the Stratford-upon-Avon Railway Company, a Mr Reginald Adkins, gave evidence, as did some of the key shareholders in the railway, including a Member of Parliament, Sir Francis Throckmorton.

'That's interesting,' commented Mr Walker. 'Call me cynical, but with high-powered shareholders like that, it does make you question how much sway the railway company had over the jury's verdict.'

'Exactly!' agreed Kelly, who had been reading ahead. 'And look there. It says that no one cross-examined Mr Adkins. He could have said anything he liked!'

Kelly and Mr Walker looked at one another quizzically. Then they resumed reading. In spite of the fact that none of the victims' families had attended the hearing, the railway company had offered an undisclosed sum to the victims' families, but it had been made clear that this was in no way an admission of guilt. Rather it was simply in lieu of the bonus which had been promised to these men on the completion of the line.

'So they came out smelling of roses and paid off the families to keep them quiet, by the sounds of it,' remarked Mr Walker.

'I wonder if that's why the families didn't put anything about the cause of death on the joint gravestone—or even any full names,' mused Kelly. 'Perhaps they were told to play it all down.'

'Maybe. Who knows?'

Kelly sat back in her chair and shook her head. 'I can't believe it. It's so wrong. Those poor men. Their poor families.'

'I know. But workers' rights were very low on the agenda back then, Kelly. Just think of all the children they sent down the coal mines. They didn't stop that until 1841. And deaths in the railway construction industry were quite common. A lot of people paid a high price to get those lines laid all over the country. Believe me, this accident is small fry compared to some. There's a famous viaduct up in North Yorkshire, the Ribblehead Viaduct. It's got twenty-four massive arches, towering over the valley and the River Ribble. Hundreds of people died building that. There were accidents, and there was lots of disease among the workers, too, as they were living so close together. There was a smallpox outbreak and so many died that they filled all the graveyards and the railway company had to pay for a new one to be built nearby.'

Kelly was shocked. For once, she didn't know what to say. Behind her, a few of her fellow tutor group students had started to file into the classroom ready for registration.

'I'll print this off for you, if you like,' said Mr Walker, nodding at the screen. 'But I think you've got the gist of it. Hey, wait a minute, did you read this final paragraph?'

Kelly peered at the screen. A footnote mentioned that the opening of the Stratford-upon-Avon to Hatton railway line went ahead the day after the tragedy, despite local people's calls to postpone the ceremony out of respect for the four men who had died. The line, it explained, would not only provide passengers with vital links between Birmingham and Oxford but was also the new life-blood of the Wilmcote Lime and Cement Works, which was supplying stone to the late Sir Charles Barry's Westminster Palace project.

'The *late* Sir Charles Barry!' remarked Kelly. 'I wonder what happened to him? He must have died before the building was finished and he'd been working on it for years. I wonder what he died of.'

Mr Walker was already heading over to the printer. 'Well, it looks like you've got plenty of good material for your project now, Kelly.'

'Yes, thanks, Mr Walker,' said Kelly, taking the print-out from him. 'There's just one more thing I'd like to find out, if I can.'

'What's that?'

'William Denton. I want to know how he's related to my friend.'

'That should be easy enough to find out. You just need to ask his family.'

'Funny you should say that,' laughed Kelly. 'I've got an invitation to supper tonight which might just give me the chance to do that.'

Chapter 33 – 28th September 1860

Sitting on her own in her kitchen, the whole cottage empty and eerily quiet, Alice was numb. When she first heard the news, she had felt dizzy and unable to breathe. She had heard someone hammering on Mr Greenslade's front door and had rushed to open it, only to see a distraught Lucy Sherwood, tears streaming down her face, stammering something almost incomprehensible about Ted and the others. But the gist of it was clear. Four men, William included, were dead.

Hearing the commotion, Mr Greenslade had steered the two ladies into the kitchen where his wife had made them both cups of strong tea, her kindness being rewarded by wracking sobs from Lucy and a shocked silence from Alice.

Alice had insisted on going home, refusing to let Mr Greenslade or his wife accompany her. She had wanted to be alone. Besides, Billy would be home from school soon.

Now that she was alone, Alice wasn't sure what to do with herself. What were you meant to do when you had just heard that your husband had been hit by a train? It didn't seem real. She didn't feel anything.

Looking about her, she noticed that the kitchen was unusually tidy. Neither her husband nor her son was very good at clearing away the breakfast things, and there was always something left out on the table or by the sink when she got home from work. But not today. Perhaps she should make a start on supper. She and Billy would have to eat, no matter what. At the thought of breaking the news to her son, Alice felt her stomach contract.

She had just started peeling some potatoes over the basin when there was a knock at the door. The unexpected noise made Alice jump and the peeler slipped, taking a slice of skin off the side of her thumb.

'Blast!' she exclaimed, sucking the blood from her finger as she went to answer the door. She was surprised to find tears in her eyes. It was only a silly nick, after all.

For a moment she wondered if it was Billy, home from school early, but Billy would never knock at the front door like that. He always let himself in through the back door from the garden.

It was William's foreman, holding a damp cardboard box with her husband's name scrawled hastily on one side. Alice had seen him in church many times and he always acknowledged her and Billy, so she had him marked as a good man. Well-mannered at least. For church he wore his hair neatly slicked back, and his clothes were clean and freshly pressed. Today he looked altogether different. The colour was drained from his face and his eyes were red-rimmed and blood-shot. He was soaking wet and filthy too, and Alice recoiled when she noticed what looked like a smear of blood on his sleeve.

'I am so sorry about your husband, Mrs Denton,' he stammered. 'He might not have been the best timekeeper, but he was a good worker and he was popular among the lads. It's just terrible. They couldn't hear anything you see, 'cos of the southbound train.'

Alice held up her hand to silence him. She wasn't ready to hear it yet. Besides, what could knowing the details change?

'What's that?' she asked, pointing to the box.

'It's a couple of William's things. They have taken the...' the foreman swallowed, '...the bodies to the mortuary in Stratford-upon-Avon. But there were a few clothes and things, scattered about. I thought I should gather them up and return them to the families straight away.'

'The mortuary?' asked Alice. 'Can I go and see him?'

The foreman looked down at the box, searching for the right words. 'The doctor said the bodies would be taken straight from there to the undertakers and put in closed coffins. They were... well, the train hit 'em pretty hard, Mrs Denton. To be truthful, they had trouble recognising who was who.'

Alice swayed, falling against the door frame. The foreman lunged forward to catch her arm, dropping the box as he did so. 'Oh, Mrs Denton, I apologise. I've said too much. Let me take you to a chair.'

'I'm all right,' Alice reassured him, regaining her balance and touching her brow with a trembling hand. 'Don't worry about the box. I'll deal with it. Please, please, just leave me be.'

The foreman still lingered, his face lined with worry. 'Are you on your own, Mrs Denton?'

'My son will be back any time now. Really, you can go. I'll be fine. Thank you for bringing William's things.'

The foreman retreated, and Alice bent down to pick up the contents which had spilled from the box onto the floor. A few coins in a small leather money purse which William always kept in his jacket, a door key, his left boot and his cap. Was that it? Was that all she had left of him?

Alice slipped the purse and the key into the pocket of her cardigan then put the boot back in the box and slid it gently under the hall table. She carried the cap into the kitchen with her, sank down in the chair and stared at it in her lap. Some of the blood from her finger had seeped into the material on the peak and she absent-mindedly rubbed at it with her sleeve.

'Trouble recognising who was who,' the foreman had said. Alice closed her eyes and tried to block out the horrific image that kept appearing in her mind. Suddenly she didn't want to be on her own any more. She needed Billy to come home.

She listened to the clock in the sitting room ticking off the minutes from the end of the afternoon. Billy was normally home by now. What if someone had stopped him on his way back from school and told him what had happened? Panic rose in her chest. She didn't want her son to hear the news from anyone but her.

Her unease growing, Alice became aware that she was wringing Willliam's cap in her hands. She checked herself, and gently smoothed out the cap on her knee. It was then that she noticed the initials which, months ago, she had so carefully embroidered on the inside to stop William from moaning that

241

he kept leaving for work with a cap that was too small. She went cold. She was looking at the letters B T D.

William must have picked up the wrong cap this morning, Alice told herself. He was in a rush. It was early. It was dark.

She shifted in her seat. Then she went into the sitting room to check the clock. She was right. Billy *was* late.

Alice dropped the cap on the floor and ran to the coat rack by the back door. A second cap, still there. She snatched it down from the peg. Perhaps she had misread the letters. No, there, in her own neat little stitches, were the letters W T D.

The boxroom! Alice took the stairs two at a time to check the room to which she had banished her inebriated husband the night before. She threw open the door and was hit by a stomach-churning stench. There was a pool of vomit on the floor by the bed, hastily half-covered with one of her best linen towels, and she put her hand over her mouth as she tried not to retch. She took in the crumpled bedspread, the pillow knocked onto the floor. Everything suggested that William had left in a hurry.

For a moment, she felt relieved. Her theory had been correct. William must have been in such a rush to get to work that he simply picked up the wrong cap. Then she felt guilty. She didn't want William to be dead of course. But if she had to choose between him and her son...

Breathing deeply, Alice shut the door on the distasteful scene and crossed the landing into Billy's room. She was surprised to see that Billy's bed wasn't made either. Then she saw his satchel, sitting packed and ready on the rocking chair beside the bed.

The sense of dread returned. 'Please, God, no!' she cried.

242

Alice dashed down the stairs. 'William? Billy?' she called out, over and over, as she searched every room and peered out of the front window. She no longer knew what to think. In her panic, she ran blindly out into the back yard, through the side gate, and flew down the track in the direction of the railway. She didn't feel the cold wind, or notice the rain on her face. Her mind was focused on one thing alone. Finding her son.

She took the short-cut along the footpath through the wood. She knew it would be muddy, but from the other side of the trees she could pick up the canal towpath and come out on the main road just down from the station. The path was slippery and more than once Alice tripped and nearly fell, but she didn't care. She had to keep on going.

As she stumbled through the trees she came to the new shed that William and his workmates had built to store all their tools and equipment. Something about it caught her eye. The door was usually locked when no one was around. Now it was ajar and she was sure she could see a shape or detect the tiniest of movements inside. There must be someone there. Perhaps they could help her.

Slowly, yet inexplicably nervous, Alice walked up to the door and peered inside. Then she fell to her knees. Hanging from a roof beam, the knotted rope around his neck gently creaking, was William.

Chapter 34 – 28th September 1860

Y ou've heard the news, I presume?'

It was Sir Francis, his face grim as he burst into Sir Charles Barry's study.

'It's terrible,' Barry replied, close to tears. 'So close to the opening. Just dreadful.'

'Indeed, the timing could not be worse. But don't worry, my friend. It's all in hand. I have Adkins' assurance that the train has been able to continue its journey via Birmingham, and it won't delay the official opening of the branch line.'

'That's not what I meant!' snapped the architect. 'I meant how terrible it is for those poor men. It's heart-breaking that they have lost their lives at all, but at this stage of the project, after all those months of labour, when they were so close to finishing.'

'Well, yes, of course,' sniffed Sir Francis. 'Tragic. But it needn't reflect badly on us.'

'How can it not?' enquired Barry, appalled. 'What about the families of the men killed?'

'Surely they understand that railway work is dangerous.'

Barry gasped. 'Maybe they do, but everyone knows that those men have been asked to work at twice the speed. They will suspect that corners were cut. People are bound to ask why a fully-laden goods train was running on a line that hadn't yet been officially opened. They will want to know if the men were put at unacceptable risk. Deadlines or not, as shareholders we still have a duty of care. The families could have a case against the railway company for negligence or worse!'

Sir Francis paced back and forth in front of Barry's desk. 'The families might *think* they have a case, but they could never prove anything. This was just an unfortunate accident.'

Barry felt sick. 'But the driver should have been told that there were workmen on the line. At the very least there should have been a look-out, a signal of some kind. Those poor devils had no warning.'

'Well, the driver's too knocked out to say anything at the moment,' Sir Francis remarked. 'The doctors have given him something to calm him down. They say he was in a very bad state of shock. And I doubt he'll say anything that would reflect badly upon his employers—not if he values his job. The driver of the other train said he didn't see what happened. So the only other witnesses were the victims. Luckily they were all killed instantly, so they didn't have chance to blame anyone.'

'Luckily?' Barry couldn't believe what he was hearing.

'The engine made a mess of them, that's for sure, especially the two who were struck first. It'll be closed coffins at those four funerals!' Throckmorton let out a small chuckle.

Barry shot to his feet. 'This is no joking matter, Francis! These were human beings.'

'Look, my friend,' said Sir Francis, his face turning serious. 'Building railways is always dangerous. A few corners may have been cut, but you need to remember why. There are plenty of people, including everyone in that godforsaken village, who will benefit from the new railway and from that quarry staying in business.'

Beads of sweat were forming on Barry's brow, and he felt unsteady on his feet. He leaned on his desk for support. 'Will the board offer the relatives some compensation, at least?' he croaked, after a few moments of silence.

Sir Francis sighed. 'Perhaps. As long as it's without admission of guilt.' His face brightened. 'Even better if it were a settlement rather than compensation. The men were going to get a bonus anyway. We wouldn't have to top that up by a great deal, and in exchange we can ask the families to agree that no further action against the railway company will be taken.'

'Those men deserve a decent funeral. The cost of that should be covered too,' Barry insisted.

'Yes, there's no reason why we can't do that. The bodies have been taken to the mortuary in Stratford-upon-Avon, but we could arrange for the undertakers to bring them on a special train back into Wilmcote for burial. We can't do finer than that. But I shall warn the families that the deceased will get no such ceremony unless everyone agrees to the settlement.'

'I am sure you will,' sighed Barry, defeated. He mopped his brow.

Sir Francis continued, 'Furthermore, I will insist that any memorials are kept plain. We don't want everyone being reminded of the accident for years to come. And I will stipulate that no one can talk to the newspapers.'

Barry made a strange choking noise and pulled at his collar.

'Good lord, man, are you all right?' demanded Sir Francis. 'You've turned a very odd shade.'

'Am I all right?' sputtered Barry. 'No, I'm not all right. How can I be? I'm the architect of one of the country's greatest buildings, yes. But at what cost?'

Irritation flashed across Sir Francis's face. He reached into his waistcoat pocket and checked his fob watch.

Barry waved his hand at the MP dismissively. 'Yes, yes, it's late. It's been a long day. I think you'd better take your leave. I'm sure you want to start putting your plan into action. And I've heard as much as I can stomach. Goodnight to you, Sir Francis.'

As soon as Sir Francis had left the room, Barry cast his eyes to the ceiling. He had never felt under such pressure. The weight of it was sitting heavily on his chest, like a vice tightening his rib cage, restricting every breath. He lurched across the room to the circular marble table positioned in the recess of the large bay window. Sitting upon it was a perfect, small scale model of the Palace of Westminster. Almost falling across it, Barry swept the model onto the polished wooden floor, letting out a roar of frustration as the model splintered into hundreds of tiny pieces.

The old man began to sob, his breaths becoming gasps as once again he grappled with his collar. The pain in his chest was unbearable now and was shooting down his left arm. Paralysed by it, Barry collapsed onto the floor amid the pieces of the building which had been his greatest dream.

By the time his beloved wife Sarah found him, Sir Charles Barry's body was stone cold.

PART 7

Chapter 35 – April 1861

The weather on the morning of Alice's final goodbye to her son was much as it had been on that dreadful day, six months earlier, when the train had struck him down. The rain was falling in slate-grey sheets and the bottom of Alice's skirts, as she crossed the grass of the churchyard, were sodden and rimmed with mud. The small bunch of daffodils she carried, hand-picked from the garden at Stone Pit Cottage and tied with a blue ribbon, was already battered and bruised from the unforgiving wind which had swept Alice along as she walked down through the village to the church.

Arriving at the grave, Alice paused to read the verse that she, Sarah and the other wives had chosen for the headstone, its true meaning known only to their families, before crouching down in front of the last little footstone in the row of four. She pulled away the clumps of long grass which had already began to swallow the three carved initials, and placed her bouquet down next to the space she had cleared.

She traced the letters with her index finger and swallowed the lump that rose in her throat. W. T. D. No one but Alice and her father knew that the William who lay beneath the cold soil was her beloved son. Her Billy. Her rock.

As the tears spilled down her cheeks, scenes from that terrible day flashed up in front of her eyes. Her shock at seeing her husband hanging from the roof beam like a grotesque marionette in the dark, musty shed had turned to anger as she realised that William had taken the easy way out. Everything had fallen into place then. She had known for certain that the body they had scraped off the track was that of her precious son. And William had discovered that too. He had risen from his drunken slumber too late to prevent poor Billy from taking his place—from being killed in his place. William was to blame for everything. She had known it, and he had known it. But rather than face up to what he had done, William had left her to cope with her grief on her own. Just as her father had always predicted, William had brought shame on her and her family. Yet even her father, who had despised William from the moment he met him, could never have imagined the deplorable means by which he would accomplish it.

Time after time, she and Billy had stood up for William in the face of her father's criticism. He had not deserved their loyalty. And now the shame that he had brought upon her with his drinking had been compounded in his death by suicide. How could she ever forgive him for that? No, she had decided, she wasn't going to let him tarnish her family's name with this scandal. He had taken enough from her already.

That was when Alice had made the decision. No one would know.

As she knelt by her son's grave, Alice recalled the struggle to cut down her husband's body with the saw she had found inside the shed, then drag it to the disused well outside. She had found the strength, drawing on her grief and her anger, and thankful for the slipperiness of the rain-soaked grass beneath his back. She had stuffed his pockets with rocks from the piles waiting nearby to be crushed into ballast, and had heaved his corpse over the side of the well, trying not to look upon her husband's shocking purple, bloated face. Then she had let him fall, breathing heavily yet strangely calm as she watched his body disappear down into the darkness.

After the initial heavy splash, Alice had waited until she could no longer hear any more ripples gently lapping against the sides of the well. Then she had prayed that the Lord would forgive her and allow his body, and the nature of his shameful death, to remain a secret in those cold, dark, murky waters.

Alice was happy for the initials on the stone to read W. T. D. William was her son's full name, after all. They had only begun calling him Billy when he was a baby to make life easier. She and her father had told everyone that they had sent Billy away straight after the accident, to stay with family in Cornwall. The sea air would be good for him, they had said, and it was wise to put some distance between the poor lad and the horror of what had happened. Alice had claimed she was in no state to look after him, and who would question a grieving widow?

Six months is a long time when you are shrouded in grief. By now Alice was desperate to put some distance between herself and Wilmcote. Certainly there was nothing left for her in the village besides her father, and Alice was finding it increasingly difficult to live with his look of self-righteousness every time he spoke of his late son-in-law. She had been unsettled by the relish with which he had received the news of William's death. How could he feel that way about something so intrinsically linked to the loss of Billy? Alice found her father's thinly-veiled joy distasteful and un-Christian in equal measure.

But rather than leaving right away, Alice held on for the inquest. She needed to know that her secret was safe, even while part of her wished that the truth could come out and that the world could know of the brave and loyal thing that her son had done. She prayed that the railway company would be forced to admit fault and explain to the world why her darling Billy, and those three poor men, were working in the path of an oncoming train. Everyone knew that procedures had not been followed, and that the railway company had agreed to transport Greenslade's stone before the line was completely safe.

But the shareholders had closed ranks and used gold to tempt the families into silence. And so it was that the four bodies lay in a grave with only initials to mark their memory, and an epitaph that set in stone the families' pledge never to complain and made no mention of what had caused such a great loss.

Alice hadn't told her father of her plans. She knew he would try to stop her leaving. But she needed a fresh start. So she had bought herself a passage on the Castle Eden sailing to Adelaide from London in two days' time, and in eighty-eight days she would be on the other side of the world. Her money from the settlement with the Stratford-upon-Avon Railway Company should be enough to rent a home, start a little business maybe. Ironic that the first part of her long journey to a new life would be on the railway line that saw her old life change for ever.

She ran her hand around the cold, smooth curve of the top of the footstone. 'Goodbye, my brave sweet boy,' she whispered. 'Rest in peace. I may be on the other side of the world, but you will always be with me.'

Chapter 36 – September 2012

You can't come this time, Tyson. I'm sorry.' Kelly stepped down from the caravan ready to head off to Ben's for supper.

Tyson wagged his tail even harder, as if hoping he could change her mind.

Kelly gave him a hug. 'No, you daft dog. You stay here and be a good boy.'

'Call us when you want picking up, love,' called her dad from inside.

'Okay, I will. Thanks Dad. I can walk down to the main road if you like, save you coming all the way up the track to Ben's cottage. Unless you want to meet Ben's parents?'

'Yes. Maybe I will. Anyway, it'll be too dark to go wandering down any track. I'll come up to the cottage. It's the same turning off the main road as the one to Stone Pit Farm, did you say?'

'That's the one. I'll see you later then.' Kelly smiled as she set off through the campsite gate. She was thinking how far they had all come in the past year, since she started at The Shakespeare Academy. Her parents seemed so different now from the two people who used to fuss over her every move and refused to mix with the other parents in the primary school playground.

As she walked along the path towards Stone Pit Farm, Kelly went over everything she needed to share with Ben. She would soon be ready to start writing up her notes. She was just wondering whether Mr Walker would mind if she and Ben wrote the project together, when she came to the end of the footpath at the bottom of the lane that linked the farm house to the main road. If she had followed Ben's directions properly, the turning down to Stone Pit Cottage was further along, past the farm house.

She had never been this way before, so she slowed her pace as she passed the surprisingly grand set of metal gates that formed the front entrance to Stone Pit Farm. Kelly wanted to have a good look. This had been the home of the quarry owner, all those years ago, and he would have been an important figure in the community. Wealthy too. Kelly could see that the farm house was still very impressive—an imposing, red-brick building with large sash windows and a wide porch, set behind a sweeping, gravelled courtyard with a circular fountain in the centre.

The farmer who lives there now must be doing well, she concluded, for the house was in pristine condition.

Kelly carried on along the lane, thinking that she was probably walking in the footsteps of all the quarrymen who would have come this way to and from the stone pits each day.

The sun was already low in the sky. In just a week or so everyone would be turning their clocks back and it would be too dark to come over the fields much after school. Kelly sighed.

It had been a great summer. One of the best. She was so glad that she had met Ben.

Kelly reached the bend at the end of the lane and suddenly realised how excited she was about seeing Ben's cottage at last. She wondered what his parents would be like and hoped that they liked her. A flutter of panic ran through her. She had forgotten to ask Ben if he had told his mum and dad that she was a Traveller. She wasn't going to hide it. She was proud of where she came from. But you could never tell how other people would react.

However, all Kelly's worries about the kind of the reception she would get vanished when she turned the corner at the end of the narrow track and Stone Pit Cottage finally came into view.

She stopped dead and looked around her, confused. Had she got the directions right? Was this really it, or had she turned down the wrong track?

'No,' she said to herself. 'Ben said there was only one track leading off to the left. This must be it.'

The cottage before her had clearly not been lived in for a very long time. Its grey-blue stone work was almost completely covered in ivy, which had encroached upon the dusty old windows to such an extent that Kelly was certain barely any light could pass through. The front door showed only a hint of its original bottle green colour, the paint was so faded and peeling, and the wood was splintered and rotten.

A dense covering of weeds had run rampant in the tiny front garden so that Kelly could hardly make out where the path to the door began. Looking up, she could see tiles missing from the roof and one of the panes of glass in the largest upstairs window was badly cracked.

'Oh Ben,' she said out loud, although her throat felt so tight that the sound which came out was barely a whisper. Her eyes filled with tears.

Determined to quash the crazy theories which had begun to race around her mind, Kelly rushed up to the front door, clamped the doorknob with both hands and tried to wrestle it open. The door wouldn't budge.

'No!' she cried. 'Ben!'

Perhaps there was a back door. Kelly ran around the side of the cottage and through an old wrought iron gate, now hanging off its hinges, which led to the back yard. The scene there reminded Kelly of *The Secret Garden*. The wall that surrounded it was low, not like the high one that enclosed Mary's garden in the book, but the plants inside it were certainly as overgrown. No one had tended this garden for a very long time. Yet dotted here and there were hints of a time when the garden was once loved and cared for. A stone bird bath lay on its side, there was an old potting shed in the far corner, and ensnared in a mass of knotted shoots and branches were the skeleton-like frames of a former rose garden.

Built against the back wall of the cottage was a small lean-to with a glass door. The glass in the door was so mouldy and dirty that Kelly could not see through it, but she could see that it was open. Stopping briefly to look around her, she gathered herself then stepped over the threshold into a tiny boot room with a row of coat pegs on the wall.

'Who's there?'

A voice. A woman's voice, with an accent of some kind.

Kelly froze. She breathed deeply then said, in a small voice, 'It's Kelly. I'm Ben's friend.'

'Well, you're welcome to come on in, but I'm not sure who Ben is.'

As Kelly went through the next door she saw the source of the voice. An elderly but sprightly woman, dressed in jeans and a sky-blue turtle-neck jumper. She was standing in the centre of a dusty old kitchen with a large rectangular pine table in the centre. Kelly guessed that she was in her mid-sixties, and sensed straight away that she need not be scared. The lady had a kind, open face. Her skin was tanned and healthy looking, and her fair hair was cut into a neat bob, held back by a lavender chiffon scarf tied into a floppy bow which framed the top of her head.

'Ben lives here...I think,' said Kelly, her uncertainty causing her voice to sound a little shaky.

'No, I don't think so,' replied the lady. 'This cottage has been empty for years. There *was* a family who rented it and lived here during the war, but no one's lived here since then.'

Kelly's mind was racing. If no one had lived here for years, then where on earth was Ben? Perhaps it was the old lady who was confused. 'Are you Australian?' she asked.

'I am. That's right.' The lady held out her hand. 'Pleased to meet you, Kelly. I'm Alice. I've lived in Australia all my life, but this place used to belong to my great-grandmother before she emigrated. I'm named after her. I inherited the cottage when my mother died.'

'Woah,' gasped Kelly. Of course. Alice was the name on the census record, William Denton's wife.

Unsure how to read Kelly's reaction, the lady went on with her story. 'I always dreamed of coming to England one day to check out my roots. I had a feeling that now was the right time.'

Kelly inclined her head to the pots of paint on the sideboard. 'Are you going to do the cottage up and come and live here?'

The lady shrugged. 'Oh, I doubt it, I'm happy in Australia. I couldn't stand the cold winters you get here. But whatever I do decide to do with this place, I think I owe it to my great-grandmother to tidy it up, don't you? Mind you, I'm told that she didn't have many happy memories of her time here.'

'I know,' said Kelly. 'I've been learning all about it, you see, with...' She paused. 'With my friend Ben. For a school local history project about the quarry which used to be open here. And I've been trying to find out what happened when they first built the railway through Wilmcote, and how it changed things.'

'So you live in Wilmcote, then?'

'Just on the edge of the village. On the other side of the railway.'

'And you're going to write about the history of this place?'

'Yes.'

'Well, I can't tell you where your friend Ben lives, but I might be able to help you with some details on the history of this cottage. If you're going to write about it, it's important you get the story right. It's about time the truth was told.'

Kelly smiled and nodded. This was music to her ears. 'It sure is. Ever since I started this project, it's felt like a big mystery puzzle. And a flippin' difficult one!'

Alice laughed. 'Perhaps I can provide the final pieces. Would you like some juice?'

'Yes please.'

Alice opened a cool bag on the old kitchen table, and took out two cartons of apple juice. 'I came prepared,' she said with a grin. 'I guessed that there wouldn't be much chance of a cup of tea when I arrived. Here, have a seat.'

She wiped the dust off one of the kitchen chairs and gestured to Kelly to sit down. Because the light was fading fast, she also lit some candles, which cast a warm glow about the room. Then she sat on the other side of the table from Kelly. 'Cheers!' she said, lifting her juice carton in salute and taking a long pull on the straw. Kelly followed suit.

'If you've been researching the history of the railway, I take it you know about the railway accident?' Alice began.

Kelly, who was still sucking on her straw, nearly choked on her juice. She hadn't expected the old lady to come right out with that. 'Yes,' she spluttered, dabbing her mouth with her sleeve. 'I have. That was so sad, and so awful how the railway company tried to cover it all up.' She looked again at the lady across the table. 'Hey wait a minute, if your great-grandmother lived here, does that make you a Denton? Was William Denton your great-grandfather?'

'No, it's a little more complicated than that. Alice Denton *was* my great-grandmother, but she didn't marry my great-grandfather until a few years after she arrived in Adelaide. It was her second marriage, and she'd already made a new life for herself in Australia by the time she met him. She was a seamstress, you know, and my great grandfather was one of her customers.'

Alice took a sip of her juice. Kelly remained silent, trying to take it all in. She still didn't understand why Alice wasn't familiar with Ben if he was a Denton, but the old lady seemed in full flow, so Kelly didn't interrupt.

'They had my grandfather in 1875. They called him Billy in memory of Alice's first son. The one who was killed in the rail accident.'

Alice stopped speaking, noticing the surprise on Kelly's face.

'Her...her son?' Kelly stammered. 'You mean, it was Billy who was killed? He was working on the line? Wasn't he only about twelve or thirteen in 1860?'

'Just thirteen. And yes he *was* working, although he wasn't supposed to be there. I'm not surprised you didn't find that out. My great-grandmother had her reasons for keeping that a secret.'

'But I saw the gravestones. They are still there, in the churchyard,' said Kelly, breathlessly. 'The initials on the footstone are W. T. D.'

'Everyone called the boy Billy, but he was christened William Thomas, like his father. So the footstone was accurate. Everyone just believed it was for William senior.'

Kelly shook her head. She was having trouble understanding it all.

Alice leaned forwards, folding her arms and resting them on the table. 'My great-grandmother started a diary on her crossing to Australia. She had lots of time to kill on that ship. And she began it by explaining the background to her decision to move to Australia. She never spoke about it to anyone. She wanted to start a new life and put it all behind her. But she obviously wanted the truth to be recorded somewhere. My mother used to read the diary to me when I was younger, and it's mine now, of course, along with the cottage.'

'So did your great-grandmother say what happened to Billy?' asked Kelly, fascinated.

'Well yes, but a lot of the details about the accident itself were a result of her putting two and two together. She believed that Billy went to work in his father's place that day because he found him drunk and hungover from the night before. The Dentons didn't have much you see. Times were hard, and there were plenty of men ready to take your place if you lost your job. If you didn't toe the line and do a good job, your boss would sack you as quick as look at you. So turning up late because you had a hangover wasn't going to cut the mustard.'

'So, what, Billy went to work so that his father would keep his job?' asked Kelly, leaning forwards into the candlelight.

'So my great-grandmother believed, yes. Plus, the railway line they were building was nearly complete, and they were due a bonus. The only man, besides the other victims, who saw Billy on the morning of the accident was the foreman, and he obviously mistook him for his father. Then of course, after poor Billy was dead, no one could tell *who* he was...'

Kelly finished her sentence. 'Because the bodies were so badly mangled.'

'That's right. Horrible, hey?'

Kelly nodded, suddenly feeling incredibly sad. 'Your poor great-grandmother. And poor William! He must have felt terrible. In bed with a hangover while his son is getting killed to protect his job. It should have been William who was killed.'

Alice tutted. 'Exactly. My great-grandmother reckoned that William must have woken up later that morning and gone down to the railway to look for his son. When he got there, he must have realised his son had been killed.'

Kelly kept shaking her head. She couldn't imagine how guilty William must have felt. 'So what did he do then, Billy's dad?'

'My great-grandmother found him in a goods shed. It's not surprising that he blamed himself for what had happened. It wouldn't have mattered to him whether or not the railway company had been negligent. All he would have been able to think about was the fact that it should have been him, not his son, who was killed. The shame and the pain of that must have been too hard to take.'

Kelly was starting to feel a bit sick. 'What do you mean?' she asked, petrified that she already knew the answer.

'He took his own life. Hung himself. In a shed, somewhere near the railway line.'

Kelly could hear it again. That dreadful creaking sound of rope rubbing on wood in the shed that Ben wouldn't enter. The mysterious photograph. She shuddered as the memory of the chilly air inside the shed brought goosebumps to her skin. Kelly looked down at her hands. They were trembling.

'Sorry, love,' said Alice. 'It's a bit cold in here, isn't it?'

When she next spoke, Kelly had to fight to control the quiver in her voice. 'So there must be another grave somewhere. William's grave.'

'I'm afraid not,' replied Alice. 'You see, back then, suicide was considered a very shameful thing, Kelly. It was seen as a crime against the state *and* against God. For my great-grandmother, with a vicar as a father and a strongly religious upbringing, the thought of everyone knowing what William had done was too much to bear. And she was angry with him too, for what had happened to Billy.'

'So what did she do?' asked Kelly.

Alice cleared her throat, evidently feeling less comfortable sharing this part of her family history. 'My great-grandmother didn't record all the details in her diary, but she said enough to convince my mother and me that she hid the body somewhere.'

'I think I know where,' whispered Kelly, sitting back in her chair and putting her hands together and up to her mouth as if in prayer. An image of a deep, dark hole in the ground filled her mind. 'There's an old shed in the woods, between the canal and the railway. I've been there. I think that might be where Alice found William. And there's an old disused well right by it. Do you think he's down there?' Kelly gasped, appalled by her own theory. 'Urgh! What a horrible thought!'

Alice blew out. 'I don't know. He *could* be. Not that there would be much left of him now.' Then, seeing the revulsion in Kelly's expression, she added, 'Look, I don't think that hiding the body was something my great-grandma was very proud of. Perhaps that was why she could never bring herself to tell anyone, or write more in her diary about it. Perhaps it was just easier for everyone if he remained unfound.'

'So...' Kelly slowly picked up the thread. 'Alice never told *anyone* what had happened to Billy? It was covered up?'

Alice nodded. 'That's about the size of it. Keeping it all a secret was made easy for them. The railway company knew that they could have prevented that accident on the line but they had the power and the means to keep that quiet. So it was hushed up. And from Alice's point of view, there was nothing to be gained by the world knowing that William had committed suicide. What good would have come of dragging her family's name through the mud? So she told everyone that she had sent Billy away. Then one day, after the inquest, she simply disappeared. She didn't even tell her father where she had gone. I don't suppose he would ever have dreamed that she had gone to the other side of the world.'

'I can't believe it,' said Kelly, shaking her head.

'No,' agreed Alice. 'It's quite a story. But I think Billy would like it to be told, don't you?'

Kelly nodded, a lump building in her throat.

'In fact,' added Alice, 'one of the things I want to enquire about while I'm here in England is whether I can put a new stone on the grave, showing Billy's full name and age. It seems only right, don't you think? It might not be possible, but I feel I should at least try.'

'Oh, yes,' croaked Kelly, swallowing hard. 'I think he would like that. The headstone says *rest in peace*. I think he would have more chance of doing that if his life and his death were acknowledged in some way. Otherwise it's like he never existed.'

'I have a photo of Billy, you know. It was the only picture my great-grandmother had of him among her things. I think it must have been taken at school here in Wilmcote. Perhaps we could get you a copy of it for your project?'

Kelly's head shot up. 'Do you have it with you?'

'Yes.' Alice delved into the handbag hanging off the back of her chair. 'It's in here with all my legal documents about the cottage.'

She pulled out a plastic folder, opened it, and flicked through the contents. 'Here you go. It's only a photocopy I'm afraid, and the original was quite faded, but you can tell he was a lovely-looking boy.'

Kelly took the piece of paper from Alice and held it closer to the candlelight. The boy in the photograph, standing proudly by the school gate, holding what looked like a certificate in front of his chest, was Ben.

AUTHOR'S NOTE

Like Kelly's adventure in *No Stone Unturned*, this book began with a dog walk. My golden retriever Dexter and I like to walk around the edge of a disused quarry, long transformed from a sheer-sided hole to a wildly overgrown nature reserve. I always try to imagine how different the peaceful, rural scene that I see today would have looked in the nineteenth century when the quarry was in its heyday.

Then one day, while browsing through a book called *A Passage Through Time* produced by my local History Society, a fact caught my eye: limestone from the quarry was used for the flooring of the Houses of Parliament when it was rebuilt after it was destroyed by a massive fire in 1834. I was amazed that what was now a hole in the ground on the edge of a small rural village could have such impressive connections!

I was determined to find out more. So I started doing some digging of my own, into the archives, and *No Stone Unturned* was unearthed.

Sir Charles Barry was the architect chosen to design the new Palace of Westminster. Born on 23rd May 1795, Barry loved Italianate architecture, and designed many country houses and gardens and public buildings in Britain, including the north terrace of Trafalgar Square and its two fountain basins. His design for the Palace of Westminster, bearing a portcullis as a symbol, was chosen from ninety-seven entries and reflected the desire for a magnificent building in the Gothic style.

For help with his drawings and with the execution of the interior design on the project, Barry teamed up with architect and draughtsman Augustus Pugin (1st March 1812–14th September 1852). Pugin suffered a mental breakdown and, in 1852, spent time in an asylum for the insane: the Royal Bethlehem Hospital, known by Bedlam, which stood where the Imperial War Museum now is today. For the purposes of the story, Pugin's death is brought forwards in time to January 1852.

Many of the details in the story about Barry's setbacks and problems during the building of the Houses of Parliament are true. The project overran massively both on time and budget. The first foundation stone was laid by Sir Charles' wife, Sarah, on 27 August 1840, and the building was not completed until ten years after Sir Charles died, with his son Edward finishing the job his father had started.

The stresses and strains of the Westminster project took their toll on Barry and he suffered repeated bouts of illness. It is said that he died of a heart attack at home with his wife in the afternoon of 12th May 1860.

The railway accident which killed Billy in my story is based on a true event in the village of Wilmcote, but the real-life tragedy happened later, on 24th March 1922. Four men were killed while repairing the railway line. At their funeral, a special train was laid on to carry their bodies, and more than 200 railway workers joined the local people who came out to pay their respects. According to its log book for 29th March 1922, the village school closed for the afternoon 'because of the funeral of those parents killed in the railway accident'.

The bodies of the four men lie in a shared plot in my local churchyard, each marked with a small footstone bearing their initials. When I visited their grave, I had already given William his name. So I was moved to see that one of the real-life victims bore the same Christian name.

William Thomas Bonehill was just 27 when he, along with his three fellow labourers, was hit by a northbound light engine which had just passed another southbound goods train close to a bend in the track. At the inquiry, a farm bailiff walking in fields near to the railway cutting testified that he had seen some men packing the ballast on the line without a lookout, and that when the first train passed them, they did not stop working.

As in our story, the jury in the inquest returned a verdict of Accidental Death and no mention of the terrible accident which took the men's lives is made on their headstone.

Many of the places featured in the story are real or are inspired by genuine locations in and around Wilmcote and Stratford-upon Avon. I have taken the liberty of tweaking some historical details. For example, in my descriptions of the Arden Inn, some of you may recognise the Mary Arden Inn, which dominates Wilmcote's village green. However, the inn did not exist in 1839 and I invented Sir Charles Barry's short stay there. The building was originally a private residence and did not become an inn until around 1870, when it was known as the Swan Inn.

Limestone was quarried in Wilmcote as long ago as the sixteenth century but it was in the 1800s that activity in the quarry increased most rapidly,. The initial boost to the industry was the completion of the Stratford-upon-Avon Canal in June 1816, but it was the arrival of the Stratford-upon-Avon railway, which opened in 1860, which enabled the village to reach its full potential.

The home of fictional quarry owner Richard Greenslade resembles the property known today as Gypsy Hall Farm. In the nineteenth century, Gypsies who travelled to Wilmcote to work in the quarries near to the farm—which was originally called Stone Pits Farm—were given permission by the farm owner to camp in his fields near to the house; hence its name change.

* * *

So there you have it. The germs of so many fascinating stories, found within walking distance of my back door. If you enjoy sniffing out a good story, or telling a tale or two of your own, then you might not need to go far for inspiration. Take a good look around you. Leave no stone unturned. There could be something special hiding there!

Acknowledgements

I would like to thank the Aston Cantlow District Local History Society for providing the first, helpful stepping stones on the path which led to this book. Had it not been for a short snippet of information tucked away in the corner of a page about working life in Wilmcote, in their publication *A Passage Through Time in a Warwickshire Parish* edited by Brian Twigg, I would never have known that the limestone from the old abandoned Wilmcote quarry had made its way down to London and to the Houses of Parliament.

I would also like to say a massive thank you to my team of family and friends who read my manuscript at an early stage and gave me their feedback and honest opinions. That includes my mum and dad, David and Irene Watts, Merle Yeomans (who turns out to be a brilliant proof-reader) and Keith Yeomans, Carolyn, John and Adam Gallagher and my dear friend Kate Whyman. All your support and advice is invaluable and much appreciated.

Thank you too, to the Reverend Richard Livingstone for your advice on the relationship between Billy and his grandfather and for checking my facts with regards to the Sunday service.

Of course, this book would be nothing more than an idea in my head were it not for the encouragement and utterly brilliant editing talents of Kate Paice at A&C Black/Bloomsbury. Thank you once again for believing in me, Kate, and for handling my manuscript which such a gentle touch. Thank you too, to Emily Diprose and everyone else at A&C Black/Bloomsbury, including the design team who did such a smashing job on the front cover.

Thank you Dexter dog, for taking me on such great adventures around the lanes and fields of Wilmcote. And as always, huge thanks to my children Jack and Georgia, and to my lovely husband Jon, without whose love and support Kelly and Ben's story might never have made it onto the page.